the tryst list

AN ENEMIES TO LOVERS ROMANCE

KAYLENE WINTER

Jordan

Pinch me.

I'm on top of the fucking world.

The black car speeds down the Vegas strip past the kaleidoscope of neon lights. A city alive with sex, dreams, and promises, and I'm determined to make the most of my excellent mood.

Tonight, I embody every inch of the buxom pinup girls I adore so much. My hair, a cascade of blonde waves, feels like a crown. My iridescent white body-con dress skims my curves and shows off my big tits. Six-inch silver sandals make my legs look a million miles long, even though I'm barely five feet tall.

Yeah, I'm feeling myself a bit. Why not? I fucking won the top artist prize at the Las Vegas International Tattoo Show and it's been a three-year slog to get any recognition at all. Hard work. Navigating institutional misogyny. Blind faith. Determination.

My phone is pinging like mad with offers. From partnerships to guest-artist stints, suddenly I'm coveted by the most-respected shops all over the world. Someone gave a talent agent from the *mn2s* agency my phone number, apparently she wants to sign me and has all sorts of ideas on how to make me famous.

Flattering, sure, but tonight's not the night to make major life decisions. I have plenty of time to figure shit out.

Later.

Tonight is time to celebrate. I'm in an Uber on my way to the Mandalay Bay where my brother Jace's band, Less Than Zero, is playing at the House of Blues. Tomorrow, baby bro's leaving on tour in Europe for God knows how long. I decided to skip a night of doing Apple Pie shots with my tattoo friends and catch Jace's show.

Using the pass he left at the box office, I make my way through the jam-packed VIP area of the venue, which is alive with the throb of music. LTZ is already on stage, powering through an energetic set of their catchy, rock-driven tunes. My brother pounds on his drums, his long, blond hair whirling to the rhythm.

I'm fucking proud. We have a bona fide rockstar in our family.

Making my way to the rail of the balcony overlooking the stage, I raise my vodka soda high above my head and morph into full fan-girl mode. Cheering. Dancing. Throwing up some rock horns. All too soon, their set is over. It's time to get another drink and wait for Jace to come find me.

Amid the crowd, my eyes are magnetically drawn to a man at the bar. Ho-ly *shit*. He's the sexiest guy I've ever seen. Blond, shoulder-length hair, square jaw with a day's worth of stubble, muscles bulging out of his tight T-shirt, glinting blue eyes and a dangerously inviting grin.

He looks like the best kind of trouble and I can't stay away.

"Can I squeeze in?" I sidle up next to him, bathing in the heat of his gaze as he unabashedly checks me out.

"Sure." His eyes twinkle with amusement as if he's used to being hit on. "Here for the music?"

This is going to be fun. I toss my long hair back and pretend to focus on getting the bartender's attention. "Yep. My brother's the drummer in the band that played a minute ago."

His eyes skate down to my ample cleavage when I bounce on my toes to wave the elusive drink-slinger down. I'm not offended. I was deliberately giving Mr. Sexy a little peek at my beautiful girls.

They're real and *spectacular*, if I do say so myself.

With a smirk, he sticks his hand out and snaps his fingers, which immediately—and annoyingly—gets the bartender's attention. "You're having...?"

"Vodka soda." I place my order and flick my eyes over to his. "Thanks."

"No problem. Are you in Vegas to see your brother?" He swishes the golden liquid in his glass around and takes a small sip, fixing his eyes on mine.

God, I love the thrill of the flirt. For now, I decide not to tell him I'm a tattoo artist who won a huge award. I'll stick with band-guy's sister. "Yeah, I'm incredibly proud of him. Are you also here to see LTZ?"

"Nah. Happy accident. I'm attending a conference about green building materials." He quirks his eyebrow. "I'm an architect. Just started my own firm in Seattle."

"Seattle?" I flutter my eyelashes playfully. "What are the odds? I live there too. Are you my destiny, maybe?"

His eyes lock with mine and he traces a finger along my jaw. "Could be."

My entire body erupts with goosebumps from his slight touch, A zing of arousal shoots straight to my pussy. I'm going to fuck this guy tonight. No question. No apologies. It's going to be transcendent. I know it with every fiber of my being.

Our shameless flirting flows, playful and effortless, charged with an undercurrent of something—more. We're a total match.

Each word, gesture, and heated look leads us to a fate we both know is inevitable.

Eventually, Jace and his bandmate Connor stop by, only for quick hugs because their tour bus is leaving. I don't bother introducing them to this guy, since I don't know his name yet. By the time they leave, the venue has cleared out leaving the two of us, a handful of stragglers, and the cleaning crew.

"So, Mr. Architect, got any other plans for tonight?" I open my purse and slick on a light coat of lip gloss.

"It's Peter. And, it depends." He leans in close and nuzzles my neck. "Are *you* part of the plan?"

The air between us crackles. We've moved away from a flirty, casual chat. Though I've refrained from one-night stands, I'm convinced something bigger is happening here. I've never had an instant rapport with someone before. It's like we already know each other.

Sure, it's possible I'm captivated by this Peter guy's charm and the promise of unforgettable passion, but I'm drawn to the possibility he and I could be something more.

Much more.

Deciding to be bold, I grip his knee and lean into him. "I'm Jordan and I'd *like* to be."

One thing leads to another and we're at the other end of the Strip in my hotel room at the Venetian. The Vegas skyline is a glittering backdrop to our own private world. When he takes me in his arms, his touch is electric, sending shivers down my spine. His soulful kisses ignite a fire, which burns fiercely. I'm *incinerated.*

"You're stunningly beautiful, you know that?" Peter's hands trace the contours of my body. He cups my breasts, thumbing my nipples into diamond points. "My every fantasy come to life..."

I'm utterly lost in the intensity of his attention. "You make me *feel* beautiful."

Before I know it, we're naked and embark upon an endless, exhilarating night of intimacy beyond anything I've ever known was possible. Every single molecule of my body feels fused with his. When he looks at me, I'm the only woman in the world. When he's inside me, I'm complete.

Whispered endearments. Promises of more nights together.

I've found my forever guy in the most unexpected way.

We're inevitable.

For a few stolen hours, I let myself believe it.

But as dawn creeps in, the magic of the night fades. I wake up to find Peter's up, dressed, and there's a distinct shift in the atmosphere. His warmth and focused attention is gone, replaced by a clenched jaw and cool detachment.

"I have to go." He doesn't bother to look at me as he ties the laces on his shoes.

God, I'm stupid. I know I signed up for this. Doesn't make it sting any less. "Just like that?"

"It's Vegas." He shrugs, still avoiding my gaze. "What happens here..."

"Stays here, right?" I finish, angry at the bitterness creeping into my voice.

It can't be helped, though. I've been played. I'm mad—no furious—at myself. This guy's been inside my body. *Bare*. A lot.

The worst part is, I allowed it to happen. *Willingly*.

So. Fucking. Careless. I have zero excuses.

Peter doesn't answer but manages to shoot me a half smile which doesn't reach his eyes. There are no niceties. No number exchanges. Sweet sentiments and promises of forever uttered in the throes of the most mind-blowing sex of my life dissipate like vapor in the air.

Naked, amongst the rumpled bedsheets, I realize—I'm fucking *crushed*.

When the door closes behind him, my stomach churns with shame. The thrill of last night overshadowed by the hollowness of its end.

I bet he's not from Seattle. Or an architect.

God, I'm an *idiot*. A disappointment to myself and womankind.

I get out of bed and stare at the reflection of my body in the mirror. I'm a scrawny little thing with giant tits, melted makeup and tangled hair. I look like I've been rode hard, which is the understatement of the century.

The love bites dotting my neck down to my nipples are a stark reminder of the insane pleasure Peter—if that's his real name—gave me all night long. Best sex I've ever had. The way he took charge. Fucked me in positions I didn't know were possible. Made me feel like I turned him on like no one else ever could.

In my own romanticized brain, I believed with all my heart meeting him was fate.

Fuck. Maybe a touch of cynicism hardening my round edges isn't such a bad thing.

Let's face it, my brave sex-kitten persona of last night was a facade. In my professional life, I'm a confident, ambitious tattoo artist. In contrast, I've always been conservative in my personal life. The woman who puts the "F" in faithful.

Winning an award gave me a false sense of bravado. Led me down a path of recklessness. I'm not cut out to live life on the wild side. Not if it means feeling like this.

Lesson learned.

An hour later I'm freshly showered and wheeling my suitcase out of the hotel room. By the time I check out and grab a cab to the airport, last night's adventure feels like a distant dream. A fleeting glimpse of what could have been if I were a better judge of character. Or, luckier in love.

Ahhh, it's only a minor detour on my journey.

I won't let it derail me.

This is going to be my year. In a few months I'll open my own tattoo shop and staff it with the best of the best. It's not like I have time for a relationship anyway. My focus has to be on my business.

Vegas, with all its glitter and empty promises, is behind me.

I'm focusing on my future and I'm ready to take the world by storm.

Chapter One

It's a few minutes past seven a.m. and I'm running behind.

Clutching my Hydro Flask filled with Purity coffee, I arrive at work. My footsteps echo off the sleek, polished floors of the breathtaking new contemporary lobby of VA/VT. My clothes, slacks and dress shirt are made out of organic, socially-responsible fabric.

Last night, because I worked until midnight, my car wasn't fully charged by the time I'd hoped to leave this morning. Facing a full schedule of important meetings and appointments, I was forced to wait for it to finish. Nothing bugs me more than being late. Very unprofessional.

But, as a devout green architect, I'm hyperaware every choice I make—from the food I eat to the clothes I wear—is a reflection of my values. I take sustainability seriously. It's not only my brand, but my lifestyle.

Despite the time, or lack thereof, I can't help but stop for a moment. My eyes sweep the room from the half-moon reception counter to the arched bronze chandeliers to the striking curved staircase leading to the executive offices. Though the color scheme is neutral—classic grays and creams—the mixture of textures and materials give the entire space a bright, edgy feel.

It's stunning. *Truly* stunning.

I did this.

It wasn't long ago when I had a simple vision. A dream. A mission.

I was determined to build a firm specializing in designing gorgeous, sustainable net-zero commercial buildings.

My environmentally conscious design philosophy isn't unique. Unless you're living under a rock, every modern architect understands the importance of using less water, energy, and other natural resources. Most people in the construction industry are committed to employing renewable energy sources and eco-friendly materials to reduce emissions and eliminate waste.

What sets VA/VT apart, however, is *how* we're better at it. Partially because of the proprietary software I invented. The way it enables us to create healthy, comfortable and resource-efficient spaces in a cost-effective manner is unprecedented. Even better, the software seamlessly integrates with government and regulatory bodies, making permitting and inspections a breeze.

Not only do I have several patents, but I license the technology—at a very steep price—to some of the biggest firms in the world. Hence, the name of my company. VA for Vander Architecture. VT for its sister company, Vander Technologies. We're also focused on long-term impact, collaborating with governmental and regulatory bodies across the US to create policy change and incentives to build green.

Ten years ago, little did I know my unique outlook on planning, design, and construction would propel my career into the stratosphere.

As I approach the conference room where my team is waiting for me, I feel proud. It isn't an ordinary day. The decisions we make at this meeting will redefine my design career. Cement my name in history. Change my legacy for not only me but my future family.

I'll finally leave my past behind.

I'm one of three architects in the world who've been invited to submit a finalized "vision" for Project SoHo, the code name for a new pop culture museum in London. The location encompasses the entire Smithfield General Market area, which has fallen into disrepair.

Of the three contenders, my firm is the only one with less than fifty full-time architects. Yet, even though we're a much smaller company, we've made it through two long years of elimination rounds to get here.

Now, I'm a realist. There's no way we'd be in the running if it weren't for Vander Technologies and my software. On the other hand, my team's prowess in practical green design and construction is unmatched as we've demonstrated time and time again.

This next round will be no different.

"Morning, everyone." I enter the conference room to find my SoHo team, Rose, Pip, and Fabiola, huddled around a holographic display in the center of the room.

They're the best in their respective specialties from all over the globe, but even the best need direction.

My direction.

"Hello, Peter." Rose, VA's business development manager, glances up briefly before resuming tapping on her tablet.

Pip, a shy, slight man from Delhi who integrates the technology into our designs, gives me a quick, efficient nod.

Fabiola, our blue-haired creative design genius, doesn't look up from the visual display. Her slight Italian accent flavors her words. "This is the digital rendering of the SoHo Project with your directives from the last meeting incorporated into the design."

I walk around the display, running my hand through my hair, feeling its tousled length. "The next phase is critical. An independent panel of design professionals, business stakeholders, and local governmental representatives will review the next round of submissions and eliminate one contender. With this in mind, I encourage everyone to be ruthless in your scrutiny. I don't need to remind you about the exposure VA/VT will receive if we're awarded the contract. It'll change all of our lives."

The air pulses with tension. Everyone knows what's on the line. Both companies have turned down other lucrative projects to take this shot at infamy.

"As we've learned, the city wants to transform the Smithfield Market neighborhood from a rundown part of London into a vibrant, mixed-use development to reflect the history of the iconic buildings while embracing the potential of the future." Rose projects our objectives onto the wall beyond the display. "Considering the other two contenders, our thesis is "the future is green." We're the best choice."

"In my opinion, the interactive elements will put us over the top..." Pip presses a button, which illuminates vibrant colors within the display to show some of the integrations we're proposing. "This latest iteration of our software allows for an immersive experience into our design."

"Phenomenal, Pip. Way to think bigger, bolder. We can show them—not merely tell them—it's not merely a building. Or a structure. It's a statement." I pace back and forth studying the improvements I asked for a few days ago. "This rendering is exactly what I had in mind.

A presentation that evolves. It breathes. We don't only want this to be eco-friendly but eco-active."

Rose's eyes light up. "Biophilic design? Integrating natural elements not just aesthetically but functionally?"

"Exactly." I point at her. "We've created a living, pulsing piece of art, which will not only redefine London's skyline, but integrate with their grid. Think of the possibilities—tracking emissions reduction in real time."

For the next few hours, our conversation delves into the technicalities of the RFP documents. We go over the entire submission from solar panels to rainwater harvesting to the urban green spaces. Where appropriate, I guide, challenge them and push for perfection. We have another week before we submit, and it must be perfect.

Lunch arrives as we're wrapping up. My phone's been buzzing nonstop for about an hour, it's a good opportunity to find out who or what's on fire.

Fuck. Five voicemails from my mother. Probably another crisis involving either Kent or Lance, my brothers.

Perpetual disappointments. Both of them.

I delete the messages without listening and silence my phone. I can't afford distractions. I'm too close to making history.

"Peter, should we discuss aesthetics?" Fabiola tugs on my sleeve. "Do you think this updated design resonates with the city's cultural fabric?"

"I do. You've done a stupendous job taking inspiration from London's diversity, its history and culture." I close my eyes, visualizing how the desolate area will look upon completion of the museum. "It's a brilliant fusion of old and new, a testament to the city's continual evolution."

The entire team nods enthusiastically. It's heady. They believe in my vision. In the legacy we're about to embark upon if we're chosen.

As we delve deeper into the discussion, I can't help but feel the weight of my family's struggles tugging at me. I grew up in a working-class home—well, when my folks still had jobs. Dad used to be a custodian and my mother worked as a bookkeeper for a furniture store.

They always found a way to keep their heads above water, but my twin brothers, Kent and Lance... They've gone down a different path.

Just last month, I loaned my parents $10,000 to bail Kent out of jail after a brutal bar fight. Unfortunately, it wasn't the first time, and won't be the last. The lingering bitter taste in my mouth is a constant reminder of the never-ending situation. I can't seem to get out from under my family's burden.

It's a noose always waiting to hang me.

Sometimes, when I'm feeling down, I try to imagine having a family who called to check on me once in a while. A mother or a father who showed interest in my accomplishments. But, no. My family isn't like that. I'm only good for one thing—my bank account. Each and every one of them are oblivious to the hard work I put in to support everyone.

Why would any of them work, when they've got me?

"I need to step out for a moment." Standing abruptly, I make a move toward the door. At the very least, I need air.

Outside, the city hums with life. I lean against the cool, glass facade of the building. My childhood seems like a lifetime ago but the truth is, no matter how much I separate myself, they drag me back in. My guilt clings to me. Like a shadow I can't shake off.

Which is one of the reasons why this project means everything to me. Being selected is my chance to solidify my place in the world. Far, far away from the constraints of my family's expectations to clean up their messes.

The phone buzzes in my hand. This time, I pick up. "Mom? What's going on?"

"It's Lance." Her voice is weary. Defeated. "I don't think he's going to come back from this one. Your father and I have no idea what to do."

Through tears, my mother launches into a story so fucked up, so convoluted, I can't even begin to process what I'm hearing. In the background, my dad punctuates some of the more salacious details with strings of curse words. He's drunk, I can tell from the sound of his voice. When she finishes her tale ten minutes later, my mind is mush.

"What do you want me to do?" I pinch my eyebrows.

Mom screeches into the phone, "Save him. You must know a good lawyer."

"You're asking me to pay for a high-powered defense lawyer even though he already admitted everything?" I kick the sidewalk angrily. "What about accountability?"

"Don't be like that, Peter. I want my son home. You have the money. He's your brother." She says this matter-of-factly, which I'm used to. After all, in her mind I'm paying off a debt so it's my *obligation* to help.

I make a decision. "No."

"*No?*" She's thoroughly baffled by my refusal.

"You heard me. He'll get a public defender. The chips will fall where they fall." I glance at my phone to check the time. "Look. I'm wrapping up a meeting and then I have an appointment I can't miss. I'm sorry, but I'm done. If you and Dad need anything let me know, but I won't be touching this with a ten-foot pole."

"Pete—" is the last thing I hear before I click off the phone.

It's been nearly thirty minutes but everyone's still focused on the proposal. We finalize the last details and I task Rose with incorporating our collective feedback and circulating it to us tomorrow. Everyone dissipates, leaving me staring out the window at the Space Needle.

I know it's time to cut ties with my family. No, long past time.

Currently, though, I have somewhere to be. A long-standing appointment I'm sure as hell not going to miss.

My family will be there tomorrow.

But I've been waiting for this moment for years.

Chapter Two

T he hum of tattoo machines is always music to my ears. It's the sweet, sweet sound of success.

Something I don't take for granted. Hard work and fortitude is in my blood.

I've managed to turn my art degree into a gold mine. I graduated from Cornish College of the Arts many years ago, but it took a while for me to find my way. Did the starving artist thing—tried to sell my paintings while paying the bills as a server and barista. Then came a corporate stint in commercial design, which I absolutely hated. Leaving me with freelancing—a nightmare through and through.

A career in the arts seemed out of reach. Well, maybe for me. I was going nowhere.

On a whim, I sold my belongings and fled to Europe for a year-long backpacking excursion.

Within the first couple of weeks, I met a group of tattoo artists at a collective in Amsterdam. Immersing myself in their world, I changed my plan. Rather than aimlessly traveling, I apprenticed and soaked up the culture.

By the time I returned home to Seattle, I'd developed my own style and had a small following. A few months later, I won a contest in Las Vegas and haven't looked back since.

Rather than work for someone else, I presented my pops with a business proposal. It worked. He staked me with enough funds to open my shop, The Salty Siren. Jace taught me how to cultivate a social media following. Within a few months, I had a waiting list, paid back Dad's loan and bought a condo.

It blows me away how far my schedule books out in advance.

For the most part I'm happy, but recent life changes have me reconsidering a few things.

"Merc, who's on the books today? I'm pretty sure it's a long-ass appointment, if memory serves." I approach

Mercury, my best friend and shop manager. "Let me guess. Someone wants a mermaid sleeve."

Merc, as everyone calls him, with his silver hair and piercing blue eyes, shoots me a glare. "Careful. You're not exuding gratitude today. Your mermaids are *legendary*. People wait for over a year to get inked by you."

Appropriately put in my place, I flip through my sketchbook past pages of intricate flowing tails and ethereal faces. "Oh, I know, but I like to mix it up. Keep my chops up."

"Well, today's your lucky day, babe. New customer. The guy booked over a year ago." Merc peruses the shop's master calendar on his tablet.

I'm barely paying attention because my fingers pause on a page in my notebook. Amongst my designs is a list I started after Cameron and I broke up. The "Tryst List" is my secret rebellion against the monotony of my love life. Merc's eyes follow mine, and he raises an eyebrow.

"*Oooh*. What do we have here?" With a mischievous glint in his eye, Mercury's hand claps over mine, stopping me from turning the page.

I feel my face redden. "Uhhh...my plan to live a little. Or a lot." I offer a wry smile. "I'm thinking of making up for lost time, you know, after Cameron."

"Cameron. *Ugh*. Your couple vibe was definitely more cookouts and beer than fireworks and passion. Maybe it was his uniform of khakis and button-down shirts." He rolls his eyes in disgust.

I can't help but laugh. Of course, Merc would feel this way given our affinity for grommets, leather, and chunky boots.

Merc leans against the counter and his expression turns more serious. "I tried not to pry when it happened, but it's been a while. Why did you break it off? You two were together for a long time."

"Almost eight years." I exhale deeply. It's always jarring to realize how much time I wasted in a dead-end relationship. "Cameron was...safe. After my disastrous one-nightstand in Vegas, I craved stability. I wanted what my parents have. I thought Cameron would provide it for me."

"But?" Merc prompts, knowing there's more to the story.

"I was kidding myself. We weren't a match. For years, I tried to feel something...deeper, but...yeah. He wasn't my guy." I feel a weight lift at my admission of something I denied to myself and everyone around me for too long. "He wanted me to be someone I'm not. Underneath his passive-aggressive ways of supporting me, he saw tattooing as a quirky hobby, not a serious profession. God, the needling. Snarky comments about how artists were flighty. Subtle digs at my artistic skill."

Mercury nods in understanding. "Oh, girl. I've been there. Death by a thousand paper cuts."

"Exactly. It all came to a head when he started criticizing my business acumen. *As if.* I bring in easily ten times what he makes every year. After a while, I realized he was projecting. Beware of the guy who compares himself to you to demonstrate his superiority. Oh, and the sex sucked too. Do you know he wouldn't go down on me?" My hand curls into a fist. I'm annoyed with myself for how long I put up with him. "I finally got fed up. Told him we'd reached the end of the line. He wasn't surprised."

Mercury shakes his head. "Well, good riddance. You deserve someone who respects you and what you're passionate about. Oh, and some good old-fashioned, toe-curling pussy licking."

"You're right." I tap the page of my sketchbook, feeling a spark of excitement at my potential upcoming adventures. "The Tryst List is my solution. I'm craving sex like it was with he-who-shan't-be-named. I'm older, I know myself better. This time, I'll be able to compartmentalize great sex from love at first sight."

"Girl, I can't believe you're still obsessing about a freakin' one-night stand." Mercury peruses my list, his eyebrow arched with acute interest. "You realize how stupid you sound, right?"

My thighs clamp shut inadvertently at the memory of how many orgasms I had in the span of seven hours. "The guy was a lying bastard jerk, but—ohmygod, Merc. What he did to my body? Hoo-ey. That man turned me inside out, upside down, and spun me all around. It was more than physical though. I've got to get more of..." I take a deep breath. "Look, I'm reclaiming my sex life. On my terms. Hence, my Tryst List. I'm going to make all of my sexual fantasies come true."

"Holy shit, Jordan. This is some list." Merc traces down the page with his finger. "Stranded somewhere? Mile high club? Anal? Bondage? Public sex?"

"Yeah." I shrug coquettishly. "I'm owning what I want and I'm willing to experiment a little to learn what I like. It's time to stop fantasizing about a stupid night in Vegas and experience bone-shattering orgasms for real again."

Merc places a supportive hand on my shoulder. "It sounds like you're looking for some plug-buddies." He wags his finger. "Be careful, babes. You've got a wild heart, but it's still *your* heart, and considering how much this Vegas guy owns your brain, I'm not sure you're cut out for casual sex."

I nod, feeling a surge of gratitude for my friend, because deep down I wonder if he's right. "I will. Thanks, Merc."

"Okay." He claps his hands. "Your appointment will be here any minute. Show me what you've got."

I page through my sketchbook until I find the artwork I created months ago. "I'm pretty sure this client is one of those douchebags obsessed with the Roman Empire."

"Jordy, this is gorgeous." Merc stares at the full-sleeve design of ancient buildings interwoven with realistic renditions of the four cardinal virtues of temperance, fortitude, justice, and prudence.

I gaze at the drawing. I vaguely remember when this commission came in last year. The client approved my first rendition outright, which rarely happens. "Thank you, I'd nearly forgotten about this appointment. The tattoo is such a huge departure from my ordinary style, I'm actually psyched. Would you mind uploading and printing out a couple of thermo stencils while I get my room set up?"

"I'm on it." Merc grabs my sketchbook and disappears into the back office.

With a half hour to spare, I have more than enough time to get prepped. No need to rush. I'm casually scrolling through emails when the front door chimes, signaling a new arrival. Because we're an appointment-only shop and Merc is working on my stencils, I answer the door myself.

When I do, all the air whooshes from the room.

I can't believe my eyes. It's like I conjured up a blast from the past out of thin air.

"Watch my cock fuck your sweet cunt," he growls in my ear.

His bulging arms are curled under my thighs, effortlessly holding me suspended in midair. I lean back against his chest and cling to his elbows, watching us in the full-length mirror as he bounces my slight frame up and down on his mammoth dick. My pussy consumes his shaft, hungrily squeezing him with every pass.

I'm so turned on every single nerve ending feels like it's buzzing.

He buries his chin in the crook of my neck. Our eyes meet in the mirror. "I've got you, beautiful. You're weightless. Let go of my elbows and rub your clit. Can you feel every inch of my cock sliding inside your wet heat?"

I literally gush at his dirty words. One hand snakes down to my sensitive nub and I wince because I've already come half a dozen times tonight. Every part of my sex is overstimulated, but I do as he asks and rub myself.

I have to.

I need to.

His eyes are locked on where we're joined. With a feral growl, he effortlessly shifts my position so his crown hits a magic spot inside me I never knew existed. Something tells me I'm on the brink of the greatest pleasure I've ever known, so I keep rubbing.

It's incredible.

Unbearable.

A high-pitched squeal bursts free when it all becomes too much. I watch my small body impaled by his big cock in the mirror. He slams me down harder and harder. My tits bounce and jiggle. "Don't give up, baby girl. You're almost there. Look at how swollen your pussy is. Dripping wet. Jesus, you're so fucking sexy."

The dirty talk is too much.

Not enough.

My breathing comes in short spurts and my core seizes around him.

"That's it. Now, bear down like you're going to pee." I can't think. Every nerve ending is alive. I'm stuffed full of him. My nipples are tight and puckered. Am I feeling pleasure or pain? Who knows—who cares! I never, ever, ever, ever want this to end.

More. More. More.

"Fuck me. Fuck me. Fuck me!' I scream, closing my eyes and squeezing his shaft with all my might. Sucking him deeper into my body.

"Oh, fuck yeah," he moans. "Rub, baby. Rub. Faster. Faster."

Moments later a sonic blast shoots from my toes through my pussy up my channel and out of the top of my head. I let out an agonized moan. "Gahhhhhh."

"You've got to open your eyes and watch," he shouts. "Let go. Just let go. I've got you."

My eyes open at the moment I literally detonate. Splash after splash of my release coats the mirror. I'm wailing. Tears stream down my cheeks as I experience the most intense orgasm of my life. "Oh Godddd-ddddddd…"

"Fuuuuuuck. You're so fucking hot. I'm gonna come so fucking hard." His eyes squinch shut and I feel his hot release spurt inside me, over and over.

I try to squiggle and get away because I have no idea what just happened and I'm a bit embarrassed at the mess I've made, but he keeps my legs spread apart and suspended, so I have no option but to lean back against his chest as he continues to pump up into my *body. "Don't be shy, baby. I made you squirt. Watch us fuck. We're perfect."*

Electricity ripples through my body when I see our come dripping out of me, down his cock, pooling on the floor. His eyes are half-mast, but he's gaping at me in the mirror like I'm the sexiest goddess on the planet.

I'm gone. Again. My pussy clamps down on his cock and I scream bloody murder when another orgasm tears through my body like an exorcism.

"You're so fucking beautiful. You're mine." He bites my earlobe. "Say it."

I'm nearly passed out from pleasure but can't take my hooded eyes off his cock still buried to the root. "I'm yours."

"Hi there." The familiar, deep voice snaps me back to reality.

Standing before me, in all his brooding glory, is the asshole from Vegas.

The man who's haunted my dreams—and is still the subject of my every fantasy.

Chapter Three

She remembers.

I'm sure of it.

Well, *sort* of sure of it. The distinct flush on her face briefly gave it away before she caught herself and smoothed her expression into a mask of professionalism.

Either way, I remember our night and I'm hard as a fucking rock. There's no hiding it.

The woman before me is perfection. She wears a black-leather corset, clearly custom made by the way it cradles and pushes up her unbelievable tits. Barely five feet tall, her legs are long and lean in tight black jeans stuffed into thigh-high black suede boots. Blonde hair tied up in a messy bun. Peaches-and cream skin adorned by the most colorful, dimensional flowers winding up and down her arms. A dusting of freckles across her nose. Huge green eyes. Pillowy lips.

It wasn't hard to track her down, considering her brother's the drummer for LTZ, the biggest band out of my hometown.

"Jordan Deveraux?" Her name rolls off my tongue, though my skin prickles with anticipation of hearing her voice.

I wonder...does she remember me?

"Yes. And you are?" Jordan's pleasant smile gives nothing away.

WTF?

"I'm Peter Vander. I have an appointment today. A new sleeve on my left arm." Smiling broadly, I extend my hand toward her, knowing my name will jog her memory.

Jordan places her dainty hand, tipped with blunt, groomed nails, in mine. Electricity sparks as I knew it would. Her eyes flick up to mine briefly before she withdraws her grip, spins on her heel and makes a beeline for the reception desk.

She taps into a tablet and glances in my direction. "Oh...right, you're the guy with a Roman Empire fixation. The design you approved is quite the departure from my usual art, what made you decide to book with me?"

Ahhh. She's gonna play it like this.

Interesting.

"I've heard you're the best." I flash her the same wicked grin that led to the greatest night of my life all those years ago. "For the record, the design is inspired by Florence not Rome. It's got special meaning to me."

Unmoved, she hands me a clipboard. "You're a little early. Please fill out this release form while my assistant finishes up your stencil."

My mind races. There were a million ways our reunion could have gone, but I didn't count on this.

I fill out the form and sign the release. "All done." I hand the clipboard back to her.

"So, you're an architect?" She scans the sheet without looking up. Like I'm any other client. Like I haven't been inside her body.

"Yeah. I run VA/VT. We specialize in green building designs and technology." I wonder if tossing in the reference to my specialty will jog her memory.

I don't get a chance to find out. A tall man with long cornrows wearing a jumpsuit made of various types of buckles emerges from the back. "Jordan, your stencils are done."

"Thanks, Merc." Jordan takes the folder from him. "Mr. Vander is early."

Merc crosses his arms and flashes me a toothy grin. "Ahh. Mr. Roman Empire, amiright?"

"*No*. Florence." Perturbed, I roll up my shirt sleeve to show them the ink on my right arm—busts of Roman gods intertwined with laurel through a realistic rending of the ancient structure St. Peter's Basilica and the modern Maxxi museum building. "It'll be the companion piece to this."

"Impressive." Merc examines my arm. "This looks like Ruben Riksfjord."

I raise an eyebrow. "Yeah. It is. I got it in Copenhagen. I was there for work on a multiyear project. I'm very pleased."

"So, you're still good with my design? I'm not the type of artist who copies my colleagues' art." Jordan defiantly stares me dead in the eye.

I'm already irritated she's pretending not to know me, so the insinuation offends me, as does her bluntness. She's not the flirty, submissive sex kitten I remember, apparently. "I wouldn't be at The Salty Siren if I wanted a hack job and I certainly wouldn't have waited over a year for an appointment with *you* for a replica."

"Hold on." Jordan peers at me and holds up a finger. "Shitty attitudes are not tolerated in my establishment. I'll give you the benefit of the doubt. Once." She studies one of the stencils. "For the record, you're about to spend about thirty hours getting permanent ink on a highly visible part of your body. I'm going to ask questions and you're going to answer them because I'm a professional. If my approach doesn't work for you, I have a lot of very nice, appreciative clients who'd be thrilled to move up the list."

I nearly have to hold my jaw to keep it from dropping open. I reaffirm my previous assessment. Jordan's not afraid to set boundaries. Few people are able to put me in my place anymore and frankly, it's fucking sexy. "I apologize. In my defense, I'm an artist too and I wouldn't ask you to copy someone else's style. I made the appointment with you because of *your* talent."

"Good to know. Let's get the party started. I'll need about ten minutes to get my station set up. Afterward, we can work on placement." Jordan disappears into a room behind the counter.

My eyes linger on her heart-shaped ass as she walks away. Holy fucking hell. I can still picture Jordan's bare cheeks jiggling from the force of my thrusts when I fucked her upright against the hotel window. Unfortunately, my dick twitches at the memory and my jeans grow even tighter.

Merc snaps his fingers in front of my eyes. "Eyes off her caboose, Romeo. I need a credit card for the deposit."

"Uh...sorry. I mean, uh...sure." Flustered at being caught staring—and picturing her naked, no less—I fish out my card and tap it on the terminal.

"Don't take it personally." Merc hands me a receipt. "I look out for her. As you might imagine, Jordan gets hit on a lot. She's a knockout so it's understandable—but get yourself together before you go back there." His eyes flick to the bulge in my jeans before meeting my shocked gaze. "It's a lost cause anyway, she doesn't fuck her clients."

I nearly choke on my own spit.

There's no chance to recover because Jordan beckons me from the doorway. Her smirk indicates she overheard Merc read me for filth. "Mr. Vander, please come in."

"Peter." I straighten my shoulders, take a deep breath and stride toward her, trying to regain some semblance of equilibrium. When I peer inside the room, I'm stunned. It's more high-end spa than tattoo parlor. "This isn't what I was expecting."

"At The Salty Siren, you get white-glove service and a five-star experience." Jordan ties a pink bandana round her hair and rattles off her spiel. "I'm assuming you know about prep since you're not a novice to a full sleeve, but as a reminder I'll need to shave and clean your entire arm with antiseptic. Then we'll focus on placement of the stencil. Once you're satisfied, I'll focus on the outline today and we'll schedule additional sessions for the shading and final details every couple of weeks or as your schedule permits. I'll step out so you can take your shirt off."

"No need." I pull off my sweater and T-shirt. "I'm ready."

Jordan's eyes widen as she takes me in. I work hard to keep a taut six-pack and cut arms. All the better to show off my body ink, which she hasn't seen yet. My torso—save my stomach and left arm—features artwork from three amazing tattoo artists.

"Incredible." With her finger, she traces the intricate Japanese design on my back featuring dragons, koi fish, and lotus flowers interwoven with a mosaic pattern of glass, metal, and solar panels invoking the Besançon Art Center, designed by my most-cherished mentor, Kongo Kuma. "If I'm not mistaken, this looks like Haruto Ito's work."

I'm stunned. "You're familiar?"

"Of course. I've not met him in person, but I'm a fan." Jordan's eyes scan the smattering of small but intricate designs on my right pec.

With her sparkling green eyes perusing my body, my cock remains painfully stiff. Discreetly, I hold my sweater in front of my erection. I don't want her to feel threatened by me, but I have little control over my dick where she's concerned.

"Well, let's get you shaved." She snaps back into all-business mode. "Follow me."

Fifteen minutes later, my arm is hairless and swabbed. Jordan holds up the stencil against my bicep, her eyes furrowed in concentration. "I like to take my time at this stage to make sure the design fits around the anatomy of your arm. It's important to position it correctly."

"I like your style," I hear myself blurt out as she peels off the stencil. "Not just your artistic talent. You have a certain...aura about you."

Her expression remains passive, disinterested. "Thanks. Let's look at the three-way mirror."

She spins me around and holds my arm up at various angles. I can't really make heads or tails of the design in its current state, but I trust her. I've followed her work for years. "It's perfect."

"Good. Let's get you comfortable." Jordan helps me recline on her special chair and positions my arm on a table she slides out. "It can get cold in here." She drapes a light blanket over my chest and pants.

Shit. She noticed my boner.

"You ever been to Vegas?" I can't seem to stop myself from speaking after she starts on the outline. I want some sort of reaction from her. Anything to let me know she remembers me.

Her hand hovers above my bicep for a fraction of a second. "Lots of times."

"Fun place," I toss out. "I've had some wild experiences there…"

Her eyebrow winches up and her nostrils flair slightly, but she keeps her composure. "I'm sure."

For the next couple hours, we fall into silence. The only sound is the buzz of the tattoo machine. I'm sure Jordan can feel my eyes on her, but she her keeps focus on my arm. Every fifteen minutes or so she asks how I'm doing and offers me water and snacks, which I turn down. As the session continues into the third hour, I'm lulled into an almost trancelike state.

I love the feel of a tattoo needle, even on the sensitive parts of my arm.

Sweet, sweet relief.

Throughout our session, Jordan gives no indication she has any idea who I am. *None*. She's laser focused, barely blinking as she concentrates on the outline of my intricate design. When we finish for the day, she cleans me up and we stand examining her work in the mirror.

"Impressive." I meet her eyes in the glass. "You're worth the wait."

Her cheeks pinken, the only indication I've affected her in any way. "Well, thank you. It's always nice to hear."

She wraps my arm, helps me into my sweater and spends a few minutes on aftercare instructions. The next thing I know, she's handing me off to Merc. "I'll see you in about two weeks. Make sure to get an appointment on the books. I keep openings on my calendar for follow-up appointments."

"Look forward to it." I wave, but she's already gone without a backward glance.

Merc suppresses a grin and hands me Salty Siren specially formatted CBD soap. "You, sir, are a glutton for punishment."

I'm not going to be baited into a discussion that's none of his business. Instead, I pull out my phone to block my own calendar for our next session and leave with a lightly bruised ego and slightly sore arm.

It's taken me a long time to connect with her. *Too long*. Jordan may be pretending not to know me, but her facade won't last forever.

I won't be deterred.

With twenty-two hours of unencumbered time ahead of us, there's plenty of time to jog her memory.

By the time my tattoo's finished, Jordan Deveraux is going to be mine again.

Chapter Four

P eter Vander.

Huh.

Vegas guy has resurfaced after all this time. What are the odds? I show Merc my Tryst List one minute and poof! It's like I manifested him out of thin air. Somehow, he's my customer to boot.

Still as arrogant as I remember. Still as devastatingly handsome.

More professional, though. His blond hair is a bit darker and shorter, though it's still long on top. He's more ripped than I remember, the years have only made him hotter. His clothes and shoes are clearly designer, though not ostentatious. When he spoke, his low, growly voice sent trembles of desire racing through my body.

Instantly conjured up memories of him ordering me to get down on my knees and...

No!

No. No. *No*.

I'm not going down this path. Peter Vander may have been the best lay I've ever had but he left me high and dry in my Vegas hotel room after a night so fucking magical I was picturing our wedding. Which is stupid and immature, I know...but it hurt really fucking bad when he left. Just like it hurts today.

He *knows* it's me—the Vegas innuendos couldn't have been by accident—and yet he didn't say a fucking word. Didn't apologize for how he treated me. Didn't bother to be sufficiently embarrassed and humble.

Nope. Instead, he *smirked* at me, sporting a huge *bulge* in his pants.

What a *disgusting* sicko.

At the same time, he's a sicko who's paying me fifty thousand dollars for a sleeve. It's no problem for me to suck it up and decorate him with my art. It's kinda ironic, actually. I'll put a little piece of myself on his body to make sure he won't ever forget me again.

Meanwhile, I'll continue to ignore him. Pretend I don't remember.

There's no time to think about it now, though. I'm running late.

On my way out, I stop for a quick second. Look around. Try to see The Salty Siren through Peter Vander's eyes.

A sense of pride washes over me. Creating this space was more than opening a business; it was about breaking barriers in a field where female tattoo shop owners are still a rarity. Every detail is my vision come to life—from the white marble flooring to the dark, modern furniture to the paintings I created for the walls.

My goal was to elevate the tattooing experience for my clients and make it feel more like a luxury service, which is why I opted for private spa-like tattooing rooms with ambient lighting. I've invested in the most cutting-edge gear available and use only the finest vegan ink to ensure my shop provides the highest quality and longest lasting body art.

The work's paid off. My reputation in the industry is pristine. Kali Nighthawk, Ryuji Takahiro, and Luna

Marquez, three of the best artists in the world, have made my shop their permanent home. Others are guest artists for stints between six months and two years.

My shop kicks ass. I wonder if he's impressed?

No!

You don't care if he's impressed.

Annoyed about Peter Vander fucking with my mind, I'm ready to get outta here. My hand is on the door-knob when Merc steps in front of me.

"Not so fast." He rests his hands on his hips. "Ro-man-tattoo man was hot. As in young David Beckham hot."

I roll my eyes and reposition my cross-body bag over my corset. "*Meh*."

"Uh...don't play me, boo-boo. You seemed a bit, uh...tense around him. Maybe it was his ginormous crotch rocket. Is there something I should know about?" Merc's eyebrow is arched up to the sky.

Crap. Nothing gets past him.

I decide to come clean. "Peter isn't some random client. He's the guy from Vegas. The one-night stand."

"No fucking *way*!" Mercury's eyes widen in disbelief.

I wince, frustrated and a touch embarrassed. "Yeah...it took me by complete surprise. I can't believe we were talking about him and he showed up a minute later. Merc...I'm *sure* he recognized me, but he didn't acknowledge who I was. I've thought about a million things I would say if I ever saw him again, but I never thought it would be at my shop. Embarrassingly, rather than telling him off, I wussed out and pretended not to know him."

"Don't be embarrassed, that's a boss move. JFYI, I had to reprimand that pervert from staring at your ass. And for being hard as a rock." Merc swooshes his hand in a circle.

I can't help but roll my eyes. "Well, a lot of guys get boners when I tattoo them."

"What the hell do you put in your ink, girl?" Merc dramatically fans himself.

"Shut up." I shake my head, laughing. "Seeing him in the flesh has one positive benefit. It cemented my Tryst List plan. He fucked with my self-esteem, Merc. I'm not allowing this Peter guy to get under my skin. No fucking way."

Merc leans against the wall. "Well, if you ask me, there's still something there, amiright?" He wiggles his fingers. "The air was *thick* with sexual tension."

"Oh, there was tension, but not what you think." I tap my finger on my chin, trying to explain. "Truthfully it's more like...resentment. Back then he made me feel like I was something special, only to discard me. Today, he acted like he didn't know me. He's a player to the core and I want no part of him."

Merc boops me on the nose. "Well, my dear. Sounds like you're playing the game right back."

"A game?" I shudder. "Ignoring him isn't a game, it's protecting my heart."

Merc cocks his hip. "Tell yourself anything you want, babes."

I cross my arms in a flare of annoyance at his remarkable perceptiveness. "Why poke the bear? He either didn't remember me, or if he did, he didn't deem me worthy enough to say anything."

"Maybe you should keep an open mind. You're a fierce, intimidating woman." Merc fixes me with a look. "It could be he was as shocked as you are. *Let. Go. Of. The. Grudge.*"

"There's no grudge. I simply hate people like Peter. They don't change. Their bullshit deepens with age." I open the door to leave. I love Merc, but I'm over this discussion.

Merc grips my shoulder. "I get you're hurt, Jordan. But maybe this weird twist of fate is your chance to rewrite the ending. Don't you think it's time to finally move on?"

"Uh..." I ponder his words for a moment and shake my head. "No. This isn't a romance novel. This is real life. And in real life, guys like Peter Vander are best kept at arm's length. Look, I've gotta go meet the ladies."

Mercury nods. "Alright, I won't push it. Whatever you decide to do about him, I've got your back."

I manage a small smile, grateful for his support. "Thanks, Merc."

On the Uber ride over to the Gemini Room, I'm finally able to relax. Peter Vander may have walked back into my life, but he's not going to shake my world. I won't let him. There's a reason I broke it off with Cameron to go live life on my terms. Nothing's going to sway me. Not even the hot Vegas asshole.

By the time I arrive, my almost sister-in-law, Alex and two of the other LTZ wives, Zoey Rainier and Fiona

Rocks are sitting in oversized silver-grommeted chairs in the main lounge sipping their drinks. The atmosphere is quiet and reserved, perfect for a night of gossip without prying ears. I give the server my order and settle in.

At first, the discussion centers around LTZ's new truncated touring schedule. Everyone in the band has kids. Two-year mega-tours are a thing of the past, thank God. Fiona gives us an update about the opening of her restaurant, Gus, and its sister nightclub, The Mission.

I try to pay attention, but my mind keeps wandering to my encounter with Peter.

"So, spill it, Jordan. Who are you fantasizing about?" Alex playfully pokes my arm, jarring me back into the conversation.

Argh.

Divert. Divert. Divert. "Okay. Fine. You're all happily married, so remember I'm recently single. Tell me what you think—I started a thing for my own amusement. A Tryst List."

"What's a Tryst List?" Zoey eyes widen. She's married to LTZ's sex-god lead singer. By all accounts, she and her husband are world-class trysters.

"Okay. Hear me out. After years of lackluster sex with Cameron, I made a list of sexual adventures and experiences I want to try." I swirl my cocktail. "My plan is to do everything on the list before I settle down again. Merc says I want plug buddies. I looked it up and apparently it's a thing."

Fiona leans in, her interest piqued. "Plug buddies...sounds intriguing. I'm into this idea, big-time. Tell us more."

"I need to shake things up." I can't help but think about the intense sexual connection Peter and I shared. "Get my groove back. I think it'll be easier if I find some well-hung dudes to have sex with and avoid the obligations of a serious relationship. Merc thinks I'm not cut out for it, though."

Alex leans back, smiling. "I wasn't either. Exploring my options was my entire gameplan for my first trip to Europe. Your stupid brother thwarted it, though. Ruined me for everyone else with his big dick...*uh*, energy."

"Ew." I point at Alex. "I'll confess something to you ladies. A long time ago in Vegas, I hooked up with an architect I met at an LTZ show." I flick my eyes nervously to each of the ladies. "Best sex of my life. A lot of talk about destiny and seeing each other in Seattle but he left the next morning and ghosted me. Coincidentally, the ghost walked into my shop for a tattoo today."

Their eyes widen in unison.

"The same guy? After all these years?" Zoey's astonished.

"Yep, and he's a total player." I touch her hand. "While I don't want to revisit anything with him, I *do* want toe-curling sex. Hence, the Tryst List. My inspiration to find plug buddies."

Alex regards me skeptically. "Jace isn't going to like the idea of his big sister having sex with random guys. And if I tell him you're calling them plug buddies, I don't even know what to say."

"Excuse me?" My jaw drops open. "First of all, this is sacred girl space. You aren't allowed to tell him anything. Second, my brother has no room to talk, he banged—"

Zoey holds her hand up. "Nope. Gotta stop you."

We all laugh, but I'm mortified I almost snarked about my brother's whorish rockstar days in front of his fiancé. Clearly, my mind's a noodley mess. "Sheesh, sorry. Uncalled for."

"Zaney and I agreed to do something similar when LTZ first went on the road. I couldn't go through with it. His dick ruined me for life." Fiona waggles her eyebrows. "Sexual freedom sounds empowering, but be careful. Merc's right. You're a relationship girl and I don't want you to get hurt."

"Please don't worry. I'm determined to keep my emotions out of it." I suck in my lips.

Everyone looks at me like I'm a cute animal in the petting zoo.

"What?" I throw my hands up. "I'm a badass tattoo shop owner. I *should* be living life on the edge."

Zoey, who's nursing her infant son, Oliver, sips her cranberry juice. "There's no reason not to enjoy being single, Jordan. Just remember, whenever you're ready to settle down, rockstars, architects, it doesn't matter. You can have it all. A committed relationship and hot sex are not mutually exclusive. Trust."

I look at my girlfriends, all of whom are younger than me by a few years, and feel a bit emotionally stunted. I guess that's what you get for entering the dating world a decade after settling for a guy because good enough seemed better than taking a risk. "How do y'all do it? Have a killer relationship and a thriving love life?"

"Confidence, Jordan. We love our men, but we work hard not to lose ourselves in their lives. Equality is key, even if there are periods of imbalance." Alex leans back in the booth. I love her attitude so much. She gave my brother a run for his money until he wised up and put a ring on it. I can't wait for their wedding.

Zoey, who's had her own ups and downs with her husband, Ty, chimes in, "Communication. No holding anything back, no matter how intimidating it might be."

"Don't forget, *you're* the catch." Fiona, who's known her husband since birth, grips my hand. "Any man would be lucky to have a tryst with you."

With all this sisterly love, I feel a renewed sense of purpose.

"So, what's first on this list of yours?" Zoey tries to cover her mischievous grin.

I laugh, feeling lighter already. "For me to know and hopefully for none of you to find out. But trust me, it's going to be tantalizing. You'll know from the glow on my cheeks."

The night continues with more laughter and more secrets shared. I realize how lucky I am to have these women in my life, each strong, independent, and unapologetically themselves.

As we say our goodbyes, my mind is clear.

Peter Vander may have reentered my life, but he doesn't control it. I'm about to embark on a journey of my own making, one tryst at a time.

And this time, I'm playing by *my* rules.

Chapter Five

Outside The Salty Siren, the anticipation of seeing Jordan has my entire body buzzing.

In a few minutes, I'll be under her skilled hands, completing the next phase of the tattoo, which means considerably more than ink on skin. It's a bridge to a past I thought I'd lost.

My phone vibrates. I glance down to see my mother's name flash on the screen. *Fuck*. Her timing is impeccably bad. Taking a deep breath, I press the green button, bracing myself for the usual family drama.

"Peter, thank God you answered. We need to talk about your brothers." She's frantic, but that's nothing new.

My temples throb with aggravation. "I told you I was done."

"It's not only Lance. Kent's involved too." The phone is silent until she whines, "I didn't want to call, but there's nowhere else to turn."

I clench my fist, trying to keep my voice steady. "Mom, I'm not bailing them out. They're grown men. They need to face the consequences of their actions."

"But they're your *brothers*, Peter. You can't abandon them." Her desperation tugs at my heartstrings.

Except, I can.

The risk of being affiliated with them is too great. The background check for Project SoHo is insane, including financial transactions over the past few years. I don't want anything to tie me to my hoodlum brothers other than the blood we, unfortunately, share.

For once, I've got to put myself first.

"Family?" I pound my fist against the side of the building. "Those two make shitty life choices time after time and my own mother expects me to come to their rescue. No. *Fuck* no. I'm not doing it."

There's a pause on the line. I can almost hear her seething. "You think you're too good for us, don't you, Petey?"

"Oh, you're onto the next tactic. *Great.*" I roll my shoulders back. "Here's what I'm willing to do, Mom. I'll deposit two hundred and fifty thousand dollars into your bank account in exchange for putting an end to this fuckery once and for all. Use it however you want. Bail Kent and Lance out of whatever trouble they're in, I don't give a shit. If you're smart and save it, you'll have a slush fund. I'll have my lawyer send a contract tomorrow."

I hang up and set my phone to silent.

The weight of the conversation settles heavily on me. Although I know it's what's best for my own mental health, cutting them off for good means I won't have a family. I wish the decision gave me some relief, but it makes me sad.

On the other hand, this constant cycle of drama has pushed me to my limits. It's interfered with every major milestone of my life and I can't let it continue.

I'm in a no-win situation.

Glancing inside the tattoo shop, I see Jordan chatting with Merc. She's delectable in black leggings and a gray V-neck t-shirt hanging off her shoulder. She leans over the desk and—holy hell—I can nearly see her nipples through a tantalizingly plunging sheer pink-lace bra.

Goddammit. I was hoping to be a bit more respectable for this session and I'm hard as a fucking rock.

Again.

I wonder if she'll acknowledge me today. Or, if I should be upfront about my intention of reconnecting. Thinking back to Vegas, the last thing on my mind was meeting the woman of my dreams. I was supposed to be there for a simple conference. I treated myself to the LTZ concert with my last hundred bucks.

Then a tiny blonde dynamo slinked up to the bar and rocked my entire world. Anything seemed possible when she looked at me. Our chemistry...fucking *insane*. Every time our bodies fused it felt like our souls followed. Maybe it was the other way around, all I knew is I wanted to be with her forever. What happened between us was sublime. Deep. *Ethereal*.

Watching Jordan sleep against my chest, I actually envisioned whisking her away to a chapel to get married by Elvis. Thought we'd live happily ever after, or some shit.

The next morning, my mother's call burst my bubble and snapped me back to reality. My brothers were busted for dealing drugs a few weeks before their high school graduation. Not only were they expelled but faced serious felony charges.

Dad tried to take out a loan to pay for a lawyer and was rejected. The stress took a toll. He had a heart attack and nearly died.

It was a mess. Partially my fault. I had no choice but to leave her and fly home.

At first, I planned on getting Jordan's phone number. But I looked over at my blonde angel peacefully snoring in the bed and I couldn't do it. She was beautiful, kind and perfect and the sex...Jesus.

How could a piece of shit like me drag this goddess down? Jordan Deveraux was too good for me. Too decent to bring into my family's mess.

All thoughts of a future with her crashed down around me. She deserved more than being tied to me and my fucked-up situation.

I vowed to find her once I was worthy. However long it took.

Youthful immaturity took over. I tried to slip out undetected, but she caught me. I was a total dick to her because I was pissed and too emotionally stunted to have a conversation.

By the time I got my head out of my ass a few months later, I tracked Jordan down. It wasn't too hard finding her, considering her brother is so famous, which led to me figuring out her dad is one of the biggest tech entrepreneurs in the Pacific Northwest.

Jordan was all over Instagram. Her tattoo work. Podcasts. Appearances.

I knew how incredible she was but finding out more about her day-to-day life...*shit*.

This woman was so completely out of my league it wasn't even funny.

A few hours of online stalking later, I was crushed, but not surprised, to learn Jordan was already taken. Her boyfriend was some executive-type asshole named Cameron.

Didn't keep me from being obsessed with the girl, even though it seemed like our night didn't even matter to her.

My coping skills sucked. I couldn't exactly blame her for settling down with a guy she had more in common with. In many ways, losing her fueled my unrelenting drive and determination to build VA/VT into billion-dollar businesses.

I wanted to be *worthy*.

For a while, I tried to forget her by fucking my way through Seattle.

It was useless. No woman could ever compare to Jordan Deveraux.

As luck would have it, a couple years ago, LTZ's guitar player, Zane, and his wife, Fiona, offered me the job to design their club and restaurant. The project itself was pretty small, but I took it anyway on the off-chance I'd overhear some news.

One day, Jordan's brother, Jace, was helping Fiona go over some paperwork and I overheard him talking about his sister. Without a second thought, I booked an appointment, even though it was over a year wait.

I *had* to see her again.

Over the next year or so I lurked on her socials and picked up bits and pieces about her life and was delighted to learn she broke it off with Cameron. Jordan was finally single. When I came in three weeks ago, I had no idea how she'd react to seeing me. I certainly had no idea she wouldn't remember...or, if she did remember, ignore me.

Fuck it. She's going to see me outside creeping if I'm not careful.

I push open the door. Jordan and Merc greet me, and she leads me back to her room. We barely exchange two words as she shaves and cleans my arm. I lie down on my stomach because she's working on the underside of my arm. Soon the familiar sound of tattoo machine lulls me into a state of Zen.

Determined to make this session different, I decide to break the ice. Ease my way into reconnecting. Perhaps if I can jog her memory, I can apologize about Vegas. She may not remember, or even care. But I do.

I treated this goddess like shit and I want to make it right.

"Hey, Jordan." I look up at her, trying to sound casual. "The CBD soap is bomb."

Jesus. *Bomb?* My mojo is *waaaaay* off.

"Yeah. It's good stuff." She glances at me. Raises a judgy eyebrow and goes back to concentrating on her art.

Shit. "Yeah, well." I try again. "I've been looking forward to today."

Nothing. No reaction. The hum of the tattoo machine fills the air. I steal glances at her, wondering how to breach the wall of silence between us.

"About the design." I make another attempt. "It's really something special. You're incredibly talented."

Her lips curve into a hint of a smile but she doesn't look at me. "Thank you. I try to put a piece of myself in everything I do."

"You know, I did my research, I knew I had to have your art on my body." I take a deep breath, deciding to dive in. "There's something about your aesthetic that resonates with me."

Her hands still. "Oh?"

"Yeah." I can practically feel the tension emanating between us. "It'll be worth every penny."

Jesus. I'm so tongue-tied around her; I sound like a *dick*.

Jordan barely contains her eye roll and resumes working. "Well, I'm glad you like it."

As the session continues, I find myself babbling. Telling Jordan about my business, projects I've worked on here in Seattle, hoping she'll engage in conversation. I'd give anything for the chance to maybe, just maybe, reconnect emotionally with the woman who's haunted my thoughts for years.

But no, she's preoccupied and doesn't take my bait.

A few hours in, we take a break. I sit up and shake out my arm, watching her tidy up the station and refill her ink pots. "Is everything okay, Jordan? I've been chatting away and you've barely said a word."

"What?" She stops what she's doing and offers me a brief half smile. "Oh...yeah. Just a lot on my mind."

Aha. An opening. "I'm a good listener."

A strange expression passes across her face. She opens her mouth to say something, but Merc pops his head in the door. "Jordan, sorry to interrupt, but you've got an urgent call."

"Okay." Jordan's halfway out the door. "Peter, do you mind?"

"No problem at all. Take your time," I say to the air because she's already gone.

Left alone, I glance around the room. My gaze drifts to her sketchbook lying open on the counter. Driven by curiosity, I take a closer look. The pages are filled with intricate, colorful realistic mermaid designs that practically swim off the page.

There are plenty of other sketches. Lifelike faces. Floral filigrees. Landscapes. Each more impressive than the last.

The mermaids, though.

As an artist myself, I'm struck by the depth of her talent. Very few people are able to capture something essential. Something *real*. Not like her.

I continue to thumb through the pages and stumble upon something I instantly know I'm not supposed to see. It's a list, written in scrolly, calligraphy-like penmanship. At the top it says, *Jordan's Super-Secret Tryst List.*

Intrigued, I can't help but read through it. My desire to get some glimpse into her mind is too tempting, even though I'm invading her privacy.

1. *Stranded Somewhere*

2. *Public place...Dressing Room? Bar or Restaurant?*

3. *Mile High Club*

4. *Yacht*

5. *Make Video*

6. *Washing Machine*

7. *Abandoned Building*

8. *Balcony*

9. *Conference room or Office*

10. *Nature...Under the stars? Picnic?*

At first I'm confused, but I continue reading.

Willing to try: Anal (DP?), Bondage, Toys – experiment a little! Figure out how to squirt like Vegas. Hard no: Sex club. Threesomes.

Holy fucking shit. This is a goldmine—a Jordan Deveraux sexual instruction manual! She's created a list of places she wants to fuck and how she wants to get fucked.

At the bottom, in bold red letters, it says, "Stay single until you're through the list."

A realization hits me—Jordan is not only free from Cameron—she's on a mission. A mission to explore her sexuality with other men.

An impulsive and perhaps desperate plan forms in my mind, a bold and daring idea. It's a crazy thought, but it excites me unlike anything I can remember.

Jordan Deveraux, the woman who's been on my mind for years, is seeking adventure.

I take out my phone and quickly snap a picture of the list.

Because I'll be damned if I'm not going to help her check off every last item.

Chapter Six

I take a deep breath and rap on the door before entering.

Peter looks up, his expression hard to read. There's no denying the chemistry between us anymore. It's been bubbling stronger and stronger with each session.

Except, we're still playing this stupid game. It's our fourth and final appointment. Each time, he's danced closer to the flame of admission. I've held strong to revealing nothing.

If he doesn't cave today, I'm going to read him for filth. I'm sick of playing stupid, childish games.

"Good morning, Peter." I shake out my hands and pick up my tattoo machine. "Ready to finish this up?"

"Always ready for you to work your magic, Jordan," he replies with a smile.

Despite the weirdness surrounding our standoff, the hard edges of my initial resentment have softened. Peter's been nothing but courteous during his visits. His skin has been the ideal canvas for the intricate and expansive tattoo I've nearly finished.

"Let's get started." I motion to the chair. "Lie on your back."

"I like the sound of that." He winks at me.

Yeah. The flirting and innuendo between us has amplified. Taken on a life of its own, if I'm honest.

I start the machine and as the needle touches his skin to complete a detailed section of shading on the cathedral, our usual back-and-forth begins. "So, Peter, got any more big buildings you're planning to throw up around the city next year?"

"Just a few. It's important for me to make the skyline more interesting." He grins.

I can't help but glance at his crotch. Sure enough, he's hard.

Which makes me wet.

Refocusing on the design, I hope he didn't notice me ogling him. "Are you planning on adding some color? Seattle's gray enough as it is without more modern, steel monstrosities."

"I'll consider it." He cocks an eyebrow. "Only if you promise to design some mermaids for me to incorporate into the foundation of the new Amazon building."

"I don't mix my mermaids with concrete. They prefer the open sea," I retort, smiling despite myself.

He watches me shade a sensitive area on his inner arm. "Fair enough. But if you ever change your mind..."

"Thanks, but I'll stick to skin. It's more...pliable." I resume my focus on my art.

We're silent for a long time as I continue working, the buzz of the tattoo machine a constant undercurrent to the mounting tension between us. With only another couple of hours until the piece is completed, my stomach feels hollow. Despite our banter, I hate what he did to me then. I also hate how dishonest we're being with each other now.

On the other hand...

I don't want this to end.

"How'd you get into tattooing?" Peter keeps his eye on where the needle decorates his skin.

"It found me more than I found it," I reiterate something I said practically verbatim to him in Vegas. It's become my go-to explanation in any interview I do, so it comes in handy when customers try to make small talk. "Art's been my thing since I could hold a crayon. Tattooing is a natural progression. A way to make it more accessible to the masses."

Our eyes meet. We both stare at each other for easily a minute. Understanding passes between us.

I know. *He* knows. It's all out there.

I wait...

But he looks away and the moment dissipates into thin air. "Makes sense. Your talent certainly speaks for itself."

Fuck this. *Fuck* him. He had his chance...

I resume my shading, determined to finish with him as quickly as possible. The sooner I'm done, the sooner I can move on with my life. "Thanks. But flattery won't get you a discount."

"I wouldn't dream of it." His voice is somewhat cautious. "I value the artist too much."

I roll my eyes when I'm certain he's not looking. What a fucking crock.

As the session winds to a close in silence, I realize I'm not going to say anything. I'm going to let him get up and walk out the door like he did in Vegas. This time, however, I'm not going to jump into an unfulfilling relationship to try and forget him.

The Tryst List beckons, after all.

I finish his tattoo, wipe his arm off and set my machine down.

"Jordan..." Peter peers up at me, a knowing glimmer in his eye. "*Deveraux*. Any relation to Jace Deveraux from Less Than Zero?"

I stiffen slightly. Holy shit, is he finally going to acknowledge he's Vegas guy? "Yeah, he's my brother. Why?"

"Just curious." He swallows, his eyes shifting between me and his arm. "I...uh...we have mutual people in common. I designed The Mission and Gus, Zane and Fiona Rocks' businesses. Will you be at the opening?"

I nod, trying to keep my composure. "Of course. I'll be there with my family."

We stare at each other.

I straighten my back and narrow my eyes defiantly, daring him to continue.

Peter sucks his lips through his perfect, white teeth. Lets out a heavy sigh. Then smiles. Feebly. "I know it's you, Jordan."

I freeze. My heart flutters like a hummingbird's wings. I knew it. I fucking *knew* it. All this time, through niceties and flattery, he's been toying with me. The realization leaves me disoriented and speechless as he continues speaking.

"Just like you know it's me. How could we ever forget the greatest night of our lives?" He sits up in all his muscled, shirtless glory.

His eyes search mine for a reaction.

My jaw sets. I break eye contact. I'm fucking pissed.

Greatest night of our *lives*? What an asshole. If it was great, why did he leave so abruptly? How has he sat in my chair for nearly thirty hours without apologizing for what he did?

Every single ounce of hurt and embarrassment I felt rushes back tenfold.

I won't show him though. Methodically, I clean and bandage his arm without responding to his big reveal.

I need to regain my composure. Behave professionally and complete this job.

Because I'm not putting myself through this. I need him gone. "Peter, I'm not sure what you mean. While it's nice you've finally acknowledged me, I think you have a very skewed memory. Your greatest night happens to be my worst. Every second you've sat in this chair has been torture. Now, I've done my best to be polite and endure your innuendoes and veiled references because it's my job. But I'm ecstatic today is your last day." I take a deep breath and continue, "After you walk out the door, you're no longer welcome at The Salty Siren."

Peter's face crumples with each word I say. By the time I'm done speaking, he's looking at the floor like a shamed child, his fists flexing and releasing by his sides.

I turn back to my station and clean up, ignoring him as I bustle around the room. I can feel him watching me, but I don't turn around. This goes on for a couple of minutes to the point where I'm about to ask him to get lost.

"Jordan?" His voice is quiet.

I glance over my shoulder at him. "Yeah?"

"That night was really your worst?" He's fully dressed, coat and everything. "I don't understand."

My teeth clench. Are men always this obtuse? "Do I seriously need to spell it out for you? Maybe take some time and give the situation some self-introspective thought."

We stare at each other. Well, he stares. I glare.

"I don't need to. It's because I left suddenly. With no explanation." Peter states this as a fact, not a question. No apology. No explanation.

I look up to the ceiling, count to ten then suck it up and face him. "I recognized you the second you walked in. Do you know how embarrassing it was? How hard it's been to... The man who..." I shake my head miserably at the entire situation and my inability to form a coherent sentence.

"Jordan..." He grips my shoulder.

I shrug him away. "Don't touch me."

Seconds later, the door bursts open. Merc and Angus Courie, a visiting artist from Finland, muscle their way in to check on me. Every one of my tattooing rooms are outfitted with discreet audio devices to ensure artist safety. Clients even sign a waiver agreeing to the monitoring.

"Time to go, Mr. Vander." Merc points to the door. "I warned you on the first day Jordan does not date her clients. As she said earlier, you are not welcome anymore. Please leave or the police will be called."

I can't help but notice Peter's white as snow. His eyes are haunted and it looks like he's about to throw up. "I'm so, so sorry, Jordan. I didn't mean to make you feel unsafe. I'm sorry about—everything."

Then he's gone. Poof. Just like I wanted.

Merc enfolds me into his arms. "You okay?"

"Yeah. I'm assuming you heard everything." I cling to him and bury my face in his chest.

He pets my hair. "I have to wonder what his angle was. It's all incredibly strange."

"Did you think he was hurting me?" I pull away and move toward the open door, watching Angus make sure it's locked.

Merc stands beside me. "Only your heart, babes. I don't think he's a physical threat."

"No, he's not," I agree. "You've nailed it, as always."

"Well, the tattoo is done and so is he. Are you relieved?" Merc throws an arm around my shoulders. "Maybe we should go out. Take your mind off things."

I lean into him. "You're the best. Thanks for looking out for me. I think I'd rather go home."

Ten minutes later, I'm driving to my condo in my Mercedes GLE Coupe, reflecting on how the day turned to shit. Wondering how to reconcile the immense sense of loss currently invading my body.

It's hard to believe the Vegas Guy chapter is finally and permanently closed. No more grudges. No more what-ifs.

No more anything.

It's for the best.

Having Peter as a client was too distracting. I stagnated. Constantly thinking about him. Obsessing about whether he recognized me. Making excuses for not embarking upon my Tryst List.

Everything changes tomorrow.

He may live in my fantasies, but I'm not going to let anything about that man interfere with me.

Ever. Again.

That's a promise.

Chapter Seven

"Take them off."

My voice echoes in the hotel suite as I approach beautiful, sassy Jordan from Seattle. My every fantasy come to life. Huge natural tits. Tiny little thing.

God, I can lift her with one arm. The positions I'll be able to fuck her in has me nearly coming in my pants.

Her hip rests against the arm of the couch. One bare leg is crossed over her knee. Discarded spiky silver sandals are haphazardly tangled on the floor below her.

She bites her finger. "Take what off?"

I stand in front of her, push her hair behind her shoulder and kiss her neck. "Actually, I'll do it."

"Do what?" She grabs my T-shirt, pulling me toward her. Uncrosses her legs. Smiles at me wickedly.

My hands run down the length of her waist, past her hips to the hem of her silky, white dress, which I grip and yank up, exposing her thin, muscular thighs and a hint of her white thong. "This."

"Hmmm. That's all?" She loops her arms around my neck and hovers her pink lips against mine. Widens her legs and hooks them around my thighs to draw me toward her.

"Not even close," I whisper and press my mouth against hers.

A ragged moan escapes as our tongues meet. I glide my hands between her legs and slip my thumbs under the sliver of her panties finding her soaking wet as our mouths mash hungrily. She clings to my shirt and cries out when I find her clit. I kiss down her neck and wiggle my thumb until she's squirming and panting, squeezing her thighs around my hips.

Hooking my fingers on her thong, I step back and slide it down her legs and toss it somewhere behind me. Gripping the edge of her dress with both hands, I tug it up and over her head. Her delectable breasts spill out. Groaning, I cup them and stroke her already taut, brown nipples into puckered peaks.

"You're fucking perfect," I rasp and kneel before her, gazing up into her emerald eyes.

She brazenly spreads her legs and rests her dainty, red-tipped toes on each shoulder. "No, I'm fucking wet."

"Yes, you are. And you smell delicious." Her pink pussy is inches from my face, glistening with arousal.

I lean over to lick her slit, drinking down her sweet nectar before settling in for my feast. She threads her fingers through my long hair and winds it around her wrist, keeping my mouth captive against her folds. I lap, suck and taste every part of her as I grasp her hips to hold her in place.

"Ohmygod." Her legs are draped over my shoulders, and she leans across the back of the couch, watching me eat her out. "You're so good at this."

She pinches her nipples and my cock nearly explodes, but it's not my time yet. I need to get her there first. I suck her swollen clit between my lips and flick my tongue back and forth against it, occasionally humming for good measure. It's not long before her thighs start to quiver and her breath is labored in short little spurts.

I slip two fingers deep inside her and stroke her spongy little nerve bundle while I continue to devour her. Always watching to make sure she likes what I'm doing as I learn her body. She gasps and winces beautifully, bucking against my lips, seeking her pleasure.

"That's it, sweetheart. Do you like this?" I kiss her clit and swirl my tongue against it. Plunge my fingers inside her.

"God, yes. Don't stop." She holds my face against her pussy. "Never stop. Oh holy shit."

"I could do this all night." I nearly weep at how stunning she is.

On the brink of nirvana, Jordan writhes unabashedly. Her chest rises and falls erratically. She scrapes her nails along my scalp as her heels dig into my back. Her blonde hair is tangled and disheveled, makeup is smeared under her eyes. I add a third finger and her pussy grips them like a vise. With my free hand, I push her thigh up and out and bury my face in her, lapping and feasting until cute little mewls morph into high-pitched wails and she lets go—convulsing around me.

I'm pretty sure the entire hotel floor can hear her.

I withdraw my fingers but pepper persistent kisses on her clit as she comes down and her breathing calms. My cock strains against my jeans, aching to find its way inside her, but there'll be time for that later. I know staving off pleasure will make my release all the more spectacular. Something instinctive yearns to show her how to do the same—push her to her limits. Help her know what her body is truly capable of.

Standing, I smooth my hands up her thighs and step in between her legs. She watches me strip through hooded, satiated eyes.

My voice is strained as I seek permission from this gorgeous woman. "Is this okay?"

"Yes." She leans up on her elbows. "It's your turn."

Pumping my cock from root to tip, she watches me tap the crown on her lips. "Take me all the way to the back of your throat."

"It's not going to fit." Her wide eyes flick up to mine. "You're too big."

"You can do it." I feed it to her and her lips stretch around me until she gags.

Her hot, wet mouth is like liquid velvet. Fuck, what she's doing with her tongue...holy fucking shit. God, she's swallowing the head of my cock...

My eyes practically roll back in my head and all thoughts of withholding my orgasm fly out the window. I grip her cheeks with my palms and fuck her mouth and she takes it. Her hands cup my ass, she pulls me to her and I'm done...

*B*UZZ. BUZZ. BUZZ.

BUZZ. BUZZ. BUZZ.

I'm jolted awake from my vivid dream by an ungodly sound with my hand wrapped around my wet cock. Jesus. I've made a mess.

BUZZ. BUZZ. BUZZ.

What the actual fuck. Is someone at my door?

BUZZ. BUZZ. BUZZ.

Yep. Someone's trying to reach me. I'm going to kill the doorman for letting them up.

After cleaning the sticky mess off my hand and dick with the sheet, I reluctantly get out of bed and throw on some joggers. Memories of fucking Jordan in Vegas give way to reality and the weight of yesterday's events presses heavily on my chest.

Our conversation—if you could call it that—took a turn I didn't expect.

My big reveal was incredibly clumsy and about as far away from how I'd pictured it. In my mind, I'd out myself, we'd have a chuckle, reminisce about crazy nights in Vegas and I'd ask her out. Use her Tryst List as a key to fulfilling her fantasies and make her fall in love with me.

Because I'm hopelessly in love with her.

In retrospect, it was a horrible plan.

While I've always been ashamed of how I left her all those years ago, I had no idea how deeply my actions hurt her to the core. For years, I've been pining for Jordan while her resentment toward me has been building. Then I show up for a tattoo and expect—what? A glorious reunion?

Fuck. I've handled this situation terribly. Something magical could have blossomed between us and I've only made everything worse.

Fuck times two. I leave for London tomorrow and I won't get the chance to apologize before I go. Although,

I doubt she'd be amenable to seeing me after throwing me out of her shop.

Doesn't mean I'm giving up.

Fuck. What do I do?

The sharp buzz of the doorbell reminds me of why I was rudely wakened from my favorite wet dream about her. Glancing at the video feed of my security cameras, I'm perturbed to find my mother on the other side. Jesus Christ. Taking a deep breath to steel myself, I open the door.

"Peter, this contract you sent, it's ridiculous! You actually want all of us to stop contacting you?" Mom, who looks like she's aged a dozen years since the last time I saw her, bursts through the door, clutching the settlement agreement I had drawn up in her fist. "I'm not signing this."

I pinch the bridge of my nose with my fingers. "Then don't sign it. It's your choice. I'm not giving you or anyone else in the family money without some conditions."

"You don't trust your own family?" She's righteously aghast.

"It's not about trust, Mom. It's about accountability." I fold my arms across my bare chest. "Lance and Kent are adults. They need to take responsibility for their choices. So are you and Dad. This 'use Peter for his bank account' can't continue. I won't be part of it."

She glances around my open-plan condo, which is located in a building I designed. Through her eyes, she sees wealth and opulence, but every single thing in my place—from the natural reclaimed materials to the non-toxic paint to the bio-ethanol fireplace is a testament to sustainable luxury.

"You live like a king and you want to keep us down. Is that it?" She throws the agreement on the floor. "Look at this place."

I'm mentally exhausted from having this same conversation over and over. "I work hard for what I have and I'm about to give you a quarter of a million dollars. How is that keeping you down? Oh, and since you asked, yes...I have the money because I designed this building and have developed technology that's changing the world."

"You think you're better than us, don't you?" She slides her hand up the wall, unimpressed.

I need her to go. Already feeling like shit about how I handled things with Jordan, I don't need my own mother to drag me down even further. "I'm not going down this ridiculous path. If you want the money, it's on my terms. It's that simple. What's it gonna be?"

"Fine, I'll sign your damn contract. Don't think this makes you a good son, though," she sneers, making me wonder why the hell I'm doing this in the first place. She snatches the agreement from the ground. "Gotta pen?"

I grab one from my junk drawer. "Here."

We both sign it and I tuck it into my laptop bag. Then I open my bank app to make the transfer.

"I'm taking that contract with me." She reaches for my bag.

I bring my hand down to stop her. "No, I'll send a copy when I'm in the office."

"Owww." She yanks her arm away. "That hurt."

"I didn't even touch you." I set my phone down because warning bells go off in my head. I've learned to trust my gut and it's practically screaming this is all a bad idea. I shouldn't need to get an agreement with my own mother to stop her from asking me for money.

But what's done is done. She signed it.

"Did you wire the money?" Mom rubs her wrist, as if she's in some discomfort.

I pick up my phone and click send. "It'll be in your account by tomorrow."

"Thank you." She grabs her purse and moves toward the door. "It didn't have to come to this, you know."

"Come to what?" My shoulders tense, on edge every time I'm around any of my family.

"Nothing. Never mind." She practically sprints toward the door and slips out.

This conversation with my mother—like all conversations over the past decade—leaves me drained. In some weird way, it's also solidified my resolve.

Instinct tells me to give Jordan some space.

After London, I'll find a way to fix things.

My only hope is she doesn't start on her Tryst List before I return.

I wouldn't forgive myself if I pushed her into another guy's arms.

Again.

Chapter Eight

It's weird being single during the holidays.

I broke up with Cameron not quite a year ago. Sadly, the only thing I miss about him is having a date at family gatherings. He was courteous, polite, helped in the kitchen and loved all our little traditions.

Too bad he sucked as a partner and was horrible in bed.

God, I'm a bitch.

No, I'm not.

I'm crass, but it's all true. We didn't work. Cameron wasn't in love with me, he wanted to be near my pops. Every tech nerd in Seattle loses their shit over him, I was merely his liaison.

To be fair, my mind was always elsewhere.

Vegas.

"You look beautiful, sweetheart." My mom, Grace, brushes a piece of lint off my charcoal sweater dress, which I've paired with knee-high black boots.

She's always stylish perfection. Tonight, she wears a rust silk shirt paired with black wool slacks. Not a speck of food on her, though she and my sister Jen have been cooking all day. "Everything looks fantastic, Mom. My stomach is growling."

The Thanksgiving table at my parents' house is, as always, a masterpiece of modern opulence. A reflection of my mom's superior interior design skills. The centerpiece is a stunning arrangement of vibrant chrysanthemums, delicate dahlias, and exotic orchids artfully arranged in a sleek, geometric vase. It's flanked by slender, elegant candles in minimalist holders, which cast a warm, inviting glow.

As we gather around the dining table, I find myself unexpectedly gulping back tears. It's been such a transitional year; I really needed this day off with my family. The tantalizing aroma of my mom's cooking is comfort personified—a blend of familiar scents that always signifies love and togetherness.

"You've outdone yourself, Gracie." My pops joins us and admires the golden-brown turkey surrounded by dishes of creamy mashed potatoes, green beans, fresh-baked rolls and my favorite—the traditional Deveraux sage stuffing recipe passed down from my grandma.

Mom pours him a glass of wine. "I'm happy to do it, it's my favorite time of year."

"How in the heck do you fold these, Jason?" Becca holds up the gold linen napkin, which has been twisted into some sort of sleek, geometric shape. "Every year, it's something new."

Dad laughs. "Trade secret, my dear. I'm not about to lose one of my holiday jobs."

"You're such a geek, Dad." I lean over and kiss his cheek. For a man as influential as Jeff Bezos, he's about as down-to-earth as it gets.

Unlike Jeff Bezos, who dumped his first love for an actress, he loves my mom with all his heart. Their marriage is one I aspire to.

I look over at Becca and Jen, who've been happily coupled for years. Though they're not with us today, my sister Jaylynn married her high school sweetheart years ago. Jace and Alex, who've had a rough year, decided to recuperate in Italy with their daughter for a few weeks.

Suffice it to say, as the only single person in our clan, I'm lonely, even though I'm amongst people who love me.

"Jordan, will you please pass the cranberry sauce?" Mom wiggles her fingers at me from across the table.

"Sure." I hand her the bowl, mustering a smile.

My mind drifts to Peter. I wonder what he's doing today. Probably spending time with his own family. I shake my thoughts of him away, annoyed by the unresolved feelings, which seem to consume my every thought.

I'm smarter than this.

Dad carves the turkey with practiced ease, distributing slices onto each plate. "So, sweetheart, how's the shop doing? Any interesting clients lately?"

"It's good. Me and everyone else are booked months in advance." I force a smile. "I've had some interesting projects, yeah."

My sister Jennifer, or "Jen," as she prefers to be called, is my most staunch supporter. "Tattooing is such an intimate art form. Your work gets better every year."

I nod. "Thank you. I appreciate you saying that. Every tattoo has its own story. One of the best parts of the job is getting to know the clients and learning the reasons behind the art. Although, most people want mermaids..."

"Your mermaids are stunning. They made you famous, but it's always nice to keep your creative juices going." Dad kisses my temple. "I saw the latest feature in *Inked*. I'm proud of you for being modest, but I'm also going to toot your horn." He looks around the table. "Our Jordan is the third highest-paid tattoo artist in the entire world. Her waitlist is well over a year."

I hold my hand up. "Stop, Dad. Seriously."

"He's proud, sweetie." Mom beams at me. "We all are."

"How's everything going at the ranch?" I gesture with my fork at Jen, hoping to divert focus off me.

It works. As we eat, Jen and Becca excitedly fill us in about their latest project on Jace and Alex's property. My folks talk about plans to visit my grandparents in Sweden next year. I'm listening, but admittedly, my mind wanders to Peter.

He's got a hold on me I can't explain.

Once the table is cleared and the dishes are done, I decide to take a quiet moment in my favorite spot at the house—the expansive covered back porch overlooking Lake Washington. Sitting under a heater and wrapped in a cozy blanket, I take out the page I tore out of my sketchbook, unfold it and look it over.

My Tryst List. It feels like forever ago when I came up with this scheme. Before Peter walked back in my life and shook it up, much to my annoyance. Everything had been going to plan. I was feisty and ready to reclaim my sexuality and live life by my terms.

He shows up and I'm back to fucking square one.

What's wrong with me?

I lean back, shut my eyes, and memories of the night consume me.

The neon lights of Vegas glow through the curtains as I lie next to him, tangled in the white sheets of the hotel bed. The air is heavy with the scent of our passion. My skin tingles from hours of him touching, kissing, and worshipping every part of my body. Despite the whirlwind of meeting him to this moment, everything feels tranquil, almost surreal.

His muscular arm is wrapped protectively around me. The warmth of his body is comforting. I'm at peace, with my head resting on his chest. I've found my person in the most cliché manner, but it doesn't matter.

We're meant to be. Which sounds crazy but feels saner than anything I've ever known.

"You know..." His voice is a low rumble. "I haven't felt like this...well, ever."

I lift my head to look at him, his eyes reflect a sincerity that sends a flutter through my heart. "Me neither," I admit, feeling vulnerable.

"There's something about you, Jordan." He carefully brushes a strand of hair from my face. "It's like you've walked into my life and turned it upside down."

I can't help but smile, my cheeks flushing with happiness and a tinge of disbelief. "In a good way, I hope."

"In the best way." His lips graze mine. "I came to Vegas expecting a mundane conference. Instead, I find you. It's like fate had a hand in us meeting."

Fate. Destiny. Could this really be something more than a chance encounter?

He continues, his voice tender yet earnest. "I don't know what the future holds, but I know I want you in it. These few hours with you have been more real than anything I've ever experienced in my life."

"I feel the same way," I whisper, allowing myself to get lost in the moment.

He pulls me closer and our lips meet in a tender kiss, a promise of something deeper than a night of sex in a Vegas hotel room.

For the rest of the night, in between making love and fucking—because we do both, he and I talk about everything and nothing. The world outside fades away. We share silly snippets of our lives. Tease each other. Learn about our likes and dislikes. Even though we don't talk much about our families or our professions, it doesn't matter. With each word, the bond between us grows stronger, more tangible.

His affection is unwavering. Peter makes me feel cherished, understood. He says everything I've ever wanted to hear, everything I didn't even know I needed.

I find myself believing in the possibility of a future with Peter. In a city known for its fleeting pleasures, we've found something rare and profound...

I barely notice Jen join me. "Penny for your thoughts?"

"You'll need a lot more than a penny." I fold the list and tuck it away. "I'm thinking about...stuff. You know, life."

Jen leans her head on my shoulder. "This about the client whose tattoo you finished last month? Peter, was it? Vegas guy."

"What a little bitch." I shake my head but can't help but smile a bit. "I knew I shouldn't have let Becca befriend Merc. He has a big fucking mouth."

She squeezes my arm. "He's worried about you. He said there was an incident..."

"Yeah." I nod, feeling a knot form in my stomach. "I kicked him out of the shop. It was a mess."

"Care to share?" she probes.

I recount what happened and the flood of emotions it's unleashed. Jen listens intently, her hand resting reassuringly on mine.

"Feelings are tricky." Jen looks off into the distance. "But sometimes, they're the best guide we have. He's touched you deeply. It's not really about him, though. It's about you."

"I'm actually confused." I glance at the Tryst List. "I made this to move on from Cameron. But I'm not sure if it's him I'm moving on from."

We stay snuggled for a few minutes, staring at the lake.

"My advice is to talk to Peter. Clear the air." Jen gets up to go back inside. "Stop all the bullshit and dancing around. You might not like what you hear, but at least you won't be in limbo. There's nothing worse."

I consider her words, but the idea of facing Peter is daunting. "I doubt he'll want to talk to me after being humiliated at my shop. It's been a few weeks and I've heard nothing."

"Well, you won't know unless you try." Jen hovers in the doorway. "The point is, there's no rush. We're knee deep in the holidays. Make it a New Year's resolution."

"Yeah..." I'm saved from answering when my parents and Becca join us, bringing coffee and pie.

We spend the rest of the evening talking, laughing, and sharing stories, though, in the back of my mind, Peter lingers. Jen's right. Of course I need to talk to Peter. I can't keep running from it.

I'm going to forget about this mess for a while and enjoy some time with my friends and family. I have a busy schedule and lots of events to attend. The last one being the opening of Gus and The Mission on New Years' Eve.

Peter will be there. I'll get some answers then.

Or closure.

Either way, it'll be the perfect way to start a new year.

Chapter Nine

Growing up in a small rural town in Washington, I was surrounded by people who had no interest in traveling.

My family certainly didn't.

The prospect of getting on a plane was unfathomable, let alone jetting off to cities all over the world for work.

When I left the country the first time, the thrill was intoxicating. There was a sense of disbelief and wonder in those early days of success—the realization I was doing what I loved, and people were willing to pay significant sums of money for my vision and expertise. Those initial trips were more than work, they were adventures that shaped me into the man I am today.

This morning, however, I'm grateful to be seated in the familiar conference room at the Seattle headquarters of VA/VT.

The London trip was a whirlwind of stress. Walking the site with the stakeholders helped me comprehend the impact Project SoHo is going to have. Not only will it change the blueprint of the historical city, my team's part in the process is substantially more complicated than designing and building structures.

It's infinitely bigger than anything I or anyone in my firm has ever worked on.

Today's an all-hands-on-deck meeting to go over every project we're working on throughout the company. Everyone is bustling with energy as my Project SoHo team and I prepare to debrief about our London trip. The staff take their seats, eager to hear about our experiences and next steps.

"Alright, everyone, let's get started." I take my place at the head of the conference table. "First off, I want to thank Rose, Pip, and Fabiola for their incredible work in London. It's been a grueling four weeks, but we've made significant progress."

On cue, Rose starts the presentation. "The panel was quite impressed with our proposal. Over the three-week period, we had several in-depth discussions about our design and the sustainable aspects we're incorporating. We were also able to demonstrate how VT software will integrate the process."

"Yeah, the feedback was overwhelmingly positive. They focused mostly on the green rooftop and the energy-efficient lighting system," Pip enthusiastically chimes in. "My take is, compared to the other contenders, we seem to have the edge because of the technology innovation we're bringing to the table."

"It's true. We've established key contacts in London who support our vision. Being there was...incredible. To think VA/VT will potentially be responsible for such a prominent landmark..." Fabiola wipes a tear from the corner of her eye. "I'm proud to be part of this. Thank you, Peter for trusting us."

I clap my hands and nod at my three colleagues. "I couldn't have done it without you. Now, the next steps are crucial. We're refining our proposal based on the feedback and preparing for the final in-person presentation in the spring. There's a lot of work ahead of us, but let's make this project a reality."

The three of us recount the long days of meetings, the opulent dinners and map out the ambitious plan to win this job. We have a long road ahead of us, but the room reverberates with energy as the presentation comes to an end.

"So, I have to share this." Fabiola has a mischievous glint in her eye as we wrap things up. "We met this British politician during a reception—you'd know who he is if you saw him. Very stiff-upper-lip. But you won't believe it, he developed quite the crush on Rose."

Rose's face turns beet red.

The room erupts in laughter and Fabiola rolls her eyes playfully. "He was *fascinated* by the concept of sustainable architecture. Kept asking her all sorts of questions because he was *fascinated*."

Pip snorts with laughter. "Oh, it was something! I don't think I've heard the word *'fascinated'* as much in my life. The way he was looking at her, I thought he was going to propose a green energy alliance right there!"

"Well, it certainly helped in getting his attention on our project." Fabiola puts her arm around Rose. "Maybe you should lead all our British negotiations from now on."

Rose clearly doesn't mind the teasing. "I'll consider it if it means advancing our cause."

"I'd love to get an update on the other projects." I'm still laughing but want to move things along. "We've got a lot lined up. I'll start. The eco-friendly residential complex in downtown Seattle is moving into the planning phase, the renovation of the old hotel on Pike Street is underway and my part in the Vegas project is nearly complete, though I'll be checking on the installation at some point next year."

As we delve into the specifics of our ongoing projects, I feel a huge sense of pride in my team. Their dedication and talent are what drive my firm forward. I'm closer to these people than I am my own family.

Before we wrap up, the conversation shifts to the upcoming opening of Gus and The Mission.

"Alright." I glance around the table at my staff. "We need to decide who's going to accompany me to the event at The Mission. It's an important networking opportunity, and I think it would be beneficial for one of you to come with."

There's a murmur of agreement around the table. The opening isn't just any event, it's a chance to mingle with some of the most influential people in the city, eat an amazing dinner and see Seattle's most famous rock band in an intimate setting.

"How about we make it interesting?" Pip waves his hand wildly. "Let's write down names and draw from a hat. Keeps it fair and spontaneous."

Fabiola nods in agreement. "I'm in. Let's do it."

Ever efficient, Rose hands me an empty box and passes around notepads. "Everyone write your name and fold it once in half."

There's a lighthearted energy in the room as I stroll around the perimeter of the conference table collecting the folded pieces of paper. I shake the box and shuffle it around.

"Okay, here goes." I reach in the box and pull out a name, unfold the paper and read the name aloud. "Rose."

A round of applause and cheers erupt from the team.

"Well, it looks like you're my plus-one for the evening, Rose." I clap my hands and pump my fist in the air.

"Me?" Rose is visibly shocked but her face steels with composure. "Cool. It'll be a great opportunity to network and showcase our work."

Fabiola shrieks with laughter. "Oh, Rose. I adore you. Showcase our work. You're going to lose your mind when you meet Tyson Rainier, aren't you?"

"Uh..." Rose blushes and sighs heavily. "Yeah. He's *dreamy.*"

I make a mental note to make sure Fiona and Zane give her a little behind the scenes LTZ experience. She's worked hard, often pulling all-nighters to make Project SoHo possible. I'm happy to be able to do something nice for someone who clearly deserves it.

On the way to my office after the meeting, my sense of accomplishment gives way to a twinge of apprehension. The New Year's Eve event is more than a professional commitment, it's a chance to see Jordan after our last tumultuous encounter.

I haven't made contact since she threw me out of her shop. It's been a few weeks now. Maybe she's calmed down enough for us to have a conversation.

Staring out at the city, my mind drifts to that night...

She fits perfectly against me, her curves melding into my side as if our bodies were engineered to lock together this way. I run my fingers through her hair, feeling a sense of protectiveness and affection unlike anything I've ever experienced.

The room is charged with an energy that transcends physical desire. We've talked, shared, and laughed, dove into conversations about our favorite sports teams, our past dating history, and the futures we both envision. With each word, the bond between us deepens, turning our initial physical attraction into something resonant and meaningful.

"I want this to continue once we're home in Seattle," I confess, surprising myself by stating the truth.

She lifts her gaze to meet mine. I see a reflection of my own unexpected emotions. "I feel the same. It's as if everything before this was leading me to this moment with you."

No one has ever said anything like that to me. A sense of profound happiness washes over me.

"You're remarkable." I trace her perky brown nipple with my finger. "You're gorgeous, of course but it's not

only in how you look. It's who you are—your passion, your intelligence. I feel like I've known you forever."

She giggles and reaches for my hardening shaft. "Right? And I feel like your cock was meant to live inside me forever."

"You're insatiable. And right. He's meant to live inside you, baby. Let's make that happen." Dawn is breaking when I raise her leg over my hip and slide inside her for the umpteenth time. "Fuck you feel so good. I wish we didn't ever have to leave this room. If only we could pause time, right here, right now."

"Yeah..." Her eyes flutter closed when I roll my pelvis against hers. "Peter, I...uh..."

"You don't need to say anything. I feel it too." I band my arm around her.

Holding her tightly against me as we work ourselves toward yet another climax, I let myself believe in the potential of our future. It's been a night of unexpected good fortune—I've met a woman who understands me in ways I didn't know were possible.

Jordan Deveraux is the one.

My memory of Vegas morphs into what happened at The Salty Siren. The aftermath hovers around me like a lingering fog. An image of her, fierce and hurt as she ordered me out of her shop, haunts me.

Opposing memories. Confusing feelings. I can't shake the profound regret of how good things could have been if I hadn't fucked things up.

Uncertain about how to make things right, I've lamented the distance between us every single day. It can't be too late. The last time I dropped off the planet, I lost her. By the time I pulled my head out of my ass, she had a serious boyfriend.

Fuck.

Fuck. Fuck. *Fuck.*

This time it could be worse. Another nagging thought is that Tryst List. What if she's indulged in her fantasies with other guys?

It makes me want to punch a wall. No, *worse.*

I'm the one who should fulfill those fantasies. *Me.*

Only fucking me.

Decision made. I'm going to talk to her on New Year's Eve. Give it another shot.

My plan is simple. Approach her with humility. She needs to know why I walked away from her all those years ago. How I've changed and grown. Most of all, she needs to understand my feelings for her are genuine.

Convincing Jordan won't be easy. She's guarded, rightfully so, and I'm the last person she wants to be vulnerable with. But if there's even the slightest chance I can regain her trust, isn't it worth trying?

My redemption arc starts at the opening of The Mission.

Everything's at stake.

I'm either going to mend what's been broken...or lose Jordan forever.

Chapter Ten

The atmosphere at Gus is unbelievable.

A curated group of Seattle elite are in attendance from famous musicians to actors to the mayor.

I'm proud of my friend. Fiona's dream is finally coming true. Gus is likely to be the first Michelin-starred restaurant in the Pacific Northwest and no one deserves it more than her.

She greets everyone before dinner service as Zane looks on proudly. From the open-plan kitchen adjacent to the dining room, aromas of a high-end feast waft about. The restaurant itself is buzzing with the chatter and laughter of guests with a distinct sense of celebration.

I'm trying to enjoy the lively scene by hanging out with my parents and Carter Pope, Zane's rockstar father. Jace and Alex are deep in conversation with Ty and Zoey. Connor and his wife, Ronni are chatting with Jen and Becca.

As cool as it to be on the band's short list, I'm unusually fidgety because I've made a rookie mistake. It's a bit humiliating at my age to attend an event like this with my folks. I should have brought Merc or Kali as my date. LTZ is a close-knit closed-rank bunch and while I adore everyone, I feel like the odd woman out.

Mom turns to me. "Jordy, you seem restless. Are you having a good time?"

"Yeah, of course. It's great to see everyone happy." I take a sip of my cocktail. "I hope we sit down to dinner soon; I'm starving."

She raises a skeptical eyebrow but doesn't say anything else. I get it. My attempts at paying attention to the conversations around me are futile. I can't stop glancing at the entrance. Peter's not here yet and I wonder if he has the balls to show up and face me. Every time the door opens, my heart races, only to settle down when it's not him.

Fiona, who's working the room like a pro, approaches and hugs her father-in-law. "You slipped in without saying hi, Carter."

"This is your night; I didn't want to bug you." He tugs on her long pink braid.

"You guys did an amazing job with the renovation." My pops gestures to the gorgeous floating bar. "Thank you for including us."

I hadn't noticed it before and I wonder, is that a detail that Peter designed?

Jesus, I *suck*. A grown woman obsessing about a man who...*argh*! What the fuck is wrong with me? I need to turn my brain off.

Fee beams. "Thank you, Jason. We're very happy with how it came out. Now, it's time to get seated, I hope you're all hungry."

She kisses Carter on the cheek and joins her brigade in the kitchen.

Fiona clinks on a champagne glass and urges us to take our seats. She's about to address the room when the door opens. *Peter*. He walks in with confidence in his stride, commanding attention in a tailored suit that fits him perfectly. His blond hair is slicked back, emphasizing his square jaw. The kind of handsome that makes my breath catch in my throat.

"Is that...?" Mom grips my wrist, her eyes following the direction of where I'm gaping at him. I'm lucky to have such cool parents where I can tell them anything and everything without judgment—even my sex life.

"Yeah. That's Peter." I tear my eyes away.

Then glance over to see where he's sitting.

My heart crashes to the ground. He's brought a date. A stunning woman with dark hair and porcelain skin who laughs at something he's saying. While they're not holding hands or acting overtly romantic, it's clear they're comfortable companions. Which stings more than I care to admit.

Who is she?

"Who's with him?" Dad's brow is furrowed when he utters the obvious question.

My attempt to mask my disappointment fails. "I don't know, pops. His date?"

Peter and the woman make their way to their assigned table, greeting people as they pass. I watch them and wish I could disappear.

"Well, he's made quite an entrance." Alex leans over. "Are you okay?"

"Sure." I force a smile and change the subject. "What time does the band go on tonight?"

Jace cocks an eyebrow and flicks his eyes between me and Alex. "An hour or so after dinner ends."

Determined to focus on the celebration, I manage to block out further thoughts of Peter by refocusing my attention on the conversation. Soon, I'm completely immersed in my own bubble with my own people. We tell funny stories and thoroughly enjoy each other's company. Not to mention, dinner is exquisite.

After the meal winds down, we make our way next door to The Mission. All the wives and family are seated front and center in the VIP area with the best view in the house. While we wait for LTZ to start, Zoey, Alex, and I sip glasses of wine as we reminisce about the band's first show at The Mission over a decade ago.

Noting the time, I excuse myself to use the restroom. As I head down the hallway toward the rear of the building, I see Peter. Before I can turn around, our eyes meet, and there's a moment of unspoken regret on both our parts. An undeniable link, strong as steel, draws us together, despite everything.

He approaches. Behind him, the pretty woman trails, looking around the room in awe. I'm crushed. Did he get involved with someone in the past few weeks?

I know I threw him out of my shop, but the truth is...he's under my skin. I hate seeing him with someone else when I know he's meant to be mine.

Make up your mind.

I'm barely able to hide my apprehension and dismay. My heart skips around like a stone on a river. Every part of me wants to scurry in the other direction, but I have to stand my ground. Pretend like I'm unaffected. Moments later we're face-to-face, though he towers over me despite my six-inch heels.

"Jordan." My name sounds like melted chocolate the way he draws it out, calm but carrying an undercurrent of something—more.

"Peter." I manage to keep my voice steady. "The place looks great, well done."

His blue eyes bore into mine. Heat flares between us. "Thanks, I can't take all the credit. Fiona and Zane made it come alive."

"Sure. Well, it's good to see you…" Suddenly, I have the urge to flee and take a step backward.

"Jordan, this is Rose." Peter gestures to the woman who steps to his side, thwarting my plan to escape. "We're colleagues. She's a crucial part of my team."

"I just got lucky by winning the office drawing." Rose extends her hand with a friendly smile. "It's a pleasure to meet you, Jordan. Peter's told me a lot about your work. I've always wanted a tattoo, but I'm too scared of needles to get one."

"You're not alone." I grasp the tips of her fingers and release them quickly.

Peter's gaze lingers on me for a moment. A myriad of emotions dance across his face. "I hoped we could talk tonight. Maybe after the band plays?"

"*Uh*…" I hesitate, unsure of trying to have a conversation with him in a public setting where emotions are bound to run high. "Let's play it by ear. I need to return to my friends, find me later."

Quickly, I make my way to my table and force myself not to look back at Peter. I rejoin Alex and Zoey on the banquette and take a gulp of wine.

"So, what was that all about?" Alex leans in.

I roll my shoulders. "He wants to talk later." I try to sound nonchalant, but my voice betrays me.

"Hmmm..." Zoey purses her lips. "He hasn't taken his eyes off you all night. Do you think you should hash it out?"

I shrug, my gaze flickering to where Peter is sitting with Rose. "I don't know."

The entire room goes black, cutting off our conversation. Around us, a high-tech light display beams LTZ logos all around the room as the smoke machine fills the space, creating a mystical feeling. Though the room is still dark, my brother's bass drum starts thumping. And thumping. And thumping. It creates a level of excitement and anticipation that's palpable.

Just when the crowd is about to lose their minds, Zane's guitar cuts through the percussion, shredding into the intro of their first hit, *Rise*. I know how much this moment means to the band, and to experience their comeback with them nearly makes me cry.

Throughout the evening, I feel Peter watching me. His table isn't far from ours, and every few minutes our eyes meet in a silent exchange. Rose, meanwhile, seems utterly captivated by the band, her excitement almost childlike as she watches them play.

At one point, as Zoey and I are dancing to *Kick It*, I glance over at him. Our eyes lock, and he mouths, "I'm sorry." The sincerity in his eyes melts away some of the resentment and insecurity I've been harboring. Not all of it, but enough to make me want to hear him out.

Alex nudges me, a knowing look on her face. "You okay?"

"*Yeah*!" I point at the band and resume dancing.

LTZ plays for nearly four hours with five encores, the last one turning into a jam session with most of Seattle's most famous rockstars getting up on stage. It's nearly two in the morning when they take their final bow.

Afterward, everyone in our group gathers their things. The band wives disappear down the secret staircase to join their husbands. My folks went home an hour ago, leaving me on my own.

I find myself both dreading and longing for the moment Peter approaches me. Part of me wonders if he'll follow through. My heart plummets when I look in the direction of his table to find he and Rose are gone.

I feel a zap of electricity when a hand cautiously touches my shoulder. "Jordan, about our talk..."

Before he can continue, Rose, who's visibly ill, interrupts, "Peter, I'm so sorry but I'm really not feeling well. I think I need to go home."

Concern washes over his face. "Of course, let's get you home." He turns to me, genuine regret permeating his gaze. "I'm sorry, Jordan. Can you meet tomorrow? Just the two of us? I owe you a huge apology and I'd like to talk about everything. Clear the air."

I'm torn, the evening's events have left me emotionally exhausted. Yet, there's a huge part of me that needs to understand what's been left unsaid between us.

"Alright, Peter. Tomorrow," I agree cautiously.

We exchange mobile numbers and he gives me a small, grateful smile before helping Rose out of the club.

Assuming Peter follows through—and, let's face it, that's a crapshoot—tomorrow's conversation seems like a pivotal moment. One that will either mend what's broken or confirm my worst fears.

With a heart full of uncertainty, I head home.

Whatever happens, I'll be ready. It's time to confront the past.

And maybe, just maybe, I can find some peace in the present.

Chapter Eleven

She's not going to show.

Well, it's 50/50.

We agreed to meet at eleven and it's twenty past. I'm about to text her to see if she's changed her mind when I see her gunmetal Mercedes sedan pull into the Bell Harbor Marina parking lot.

Jordan gets out of the car, dressed warmly in black jeans, boots, and big puffy coat. Her hair whips in the wind as she looks around until she sees me. I hold up my gloved hand and watch as she approaches. There's still a possibility she'll bail when I tell her the plan.

If she accepts my invitation, I'll have her to myself for an entire day and I won't waste the opportunity.

I'll lay it all out there.

She stops in front of me, pink-cheeked and trepidatious. Looks over my shoulder to take in the sleek lines of my Sea Ray Sundancer 320. Her eyes flick to me and she tilts her head. "This is your idea of a chat? You expect me to get on a boat alone with you?"

Aching to take her in my arms and kiss her senseless, I opt for what I hope is a sincere smile. "It's a rare, clear day. The way I figure it, we have an opportunity. New year. Fresh start. Plus, there's pizza involved in Kingston. Have you heard of Sourdough Willie's?"

"Peter..." She glances up at her car in the parking lot, probably considering whether to make an escape. Flicks her gaze to me. "I didn't expect this to be an all-day thing. What if I have plans later?"

I look deep into her glittering green eyes. "Do you?"

She sucks her lip between her teeth as if she's pondering her options before conceding. "*No.*"

Stepping aside so she can board, I palm her lower back to make sure she keeps her balance. "I bought this a couple years ago when I had a big project on Bainbridge. It was easier than waiting in a ferry line. I haven't taken it out since summer."

"It's nice." She glances around the helm, which is enclosed in a fiberglass hardtop. "Won't we be cold, though?"

I plug in the electric blankets I bought earlier. "Not with these. Have you boated before?"

Jordan sits in the passenger seat. "Sure, my pops loves boating."

Holding up the kettle, I gesture to the cabin. "I'll make hot chocolate for the ride. Will you help with the fenders before we take off?"

"I'm happy to." Jordan fidgets with her coat. "It'll give me something to do. This is fucking awkward."

Realizing my terrible communication skills are, once again, putting her at a disadvantage, I grip her shoulder with my gloved hand and feel a zing through the cloth. "Thank you for coming. I hope after today things won't seem strange."

"Fat chance." Jordan rolls her eyes but quirks her eyebrow and grins.

Ten minutes later, we set off to the north, the Seattle skyline shrinking behind us as we head toward Kingston. I pull the flaps of my wooly hat over my ears and keep an eye on my navigation settings. Jordan wraps a blanket around her and settles into her seat. Once we're on course, the hum of the engine and subtle sway of the boat create a sense of tranquility.

I decide to dive in. "I owe you an explanation. About a lot of things. I'd like to start with our night in Vegas."

She turns to me and takes a sip of cocoa, waiting.

"You were sleeping when my phone started blowing up. I remember thinking how peaceful you looked, considering." I raise an eyebrow and her cheeks redden. "Anyway, my younger twin brothers got into a shit-ton of legal trouble. My dad was admitted to the hospital. It was made clear, under no uncertain terms, I was needed at home."

"Okay..." Jordan rests her chin on her palm, her eyebrows twitch.

"I meant everything I said in every moment we had." I shift to face her, though I can still navigate. "The thing is, as much as we shared with each other that night, we didn't talk much about our families for some reason. In my case, it was and is an ongoing problem. Back then, it dominated my life. I'm not proud to admit this, but when I got the call, I felt like I had nothing to offer. I was a poor guy from a small town with a fucked-up family trying to make ends meet. It pissed me off. I was pissed at myself for not being worthy of someone like you. Pissed we wouldn't ever have a chance..." I blow out a huge burst of air. "None of this matters though. I handled everything with the highest degree of immaturity. There's no excuse other than my insecurities got the best of me. But, as cliché as it might sound, I didn't *want* to leave you, Jordan. At the time, I didn't think there was a choice."

As she listens, her semi-scowl morphs into what seems like understanding. "I had no idea. You left, and I thought... I thought it was something about me. When I thought about everything we'd done, I was... Embarrassed. *Ashamed.* I let my guard down and got burned."

"*God.* I'm sorry. I fucked up. I shouldn't have ever left you. I've replayed it over and over and how I treated you is the biggest regret in my life." I pat my heart, hoping she can see I'm sincere. "You have *nothing* to be ashamed of. Our night has stayed in my heart for all these years. What happened between us was once in a lifetime. Something I couldn't ever forget or move on from."

Jordan absorbs my words, contemplating. The boat glides smoothly over the water. For a moment, there's a peaceful silence between us filled with unspoken thoughts.

"You were icy cold that morning. I felt like discarded trash." She looks out over the water. "Your rejection stuck with me for *years*."

Her words hit me hard. "It didn't occur to me someone as special as you would even give me a second thought. Then again, with everything going on, I was too overwhelmed to see things through your eyes. Until recently, that is..."

"The things you said, Peter. I *believed*..." She blinks away tears and shakes her head to compose herself.

"I did too." I can't help myself; I stroke her cheek with my thumb. "Everything was real for me. I didn't want to drag you into my mess. I thought I was protecting you."

Her eyes glint with a mixture of frustration and sadness. "*Protecting* me? You left me alone and confused with a gallon of your come dripping out of me. I didn't know your last name or how to get in touch. We stupidly didn't use protection. What if I'd been pregnant? Or, you could have been riddled with disease. I trusted my gut, thinking we had something, and then... I was nothing to you but a Vegas whore. I was surprised you didn't toss a Benjamin on the nightstand."

Her words *eviscerate* me. I have to suck in a breath because it feels like a million knives are stabbing me in the gut. I try to formulate any sort of response—apology, anything to take her hurt away. In this moment, I realize the depth of my fuck-up is infinitely deeper than I originally thought.

"There's nothing I can say or do to ever take back what happened, Jordan. I'm ashamed of myself. You're the last person I'd ever want to hurt." I finally find my voice. "I bet you didn't know I tried to get in touch with you a few weeks later."

"What?" She scrunches her nose, confused.

Recalling her kissing the man in front of her shop, I ball my hand into a fist. "I knew you opened up the shop."

"That was two *months* later." Jordan's chin juts out defiantly.

The boat cuts smoothly through the water, the rhythmic sound of the waves against the hull filling the tense silence between us.

"You really found me again?" Jordan finally speaks. She holds the mug of hot chocolate with both hands and peers at me over the rim.

I sigh. "I did. It wasn't difficult. Your brother's in LTZ. Your dad is frigid' Jason Deveraux..." I glance over at her. "It wasn't hard to keep up with you. I knew you were a tattoo artist and there was an article about you opening The Salty Siren. I decided to show up and apologize. See if we could go out or something."

"You what?" Jordan shifts in her seat to face me. I can practically see the gears working from the movement of her eyebrows. She's adorable. Wears her heart on her sleeve. It's one of the things that drew me to her in Vegas. She's...she's...utterly authentic.

"You were out front; someone was painting the window while you watched. A tall guy came up behind you with a huge bouquet of flowers. You turned, threw your arms around him and kissed him like you meant it." I scrub at my eyes because this memory is one I hate with a passion. "You'd moved on."

"Of course I moved on because I had to. What was I supposed to do? Wait for the guy who fucking treated me like garbage?"

"No, of course not, but seeing you with that...*guy*. So soon after..." I try to shake the image out of my head. "I hated it. I also had no right to interfere. Plus, I didn't know what to think. I couldn't bear the thought of someone who wasn't me stealing your heart after what we shared that night."

Jordan sets her cup in the holder and covers her eyes with her hands. "*Fuck.*"

"Oh, there's more. I was furious." I decide to get it all out there. "To cope, I convinced myself I was the one who got played. You must have been a cheater, hooking up with me when you had a boyfriend at home. Yeah, anything to take the blame off me. I held a bitter grudge for quite a few years. Until I realized it was one thousand percent my fault. So, I started following you on Instagram and...look, the truth is I couldn't forget you. Or our night. *Impossible.*"

Kingston looms ahead and our conversation is cut short as I navigate the boat to the dock. Jordan's a good assistant, and we're tied up and locked down quickly. As we stroll side by side up the marina to the pizza place, we're more or less at ease, all things considered.

At the door, before we enter the restaurant, Jordan stops me. "Are you saying, after all this time, you never wanted Vegas to be a one-night thing?"

"Of course I didn't," I admit. "What I felt for you—with you. It was different. It was real. I meant what I said in your shop. It was the greatest night of my life."

She gazes up at me serenely. "It felt real to me too. Then again, we didn't know each other at all. There was no foundation for you to trust me with the news of your family situation. A decade later, here we are."

"Eating pizza?" I open the door with a grin.

She laughs. "Yeah. Eating pizza."

Inside, the place smells like heaven. Jordan and I on a date feels...normal. We order a Truffle Shuffle, a Cup & Char, and a couple of Cokes and take a seat across from each other at a window table to wait.

I can't stop staring at her beautiful face, wise but vulnerable. Kind but tough.

She catches me staring and blushes but looks up at me with a hint of desire I recognize from the night we met.

For the first time in years, I feel like I'm right where I belong.

Chapter Twelve

My mind whirls with confusion.

Every emotion inside me is jumbled like a tangled string of Christmas lights. On one hand, I'm furious. A simple, "I need to leave because I have a family issue," would have saved me—and him, it sounds like—years of frustration, anger, and hurt. On the other hand, I'm a big believer in fate and timing.

Was this meant to be our path?

What blows me away is that he came to find me. How could I have known? To think he saw me with Cameron...

How much time have we wasted?

Life is weird. You really have no idea what's going on with anyone, do you?

"What thoughts are reeling in that gorgeous head of yours?" Peter bites into his pizza and moans. "Good God, the hype is real. This is the best thing I've eaten, ever."

I quirk a brow and catch his eye. Smirk. Can't resist the opening he's left me. "You're sure about that?"

He nearly chokes on his pizza, but wisely doesn't answer.

After a few moments, he resumes our conversation from earlier. "If you don't mind me asking, what happened with Cameron? Why didn't you guys marry?"

"Cameron was...someone I thought would be safe." I decide to be honest without throwing Cameron under the bus. After all, I don't really know Peter. "On paper, it seemed like a match. In real life, we essentially existed. Different sets of friends. Different interests. It was comfortable, but it wasn't right, and I let it go on far too long."

Peter is thoughtful, probing. "You were together for many years."

"Yeah, we were. It went by quick. I was focused on the shop. He was focused on impressing my pops." It's hard not to feel annoyed at myself for staying with a man I didn't love. "He's not a bad guy. He's definitely not the guy for me. What about you? After Vegas, did you ever get married or settle down?"

He lets out a chuckle. "God, no. I've been building my business too. There wasn't any time for anything serious. Or complicated."

"Maybe everything happened the way it was supposed to." I take a swallow of Coke. "I've thought a lot about the 'what-ifs' of it all. After Cameron and I broke up, I decided to reclaim some of my youthful perspective. Open myself up to new things."

Something passes across Peter's face when I'm speaking, it's hard to tell what he's thinking. He reaches across the table. "Well, I may not be a new thing, but I'd like to date you."

A lightning bolt shoots through my body. Despite everything, his words are what I've yearned to hear, but I can't tell if what I'm feeling is excitement or fear. "I don't know."

"Okay." He holds his hands up, but smiles. "I've been patient this long. I have a meal and boat ride to Seattle to convince you..."

He changes subjects and before I know it, we're talking like long-lost friends. Mostly about work and the trials and tribulations we've endured over the years with vendors, employees, and clients. I find him to be insightful and fair. He's surrounded by loyal employees who share his vision.

"God, it's strange to learn that you're the Vander in VA/VT." I lean back and pat my full stomach. "Your company has such a stellar reputation in the community. My pops is a huge fan. You've done well for yourself."

Bit by bit, I realize how wrong my assumptions have been about him. Sure, what he did wasn't cool, but we were kids. At his heart, he's a good person.

Maybe my gut instinct was trustworthy after all.

"I hate for today to end because I'm having a wonderful time with you, but it's going to be dark soon." Peter seems down, almost like there's an hourglass on the time we have together.

I reach across the table and squeeze his hand. "It's okay. I've decided. We can go out."

"Oh yeah?" His entire face lights up. "You don't know how happy that makes me."

We make our way to his boat. As we get closer, I notice the name painted on the transom. *Emerald Eyes*. All the blood in my body rushes to my head and I stop in my tracks, staring.

Peter's a few paces ahead when he realizes I'm not with him and turns to look for me. "Jordan? What's wrong?"

"Did you..." I point to the stern. "Is that...?"

Peter's caught. And, embarrassed. "Oh, God. *Yeah*. It's you."

Before I can stop, I launch myself at Peter. Surprised, he barely has time to react as I throw my arms around his neck and press my lips against his in an explosion of pent-up passion and longing. A fusion of all the unsaid words and unacknowledged feelings I have for this man.

Peter's arms wind around my waist, pulling me closer, as if he's afraid to let me go. His hands slide down the backs of my thighs and he lifts me as our kiss deepens. We're a desperate dance of lips and tongues while the world around us fades into a blur as we lose ourselves in each other.

It's a moment of reckoning for me. A total surrender to feelings I've alternately buried or tried hard to deny.

When we finally break apart, gasping for air, our eyes lock and I see a reflection of my own turmoil and hope. This kiss, impulsive and raw, has changed everything. A turning point, maybe. A second chance. A promise of what our lives could be.

He leans down and rests his forehead against mine. "*This* is real."

Our lips meet, more tender this time as he lowers me down to the ground. He takes my hand and leads me to the boat. We don't say a word as we depart Kingston, but I'm no longer sitting next to him.

No. I need to be closer—I'm on his lap.

Peter nuzzles my ear. "I've got to be extra careful on the way home. We'll be navigating in the dark, which isn't ideal. Stupid long, winter nights."

"I'll get up." I kiss his forehead. "I hope I haven't made things weird. Or confusing."

Peter's smile nearly jumps off his face. "As long as there's more where that came from, I'm good."

"Let me make us another cup of hot chocolate." I plug the blanket in. "It's probably gonna get cold."

He grabs my hand before I go downstairs. "I'm glad you agreed to come with me today."

"Me too." I lean over and kiss him before making my way down the steps.

A few minutes later, the cabin air is filled with the comforting aroma of hot chocolate. Grasping the two mugs, a sense of contentment washes over me as the warmth seeps into my fingers. Such a stark contrast to the rollercoaster of emotions I've been riding since Peter returned to my life.

I'm about to head back up the ladder when the boat sputters and coasts into an abrupt halt and the engine falls silent. I rush upstairs, the hot chocolate forgotten. My stomach seizes with anxiety when I come upon Peter frantically checking the boat's controls.

Deliberately staying out of his way, I slip into the passenger seat. "What's going on?"

"We're out of fuel. It completely slipped my mind when we left." Peter is calm, though frustrated.

"It's my fault. I distracted you." My heart sinks. "Are we stranded?"

"Not exactly stranded. There's cell phone coverage. We're in a safe spot to anchor." He pulls out his phone, scrolling through something. "I need to check the traffic and marine conditions to make sure we're not in any shipping or ferry paths."

Taking a deep breath, I try to gauge the seriousness of our situation. "So, what are our options?"

"We could call for help, but it's almost dark and it's New Year's Day. Response might be slow." Peter glances at me, a hint of uncertainty in his eyes before resuming studying his phone. "Or, we could anchor for the night. It's safe, and we have everything we need on board. The batteries are all charged. We'll have heat and some light. I can call Vessel Assist tomorrow or row the dinghy ashore in the morning. We'll fuel up and still be home in Seattle early morning-ish."

The skeptical part of me wonders if he planned this to get me alone.

The romantic part doesn't care.

In all honesty, spending the night on the water, adrift yet safe, is a Tryst List-level adventure. In fact, we're stranded, aren't we? It's the first item on my list. Maybe this is one more sign from the universe. "Staying the night doesn't sound too bad, actually. It's kind of thrilling, in a way."

Peter's head snaps up, seemingly surprised by my response. "You're sure? I don't want to do anything that will screw things up with you."

"Let's call it fate." I pull the blanket around me. "Besides, we have hot chocolate."

Peter smiles and relaxes a bit, the tension easing from his shoulders. "Alright. An unplanned night at sea it is. Let me get us anchored."

Though I offer to help, the boat is pretty high-tech. Within fifteen minutes, Peter's navigated us into a quiet cove and secured the vessel. He approaches, breath visible in the winter air. Cheeks and nose are red from exertion. He's still the most handsome man I've ever laid eyes on.

I can't help but feel a sense of excitement. This unexpected turn of events, being alone with Peter after a day of confessions and revelations, feels like a new chapter in our complicated story. A new beginning, maybe.

We descend to the cabin, take off our coats and recline side by side on the galley bench cuddled under a blanket. The boat rocks in the quiet of the night. We sip the hot chocolate I made earlier, though now it's more like warm chocolate. Through the window, city lights shimmer in the distance and the stars above us are a brilliant tapestry in the clear night sky.

"So, this is quite the New Year's Day adventure." I settle against the cushion and gaze at Peter.

His arm finds its way around my shoulders. "Definitely not how I expected to start the year, but it's hard for me to complain. I've wanted to spend time with you for a long time."

In this moment, all misunderstandings between us fade away. We're two people, adrift yet connected, sharing another unexpected night. I lean into him. "Who knew running out of fuel could lead to this?"

"Life's full of surprises." Peter's voice is quiet as his forehead touches mine.

I pull off his hat and comb the top of his hair with my fingers. "You're cold."

"Warm me up?" He cups my face, eyes searching mine.

I don't answer.

My lips are too busy kissing him.

Chapter Thirteen

Is this really happening?

Do I really have the woman of my dreams in my arms again?

Jordan presses into my side as we make out. She smells delicious, like wildflowers and sea air. She tastes sweet and chocolatey. She moans and mewls as our mouths reacquaint for the second time today.

In every dream I've had of a romantic reunion, it certainly didn't go like this.

What a whirlwind. From talking about our past to her kissing me to us being stranded for the night. I wonder if she realizes this exact scenario is on her Tryst List?

It's Jordan's fantasy come true and I'm going to give her anything she wants.

Scooping my arm under her, I maneuver us on the bench seating until she's straddling me. "The moment I laid eyes on you in Vegas, I felt you were made for me, Jordan." I drive my hips up so she can feel how affected I am by her. "It isn't that you're beautiful, because you are. You're also strong. Sweet. Feisty. Funny. God, baby, I've dreamt of this moment for years. I'd almost lost hope."

"Peter. I've thought terrible things about you. *Said* terrible things about you. I haven't even begun to process everything but..." She presses her palm on my heart. Leans forward and tenderly brushes my lips with hers. "Please don't hurt me."

"Never." I grip her face with my hands and see tears in her eyes, which breaks my heart. "Baby, don't cry. We've found our way back to each other."

She nods sadly. "So many things were said that night in Vegas and I...I...believed them. Peter is it real this time? Are *you* for real this time?"

Her words eviscerate me. My younger self couldn't have predicted how my stupidity in a moment of stress and weakness affected her. Today affirms one thing—she felt what I felt. We *weren't* some random hookup.

We're destined for each other.

"Jordan Deveraux, I've been waiting for years to make amends. You've been on my mind every, single day." I scatter kisses across her face. "I want to be the best man for you. Trust me when I say, there's nothing I won't do to prove we're meant to be."

"Okay." She melts into me. "I want to see where this goes."

Wrapped together, our hearts beating on the same rhythm, I feel complete. I want her, the hardness in my jeans is no accident, but it's not only about sex. I want *all* of her and I'll bend over backward to make her feel safe.

"Should I make this into a bed?" I gesture to the table. "It'll be more comfortable. I may even have sheets, I can't remember. This is more of a commuter boat for work, so I haven't spent the night on it."

She sits up. "Sure. I'll help."

Together, we convert the eating area into a bed. Though I can't find actual bedsheets, I have a few blankets to spread out and the seat cushions double as pillows.

When we're done, I lie down and pat the space next to me. "Ready for bed?"

"Yeah..." She crawls up beside me and lies on her side. "Can I ask you a question?"

I curl my arm around her. Her cheek rests on my chest. "Of course."

"Did you want me to do your sleeve because of my skill or because you wanted to reconnect?" She traces the muscles of my arm with her finger.

"*Jordan*." I kiss her nose. "One hundred percent to both."

"You didn't have any ink before." Jordan runs her hand up and down my bicep. "Now you're tatted up. The entire time I was working on you, I wondered about your tattoos. Why you got them. What they meant. Usually it's a huge part of a conversation with a client, but..." She rolls her eyes. "We were playing our stupid game of not knowing each other. Anyway, they're so detailed and seem incredibly personal."

I shift slightly. "Should I take off my shirt and I'll tell you about them?"

"Uh...yeah. Took you long enough." Jordan swats me playfully.

Reaching behind my neck, I grab my sweater and T-shirt, pull them over my head and lie on my stomach allowing her a better view of the tattoo that spans my back. "This one is inspired by Kengo Kuma's work on the Besancon Art Center. I've always admired how he blends nature with architecture, creating harmony between the two. The dragons, koi, and flowers interwoven with the grid are a tribute to that philosophy, a reminder of the balance and fluidity I strive for in my own designs."

"It's magnificent. She traces the lines of the ink with a finger, her touch delicate and contemplative. "Ito is masterful, how cool you have a permanent piece of him on you."

I chuckle. "It took less time to book with him than with you."

"And the Roman one on your arm?" She smirks. "Merc was impressed you had a Riksfjoird."

I stretch my arm up and flex to showcase my elaborate, Roman-inspired tattoo. "In my defense, my fascination with the Roman Empire is because of the *architecture*."

"Of *course* it is." She arches an eyebrow. "Ruben's work in special. These busts of Roman gods look like they're jumping off your body. I love the detail of the laurel." Her thumb rubs the vine twined between the columns of the building.

Anytime she touches me, even during our tattoo sessions, I get hard, and tonight is no exception. Unlike earlier, my cock isn't patiently hanging out in my jeans, it's desperately trying to escape. "The buildings are St. Peter's Basilica, one of the most renowned architectural works of the Italian Renaissance. The modern building is the Maxxi museum designed by Donato Bramante.

"These really *do* mean something to you." Her palms rest on my back, she digs her fingers in and kneads.

Seconds later, Jordan slides a leg over me and sits on my ass to give me a more intense massage. She works the heels of her hands into my muscles and presses her thumbs into my pressure points. I can't remember the last time someone's taken care of me who doesn't work for me.

"God, that feels good." I mumble into the pillow.

"One of my special skills." She flushes the span of my lats with quick sweeps of the sides of her hands. "What was the inspiration behind the tattoo I did for you?"

"Giotto's Campanile, particularly the panels depicting the four cardinal virtues." I'm delighted we're finally talking about why I saved this piece for her.' "Prudence for the ability to discern the appropriate course of action. Justice for the concept of moral rightness. Fortitude for the courage to face adversity. And temperance for the practice of self-control and moderation. Each part of this design is my reminder to embody these virtues in life and in my work."

She examines the tattoo, moving my arm around as she absorbs the symbolism behind each virtue. "It's healed nicely, you're taking very good care of it. By the way? Hands down one of the coolest pieces I've ever done. Thank you for trusting me. It's more than art on your skin. It's like a narrative of your values."

"Yeah..." I feel such a sense of pride. "Your art, your talent, you're the only one I wanted to do this design. I wanted to carry a piece of you with me. There's no one on earth who captures the soul of a design like you do."

Jordan resumes her place by my side. "Wow. Quite possibly the nicest thing anyone's ever said to me. Thank you."

"It's true." I pull her against my chest and twirl my fingers through her silky, blonde hair. Lying there with her surrounded by the sounds of the sea, my affection for Jordan is deeper than words. Does she feel it too?

"Should I confess something to you?" I give her a little peck. "It's a bit embarrassing."

Jordan stiffens. "Will I be mad?"

"Only if you don't want to be Instagram stalked." My hand works its way under her sweater, my finger swiping across her taut stomach. "I know I alluded to it before, but I've sort of been following your life for the past few years. Well, what you shared of it."

Her eyes search mine. "You're for real?"

"Yeah." I grip her hip as her leg slips in between mine. "You posted about your breakup one morning and I made an appointment as soon as the shop opened. I'd been saving that design for you to do but didn't know what would happen if I just showed up. Of course I knew there'd be a wait but damn...you were booked out over a year in advance." I shake my head. "So fucking frustrating."

Jordan pokes my stomach. "Uh, you could have come in and been honest. The thing we did was weird. You've got to admit, both of us pretending we didn't remember each other was torture..."

"...yet you didn't fucking cave." I stroke her hair, chuckling. "You had me at a loss for what to do. Or say. And you were already working on my piece, I sure didn't want to do anything to piss you off until it was finished."

"I'm stubborn." She juts her chin out. "Deveraux trait. That being said, I'm a professional. I wouldn't have left you high and dry."

My lips hover over hers and the energy in the room turns from contemplative to charged. "Your stubbornness is sexy. I was hard as a rock every session."

"*Oh*, I noticed." She lowers her eyes and looks up at me through her lashes.

Our lips meet in a heated kiss, igniting a fire that's been smoldering since we first laid eyes on each other in Vegas and continues all these years later. A culmination of all the emotions we've restrained, leading to this unexpected detour forcing us to spend the night on my boat.

Jordan's lips are supple yet insistent, moving against mine with a fervor that matches my own. Her arms wrap around my neck, drawing me closer, deepening the kiss. I respond instinctively, gripping her ass and pulling her closer. Everything fades away as we lose ourselves in each other.

When we finally break apart, gasping for air, our foreheads rest against each other. Jordan's eyes open and I see a reflection of my own emotions—wonder, excitement, maybe even a hint of vulnerability.

"Peter...what are you doing to me?" She moans when I cup her breast under her sweater. With my free hand, I tug her leg over mine and press my erection against the heat of her core.

"Making you feel good." I grip the hem of her sweater and lift it over her bra. Her tits are as fantastic as I remember, full with taut brown nipples straining against sheer black lace.

Jordan rolls her hips against me, causing me to groan. Her fingers work the zipper down on my jeans. "We don't need any of these clothes. I want to be skin on skin."

The conversation about my tattoo makes me realize I need to embody the values it symbolizes. There can't be any dishonesty between us. Though there are several things we need to discuss, before we're intimate I need to disclose what I know about her list. "Jordan, I want to be naked with you more than anything. But I also want to start this new chapter with a clean slate. There's something else I need to tell you."

"What do you mean?" Her expression of desire changes to a hint of wariness, as if she was already expecting the other shoe to drop and now it is.

Talk about a mood killer.

"I found your list." I take a deep breath, choosing my words carefully. "That day you had to take a call in the middle of our session. I saw it in your sketchbook. I wasn't trying to snoop. To kill time, I wanted to see your *drawings* but there it was, and I... I looked."

"You went through my personal things?" Jordan's reaction is immediate. Her eyes flash with anger as she pulls away from me. "What a huge invasion of privacy."

"I know, and I'm *sorry*. It wasn't right but I was desperate to connect with you. I took a picture of it and thought maybe…I could give those things to you." I sit up, trying to explain, realizing how disingenuous I sound.

She shakes her head in disbelief. "You took a *picture* to remember the places I fantasized about having *sex*? How I'd like to be *fucked*? What were you going to do with it... Wait! I can't believe this. I'm so stupid. Just when I thought we were getting somewhere...we're stranded. Holy shit. You arranged for us to run out of fuel. *Didn't you?*"

"No. Jordan, please, I didn't—wouldn't—do such a thing." I reach out, trying to bridge the physical and emotional distance between us. "Getting stuck tonight was *absolutely* not planned."

She pulls away angrily, a clear sign she doesn't believe me.

Grabbing a blanket, she wraps it around her small body and curls up in a ball facing away from me.

Shit.

Just when I'd made progress.

I've fucked up yet again.

Chapter Fourteen

I'm so fucking confused.

As much as I've tried to deny it to myself and everyone else, Peter's the only man I've thought about for years. Even during my relationship with Cameron.

The guilt. The desire. The hurt. The regret. The what-ifs.

It's been emotional quicksand or, as Merc calls it, "dicksand."

Am I this big of a fool?

Cocooned in a blanket, facing the wall on the makeshift bed, I find myself struggling. The sway of the boat might be a soothing contrast to the turmoil inside me, but it sure isn't comforting.

Not at all.

Peter's presence looms in the small cabin. He's next to me but the comfort and closeness we shared earlier is tainted. For a minute there, I was ecstatic—sure we had a new chance to finally see where this would take us. All our past misunderstandings had reasonable explanations, but was I too quick to forgive?

"Jordan, I know finding your list the way I did wasn't right." Peter's voice, tinged with regret, astonishes me. "I should've respected your privacy. I'm sorry. If you don't feel safe, please let me call Vessel Assist. I promise, getting stranded is a coincidence, but considering everything I understand why you'd worry."

He puts on his sweater and starts up the ladder to the deck. I sit up, stretch my own sweater over my legs and hug my knees. "Wait. Let's talk this through."

"Okay." He stops on the second rung and waits for me to continue.

I take a deep breath. "My list was personal to me, filled with my sexual fantasies. I wasn't ready to share it. Do you still have the photo?"

"Yeah, I do." He reaches for his phone and punches his code in. "It was wrong of me. We hadn't cleared the air yet. It's just...when I saw that list, it made me...fucking jealous. I couldn't stand the thought of you doing those things with anyone but me. I want to be the man in your life, for a minute I thought..." His blue eyes, clearly remorseful, barely retain contact with mine. "Ah, fuck. No need to explain. I was wrong. I'll delete it."

It's exactly the response I wanted. Accountability. Action. Except, knowing my all-consuming desire for this man invariably clouds my ability to think rationally, I bury my face in my hands. I can't look at him. It's too confusing.

"There. Deleted," I hear him say.

I peer up at him. "Peter, given our history how do I know you and I aren't a mistake waiting to happen? You realize what a red flag this is, right?"

"I do. I can't change our past, but hopefully my being honest shows you I've grown because I didn't have to say anything. I could have deleted it without telling you and you'd be none the wiser." He reaches over, his hand hesitating in the air before resting on my knee. "I elected to be honest to build trust. I'm not the same man who walked away. You can be damn sure, if you give me another shot, I won't let you down."

I look into his eyes, searching for the sincerity I desperately need from him. "Your tattoo is supposed to embody virtues about balance and harmony. Is this you living up to those ideals? Being honest with me?"

"Yes." Peter squeezes my knee. "It is. Given everything that's gone on with my family, I'm adamant about owning bad behavior and facing the consequences of my actions. I'm a dumbass. It's a given I'll make mistakes, but I want to be a person you can rely on. A person you can trust."

"I want to believe you. I really do." I swallow the lump in my throat. "You seem sincere and..."

A shadow crosses his face. He moves closer. "I can't promise everything will be perfect. What I can promise is I'll try my best every day to be the person you deserve."

The combo of honesty in his voice and earnestness in his eyes breaks through my defenses. Despite my trepidation, I want him desperately. I *want* to take this chance. To see where this rekindled connection with Peter can lead.

If I don't, I'll regret it for the rest of my life.

"It would be a leap of faith." My voice is barely above a whisper.

Peter's hands pry mine from where they're clasped around my legs. He threads his fingers with mine, squeezing gently. "We don't have to rush into anything."

Maybe we aren't rushing. Maybe we're...continuing.

"I don't want to wait." Using the leverage of our entwined hands, I lean over and my eyes lock on to Peter's.

There's a pause, a breathless moment of anticipation, before he leans in. His lips meet mine and, once again, it's like a spark igniting a long-smoldering fire. What starts as a tender, mellow exploration quickly deepens into something urgent. Something that speaks of suppressed longing and new promises.

Peter's palms cradle my face, his touch is tender yet filled with a desperate kind of need that mirrors my own. I respond instinctively, weaving my fingers through his hair, pulling him closer as we kiss. When we break apart, breathless and dazed, any remaining hesitations on my part melt away.

I slide my hands under his shirt and drag my nails across his torso. "I want you. I'm not going to second-guess what's happening between us tonight."

"You're sure?" Peter's eyes are hot on me.

It feels essential to deepen our affection. To relieve any tension between us. To see if my memories of our bond are accurate. "*Yes*. I'm sure."

Peter smashes his lips against mine and we devour each other. He drags his hand up my side and we stop kissing long enough for him to take off my sweater, leaving me in a sheer, black bra.

"Jesus, Jordan. You're as perfect as I remember." He slips his fingers under the cup and finds my nipple. Pinches it into a tight bud, rolls it under his thumb. "You're *so* fucking perfect."

As he trails kisses from my mouth down my neck, Peter unclasps my bra, freeing my tits. He presses them together until my nipples are nearly touching and grazes one with his teeth, giving it a little tug. Pleasure shoots down to my pussy. "*Ohmygod*. Do it again."

"Oh yeah?" He smiles up at me, the other nipple between his teeth.

I watch him bite down lightly and suck it into a hard point before soothing it with his tongue. I grip both of his wrists as he drives me to oblivion. Back and forth. Back and forth. He feasts on my breasts, each nip of his teeth and each swipe of his tongue sending electric shockwaves through my core.

Without me realizing it, Peter's positioned me so I'm straddling him. Bucking against the bulge in his pants. My hand skims down his chest to his cock. It's enormous, bigger than I remember. I rub him through his jeans until he's panting. Make short work of his belt, buttons, and zipper.

"I'm taking your dick out." My hand wraps around his girth and I stroke up and down his length, squeezing his crown a bit to use his precum as lube.

Then I have an idea.

I guide the head of his cock in the channel between my tits. Fascinated, we watch as he thrusts up between them. His crown nearly reaches my lips. On his second pass, I stick my tongue out and swipe it across him, swirling his sweet-salty essence in my mouth.

"Holy Christ." Peter's head lolls back. "You have no idea how often I've fantasized about fucking your gorgeous tits." He scoots away, though, pulling his cock free. "If you do that again, it'll be all over."

"Fine." I shimmy out of my jeans and panties and toss them to the ground. "We'll save that for when you're ready."

Peter laughs, kicks off his shoes, his jeans, and boxers and leans against the cushion. "Fuck my face, baby. Let me make you come."

Delighted, and needing no further encouragement, I straddle his muscular thighs right above his knees and once again get distracted by his gorgeous, thick shaft resting against his belly. "Your cock is much bigger than I remember."

"Something a man *always* wants to hear." He grins.

Fascinated, I cup Peter's balls in one hand and tenderly massage them. He clenches his jaw when I run the palm of my other hand along the underside of his shaft. "*Fuck*...Jordan."

He's so much bigger than me, I'm not surprised when he effortlessly jackknifes up, grips my hips, lifts and places me so I'm hovering over his mouth. My knees dig into the cushion as he lowers me down and places an opened-mouth kiss on my pussy, causing my eyes to roll back in my head. Working his jaw, he tastes every part of me before sucking my clit into his mouth.

"Oh *shitttttttt*." I grab the rail attached to the wall and wail when my first orgasm washes over my body.

Peter holds me in place by cupping my tits and massaging them in time to his tongue, which he's flicking back and forth on my clit. I lose all pretense of holding myself up. I sit on his face and grind against his lips like a cat in heat. Tiny little zings morph into something insane when he pinches my nipples hard. And...I'm coming again.

Jesus. Sex with Peter is *exactly* how I remember.

Peter releases my tits and slides a finger into my soaking pussy, causing me to arch away. I can't hide my loud moans when he adds a second and third and immediately finds the bundle of nerves that haven't been triggered in years. He's relentless. Sucking and thrusting and...

"*Ahhhhhhhhhh*," I cry when the third wave of pleasure overtakes me.

Before he can stop me, I shift my position—turning to face his cock. I lean over and fist it. He thrusts up into my hand and my lips seal over his crown.

"Baby, stop. I'm too worked up." Peter bucks against me. "I don't want to come in your mouth, I've got to be inside you."

He slides my hips off his face and shifts me so I'm lying against his chest and my feet are on his knees. I'd forgotten the phenomenal sensation of being manhandled by him. Peter's able to move me into positions to fuck me that shouldn't be legal. Like this one. He guides his cock to my entrance from behind and thrusts up.

I watch his thick cock disappear into my body with fascination.

It's like déjà vu.

We fall into a steady, quick rhythm of him fucking me, holding me steady by cupping my breasts. I watch my swollen pussy greedily gobble him up until my head falls against his shoulder. I close my eyes as the bliss of our bodies merging overtakes me.

Just like in Vegas, we're most definitely fucking. Something about our bodies joining together creates pure, unadulterated pleasure—on steroids.

But it's more. It's *always* been more.

I'm probably being reckless. I'm probably jumping back in too fast.

I don't care. In this moment it's worth it.

I want Peter.

I always have.

Chapter Fifteen

Ow can this be better than I remembered?
Oh, but it *is*.

Jordan's tiny body is my wonderland. My hands span her hips as I slam her on my cock. She takes me thrust for thrust, squeezing my shaft with her magic pussy. My throat burns from the need to come, but I've got to restrain myself. I'm willing to wait until I can get her there again. Maybe twice.

Like a boss, she reaches under her thighs to hold her legs up and out. I fuck up into her, swiveling my hips, ensuring my crown rubs her G-spot. Writhing and whimpering, it's like she's in a trance, head lolling against my shoulder. Tits tipped with diamond-hard nipples bounce and jiggle as I disappear into her strawberry-red slit, which is so flushed with arousal it's the same color as her lips.

I pinch her nipple hard and Jordan's eyes fly open. "Stay with me," I order. She slips one hand between us to feel where we're joined but keeps her legs elevated. "Yessss, baby. Rub yourself. Make yourself come on my cock."

"Oh, God. *Yes*...." Jordan's fingers move faster and her moaning hums grow more frantic and, just like in Vegas when I was fucking her in a similar position, she bears down and her pussy detonates, spraying everywhere.

Unlike last time, she doesn't try to scramble away. Instead, she lets her legs drop and plants them on the blanket on either side of my thighs and laughs. She rolls her neck to look up at me. "Ohmygod, I squirted. I wasn't sure if the last time was a fluke. I haven't done it since."

"Fuck, you're incredible." My hand sneaks down to where I'm still slowly thrusting into her. I pull my cock out and tap it on her clit, causing her to squeal. I keep tapping. "You can take everything I give you, can't you, Jordan?"

She reaches up and locks her arms behind my neck, causing her tits to jut up. "I want to. God, I really do. Nothing has ever felt this good."

"Let's go, baby." I lift her and spin her around and sink back into her heat. "Ride me. I want to look into your eyes when you come this time."

With her body astride mine, Jordan wiggles until her pussy stretches around my girth. "You're bossy."

"You can be the boss this round." I release my grip on her hips and place my hands behind my head to watch her in action. "Fuck me like you mean it."

Jordan cocks an eyebrow, presses her palms against my chest and rolls her hips. Grinds her clit against my pubic bone. Arches her back and bounces up and down on my cock. "Like this?" She slithers around, gripping my shoulder, hair, arms, waist—moving and changing positions.

Her sexy little grunts and groans nearly do me in.

She leans down and fuses her lips to mine. Presses her tits against my chest and shifts until she finds an angle that pleases her. Then she rides me, slamming her pussy down on my cock, grinding, undulating, chasing her pleasure until everything in her body seizes. She tears her mouth away and presses her cheek against mine, quivering and shaking. "Your cock is like voodoo magic."

"You're the one who's magic, Jordan." Unable to resist, I clasp my palms against her cheek and devour her. Wind my tongue around hers and pour myself into our kiss while fucking up into her. My hands slide down her neck to her tits and I squeeze them roughly. Pinch her nipples until she cries out and meets me thrust for thrust.

There's no stopping the tsunami of an orgasm that I've staved off for as long as humanly possible. I reach around and clutch her ass and flip us over. I hover above her, pounding into her sweet heat. Jordan sobs out my name when I grip her ass, holding her in place as I come so viciously, it feels like my orgasm is *yanked* from the depths of my soul.

Jordan clenches around me so hard, I don't even know what to do. How to feel. What to say. I could die right now and know that I've reached the apex of pleasure. Except, I'm not done. As exhausted and satiated as I feel, I still want more from her.

I pull out and sit back on my heels. My cock is still semierect, coated with our come. More spills out of her beautifully swollen pussy.

"Fuck yourself with your fingers." I reach for her hand and bring it to her opening. "Deep inside, baby."

She slides two fingers through her folds and pumps. "Like this?"

"Jesus. Fuck." *Ahhh*, the sight of her. My semi springs to life.

Jordan looks up at me. Mascara is smeared under her eyes. Her head is tilted and her hair is a blonde, tangled mess. She saws her teeth on her lower lip as she gyrates against her fingers. Her head thrashes to the side "*Ah-hhh...*"

I pump my cock in my fist. "Stop." She obeys instantly and I pull out her wet fingers with my free hand and guide them up to her mouth. "Taste us."

Jordan stares into my eyes and parts her lips and sucks. I withdraw them and she smiles. "We taste delicious, you should try."

"I think I will." I bring her fingers to her soaked pussy and rub them against her clit.

She winces. "It's too much."

"I'll soothe you." I let her hand go and bend down and swipe the flat of my tongue along her opening. Lick up our come and suck her lower lips. I look up for a moment. "Better?"

Jordan's eyes are closed and her hands are flung over her head. He legs splay open. "More..."

"Gladly." I settle between her legs and pet her inner thighs while I bathe every part of her pussy with my lips and tongue. Now, my dick is hard as steel.

I climb up her body and lean down and kiss her sweet lips. "Mmmmm..." she purrs.

"Can you take me if I'm careful?" I whisper against her lips.

Jordan doesn't answer, she reaches between us, grips my cock and guides it inside her. "I can always take you. Your dick should live inside me, I think."

Her words nearly break me.

Wound together, this time is slow, sweet. We caress each other's body and sneak kisses. She comes first, a slight tremor. Enough to trigger me to pulse inside her, though I don't have much left. After, we hold each other's faces, blinking at each other in wonder.

"I was a fool." I touch my forehead to hers. "I'll never forgive myself for giving up even one moment like this."

She combs her fingers through the hair at my temples. "I've spent lots of time thinking I hated you, yet I don't really know you. Other than this instinctive, unexplainable tie. And the sex. My God, Peter..."

"Do you want to? Know me?" My heart thumps too hard for my liking. I hope she knows I want more from her than her body, though my cock's still snugly lodged inside her.

Jordan's eyes search mine. "Of course I do."

"Me too." I skim my hands along her body. "I want *all* of you. Your heart, of course." I press my hand against her chest. "Your *mind*." I delicately tap her temple. "Your *sweetness*." I kiss her pillowy lips. "Your *sexiness*." I thumb her nipple. "*Everything*."

She weaves her fingers through mine and clasps our hands. "Do my list with me."

"What?" Momentarily, I don't know what she's talking about.

"My Tryst List." She kisses the back of my hand, staring me in the eyes. "We've already knocked the first item off and I want to do the rest...with you. Truthfully, you're who I was thinking about when I made it. Then 'poof' you were in my shop after a decade."

"You were thinking of *me*? But you were upset about me having it." I roll over and sit up, confused that she'd bring up the photo I deleted a couple hours ago.

Jordan leans up on her elbows. "It wasn't cool you went through my sketchbook without asking. I'm not ashamed of the list or doing anything on it."

"So, you want to have public sex with me?" I skooch off the bed, grab a clean dish towel and wet it. "Make videos of ourselves fucking?"

"Yes." I turn to see Jordan circling her clit with two fingers. Her knees are bent and splayed open, completely revealing her pussy glistening with our come.

My dick fills immediately. "You're insatiable. I was going to clean you up, baby. Cuddle you to sleep."

"It's only ten. I'm not worn out yet. Put the washcloth down. Dirty me up some more then you can clean me after." She smiles wickedly. "With your tongue or the cloth. Maybe both."

Holy shit, this woman is my dream come true on every level.

Jordan grabs my hips and yanks me forward. My dick bobs against her mouth. She licks her lips "Or, I'll clean you this time," she murmurs and slides her mouth over my crown.

Holy. Jesus. *Fuck.*

Slowly Jordan draws me deeper into her wet mouth. Wraps her hand around my base as she suctions me into her heat, all the while watching me with her glinting, green eyes. Fisting a hand in her messy hair, I lose myself in the visual of her sucking me down so deep she can barely breath. She reaches beneath my shaft and cups my sack and twists to the point where I'm not sure of the difference between pleasure and pain.

My knees nearly buckle, the only thing holding me up is my grip on the sides of her face. Pumping my hips, I force my cock down her throat. Testing her. Testing my own resolve.

Jordan's eyes water, and she gags, but she's all-in, clutching at my thighs. Digging her short nails into my flesh, causing the muscles in my legs to tense.

I'm goddamn close. With every suction of her mouth and squeeze of her hand, my cock feels like it's going to burst. I'm at the point of no return when I drag Jordan's head away to free myself. My cock bobs against her swollen lips. Tears stream down her cheeks and she gasps for air.

Gorgeous.

Fucking *mine*.

Chapter Sixteen

I've lost all willpower.

I'm in the middle of a new sexual awakening and the only thing I want to do from now to the end of time is fuck Peter again and again.

And again and again.

His cock is my drug and I'm in the throes of addiction.

To think this morning all I expected was for Peter and I to clear the air.

Instead, we're at each other like wild beasts. Clawing, scraping, groping. Every part of his body covers mine as he ravages my mouth. Together, we're completely uninhibited. Free to explore anything and everything bringing our bodies pleasure. He's my ultimate fantasy.

I mean, c'mon. I've asked him to bring my Tryst List to life.

"*Ahhhhhh*," I cry out when Peter pushes my legs up to my ears and impales me. Sweet Jesus, he shouldn't know my body this well. Every time he's inside me it's like our souls seem to merge. Sex with him is intense. Overwhelming.

Terrifying.

The incredible sensation of his cock hitting my magic spot pushes all my esoteric thoughts away. Probably a good thing, I shouldn't overthink when I'm getting the pounding of my life.

"Jordan. *Baby*." Peter cages my upper body with his arms and circles his hips, drilling himself deeper. "Stop thinking. Start feeling. Your pussy is perfection, baby. You fit me like a glove. My cock was made for you."

He slips his hands underneath us to cup my ass and move my body in time to his thrusts.

Holy shit, the way he controls me is fucking *every-thing*.

Peter circles my puckered hole. Dips down to where we're joined to swipe up our wetness channel. Uses the makeshift lube to push past my rosette, triggering spasms so strong I tighten and clench around his thrusting cock. "God, baby. You're so responsive. God, I can't wait to fuck you in the ass while you fuck yourself with a dildo. I'm going to make every one of your fantasies on your list come true, including DP. One hard boundary is I won't share you with anyone. Understand?"

I nod and bite my lip. I'm filled with his cock and a thick finger; I can't imagine what it will be like with two shafts inside me.

But I *want* to know.

Because if it feels like this only better, I'm down to try it as soon as possible.

"Please...I'm close..." I buck against him, desperate.

He withdraws his finger and holds himself up, fucking me with everything he has. He reaches between us with his other hand and pinches my clit and presses on my pubic bone with his palm. It's so intense my body feels like it's been suspended in midair for a second and I nearly lose consciousness when an orgasm originating from deep inside reverberates throughout my entire body. "Ohhhhhhh. Myyyyyy. *Goooooodddddd.*"

"Holy Jesus. I'm coming. Good fucking Lord..." Through my aftershocks, Peter jackhammers into me and my head thrashes from side to side when I feel him spurt his hot come deep inside me.

I'm a babbling, blithering mess. He's turned my body inside out. *Again.* I'm hardly conscious when he cleans me up and tucks me against his side under the blanket. He cocoons me in his arms, kisses my temple and whispers things I can't comprehend in the moment.

Eventually, lying against Peter, my body and mind quiet and I feel a sense of peace. Maybe it's the rocking of the boat beneath us. Maybe it's because I'm physically exhausted from having multiple full-body orgasms.

Or, maybe it's something more.

The dim light of the cabin casts blurred shadows, creating an intimate space for us. I know the feelings I had for him in Vegas were real. I believe his feelings for *me* were real. And now? When he holds me this close and I feel the steady beat of his heart against my back, I'm convinced we're meant for each other.

Yeah. There's nowhere else I'd rather be.

Nowhere.

"You're thinking awfully hard." Peter kisses the top of my head. "Are you okay?"

I stroke his taut abs. "You've said a lot of sweet things to me tonight in between the down-and-dirty fucking."

"I mean every word." He squeezes me to him.

"So, you want us to be a couple?" I look up at him. "Or are we a sex thing?"

Peter shifts to face me. "A *sex* thing? I'd marry you tomorrow if you'd have me."

My heart thumps in my chest so hard. Is he serious?

"Aaaannnd. I've officially freaked you out." He bites his lip.

I trace his eyebrow with my finger. "Tell me more about your family. You know about mine, or at least you Googled them." I tap my finger on my lip. "On second thought..."

We smile at each other because he knows I know he's already Googled my family. Just like he knows I'll be Googling his family at some point and probably won't find anything. God knows how I've resisted until now.

"I don't like talking about my family." Peter looks up at the ceiling. "It's complicated, to say the least."

"I'm listening," I say sensitively.

Peter takes a deep breath. "Well, I grew up in Sumner, Washington, in a lower-income working-class family.

My folks always saw education and ambition as... I don't know, selling out, maybe?"

"For someone as entrepreneurial as you, it must have been hard. Growing up with a different mindset." I can't relate, my family is the exact opposite.

"It was," he admits. "I love my parents, but we don't see eye to eye. And my brothers...they're a whole other story. They've had nonstop run-ins with the law. It's funny, I've always felt like the odd one out for wanting to channel my energy into changing the world."

I can hear the pain in his voice, the sense of being an outsider in his own family. "But you've built such an amazing life for yourself, Peter. You should be proud."

He smiles but, sure enough, there's a sadness in his eyes. "Of course I am, but it's been lonely at times. From the day and hour I started VA/VT, I've felt like an ATM. None of them have any concept about how hard I've worked to get where I am. So it's a tough balance, wanting to help but not enable."

"I'm sure you're doing the best you can." I squeeze his hand. "No matter what, family dynamics are complicated."

"Yeah," he sighs. "Things are as fucked up with them as they were before. I'm trying to get better about setting boundaries."

As we talk, I can't help but feel smitten by his vulnerability, his openness.

"You know, doing the things on your Tryst List." Peter cups my breast with a playful twinkle in his eye. "You have no idea how much I'm looking forward to it."

I laugh, feeling a rush of affection for him. "Well, I'm glad you're on board. It'll be an adventure, that's for sure. But, don't get any bright ideas. I'm done for tonight. I'm sore as hell from your monster cock."

"I'd say I'm sorry but..." Tiredness etches his features though it seems he, like me, doesn't want the evening to end yet. "So which fantasy do you want to explore next? I think this counts as the yacht too, right?"

"Yep. We ticked off stranded and yacht tonight." I nestle deeper into the blankets. "I don't know, Peter. I'm excited to explore everything with you but let's not make checking off sex acts the thing that defines us."

Peter nods, his expression thoughtful. "Yeah. Of course." He kisses me tenderly. "I get it. I don't want anything to overshadow us getting to know each other. For me, it's more about the moments we share."

"Exactly." I breathe a sigh of relief. "I want us to live in the present, explore things naturally."

He reaches out, tucking a strand of hair behind my ear. "So you're open to a Vegas wedding this weekend?"

"Why wait? Let's drive to Sea-Tac after we're rescued tomorrow." I laugh.

He combs his fingers through my tangled hair. "In all seriousness, don't worry, baby. We'll take each day as it comes. No pressure, no overthinking. Oh...FYI, I'm making my own list..."

"Your own Tryst List? Care to give me a preview?" I smirk.

Peter pulls me down. "Nope. You'll know when we do it. I like to keep things interesting."

Warmth spreads through me. It's comforting to know we're on the same page, this rekindled flame won't be reduced to a series of checkmarks. The Tryst List pales in comparison to the genuine connection we're rediscovering.

Our eyes grow sleepy. Peter's arm slackens as he drifts off.

In these quiet, early-morning hours, sleep overtakes me. I find myself looking forward to spending more time with Peter.

Having unexpected and unplanned moments to share. Is where the real magic lies.

Chapter Seventeen

The early-morning light casts a serene glow over the marina.

Seattle is always beautiful, but I don't think I've ever seen the sun rise over the city at this hour. Hues of pink, yellow, and orange illuminate the downtown buildings. It's the perfect ending to the perfect night.

I got up early. Vessel Assist brought enough fuel for us to get back into Kingston where I topped up and we headed home as it began to get light.

Jordan helps me dock. We've already packed up the soiled blankets for the laundry and she cleaned up the cabin while I navigated. I'm reluctant to say goodbye, but I don't want to come on too strong and spook her. I may have said I'd marry her in jest, but there's some truth in my intentions. If I thought she'd be down, the flight would have already been booked.

Plus, I'm not completely sure, but there seems to be a subtle shift in Jordan's demeanor. Perhaps the intimacy of our night of being stranded is giving way to the reality of what lies ahead for us. I watch her closely, trying to gauge her thoughts.

"Hey, how about we grab some breakfast?" I suggest, hoping to extend my time with her, even if it's for an hour or two. "It's still early. There's a couple of great spots at Pike Place Market."

Jordan smiles, but it doesn't quite reach her eyes like it did last night. "Thanks, Peter, but I'm gonna head home. I have a lot of things to catch up on before I'm back in the shop tomorrow."

I try to hide my disappointment, badly. "Sure, I understand. Maybe we can plan something for later in the week?"

She hesitates, a waft of uncertainty crosses her face. "Yeah, maybe. Let's see how it goes."

Together, we walk up to our cars but don't hold hands or have any physical contact. Fuck, this is awkward. I rack my brain for ways to keep our rapport intact. The intensity of last night was undeniable. The sex would be incredible under any circumstances, but the fusion of our souls made it extraordinary.

At least, for me.

This morning there's a cautiousness that didn't exist a few hours ago. I certainly don't want this experience to end the way Vegas did. I've got to step up.

We're at her car. "Last night was special, Jordan. I haven't felt so happy in... Well, ever."

"Yeah..." She pauses, a complex mix of emotions flash in her eyes. "It's a lot to process, you know?"

I nod, understanding her need for space, yet not willing to let her slip away too easily. "Take all the time you need. Just know, I want more of this with you. I'm not going anywhere."

A smile blooms on her pretty face. "Persistent much?"

"Only when it comes to things I care about." I take a step toward her.

Her hand's on the door handle, but there's a moment of hesitation. Closing the gap between us, I gently cup her face in my hands. Our eyes lock, conveying unspoken feelings and a bit of trepidation. Ignoring it all, I lean in slowly, savoring the moment, and our lips meet in a tender, sweet kiss, which lasts and lasts until we reluctantly pull apart.

"Well, I guess I'll see you around," she says with a tinge of something like regret in her voice. Or is it expectation?

"I'll hold you to it." I try to keep the mood light. "Have a great day, Jordan."

"You too." She touches my face and gets into her car.

As she drives away, I'm left standing in the serene beauty of the marina with the sweetness of her kiss lingering on my lips. Hope and apprehension swirl around in my heart. Hope for a future with Jordan. Apprehension she's not on the same page.

I'm a doer though, so I get into my car to head to my condo, already plotting my next move. The drive is a blur as I think about how fucking good it felt to be inside her. Better than in my wildest dreams. Even in the light of a new day, the intense passion we have for each other is something I've only experienced with Jordan.

She felt it too, despite her standoffish demeanor this morning.

It's tough to know how to handle things. How can I balance giving her the space she seems to need while vigorously pursuing a relationship with her? Given our history, I'm determined to take any path if it leads me to her. As far as I'm concerned, last night was just the beginning.

I'm home in no time. Going through the motions of picking up my mail and unlocking my door, I'm on autopilot because I'm replaying yesterday in my mind. The boat ride. Pizza. Our intense conversations. By the time I hit the shower, I allow myself to revisit every minute I worshipped her gorgeous body. Imagine myself plunging into her sweet, tight pussy makes me hard as steel.

Beating off in the shower isn't remotely as good as fucking Jordan, but it takes the edge off.

When I'm dressed, I set myself up in my home office and realize I've missed a flurry of notifications from nearly everyone on my Project SoHo team. My mind shifts gears immediately and I get to work catching up. One of our main competitors for Project SoHo is GCBA, a well-known firm out of Spain. Last night the company was outed for using subpar materials in a high-profile project. It's turned into quite the scandal with investigations launched and executives fired. Tales of wild drug-fueled parties and orgies.

Knowing the selection committee cites family values as one of its four pillars of excellence, I'm not surprised by the most recent news—GCBA is out. Which means the competition has been narrowed down to us and Malloy & Associates from London. It's a significant development. I'm close to realizing this dream and can't afford to lose focus.

I head out to the office with a sense of urgency. Once there, I scan the report my investigator provided on Malloy & Associates, looking for any edge that we can use to our advantage.

Surrounded by stacks of architectural plans and notes, the gravity of the situation with Project SoHo begins to truly sink in. Malloy & Associates, our main competition, are renowned for their innovative approach, but they've had their share of budget overruns. This could be our chance to edge ahead. Yet, as I delve deeper into the specifics of what winning this project entails, a sobering realization hits me.

Winning Project SoHo isn't only about prestige and success—it means committing to at least 3-4 years in London.

Yesterday, the relocation issue hadn't even registered. Today? The implications of moving to another country feel catastrophic. On one hand, it's the opportunity of a lifetime, a chance to leave my mark on the architectural world.

On the other, there's Jordan.

What's happening between us certainly feels deeper and more real than anything I've experienced before. Although, if earlier today is any indication, she may only want a fuck buddy. One thing's for sure, I can't do or say anything that'll spook her. If there's a chance she and I could become a couple, well... We'll have to figure it out if I win this job.

Would she consider a long-distance relationship? Would she move? Doubtful to either.

If she won't come with me, do I go?

I think the answer is yes. There's no way I can let my team at VA/VT down. They're all geared up for this project, buzzing with excitement and ideas. If we were to back out, not only would I let myself down, but also the staff who've been working tirelessly for years. For *me*. They're counting on this project.

Truthfully? So am I.

The weight of this decision is crushing.

Fuck. How has life gotten so complicated?

Torn between professional ambition and personal desire, I don't even realize the time. Suddenly it's late afternoon and my stomach is protesting the lack of food in my system. I'm about to order takeout when my phone vibrates with a text from Jordan.

My heart leaps at her name on the screen, but it also brings my dilemma into sharp focus.

Jordan:

> Hey…I'm sorry about this morning. I was a bit overwhelmed, I guess.

I stare at her message, my mind racing.

Me:

> No worries, it was a lot for both of us. Are you okay?

Jordan:

> Yeah. Last night was amazing. I've been thinking about it all day.

Reading her words, I feel a surge of emotion. She's been thinking about me—about us—as much as I have about her.

Me too. More importantly, I haven't been able to stop thinking about you.

Would you like to meet up? Maybe for dinner?

The way my heart jumps out of my chest, I guess I have my answer. In one day, Jordan's become the most important thing in my life. There's nothing I want more than to escape my swirling thoughts and be with her.

Absolutely. How about downtown? The Pink Door?

Sounds perfect. I'm coming from West Seattle, what time?

I'll make a reservation for 7.

Cool. See you then. xoxo

Stoked at the thought of our dinner date, the reality of my situation hits me. Her reaching out means we could be taking a step toward something more—something potentially life-changing for both of us.

The restaurant is only a short walk from the office, I have time to grab a snack before I need to refocus on the competitive analysis of Malloy & Associates.

Of course it's useless. My thoughts keep drifting to Jordan. After a couple of wasted hours, I decide to head out.

Sitting at the restaurant, with a half hour to spare until she arrives, I'm stressed. The weight of the dilemma I'm facing presses down on my shoulders.

I've coveted Jordan Deveraux for a decade, and maybe, just maybe, we're going to make our relationship official tonight. Yet, the next few months are critical. I can't take my foot off the gas with Project SoHo and I'm not going to slow things down with Jordan if I can help it.

The question is, will I choose love, or will I choose my career? Can I somehow have both, or am I destined to sacrifice one for the other?

At seven, I'm immediately on the lookout for Jordan. My anticipation builds with each passing second until I finally spot her.

The sight of the stunning siren takes my breath away.

Jordan stands at the hostess podium looking around the dining area, effortlessly embodying a pinup sexy-girl vibe, yet exuding an undeniable classiness. Her red dress hugs her curves in all the right places, revealing a hint of cleavage and a lot of leg. Her hair falls in smooth waves, reminiscent of a classic Hollywood era. The boldness of her red lipstick contrasts strikingly with her blonde hair, framing a smile that lights up her entire face when she sees me.

Her green eyes sparkle with excitement and warmth as she navigates through the tables on her way over. There's grace and assurance in her steps. Jordan's the perfect blend of strength and femininity.

Mine.

I stand, hold my hand out to her and all my doubts momentarily fade away.

There's no question I want to be with her.

No. I want it all—the professional life I've worked hard for and a future with Jordan.

Tough decisions will wait.

Tonight is all about her.

Chapter Eighteen

Today's been a trip.

I knew once Peter and I returned to Seattle I'd freak out.

And I did.

Spent a good solid hour crying. The emotions of what happened last night overwhelmed me. The fact of the matter is, Peter owned me.

Body. Mind. Soul.

I'm insanely sore and stretched. I can barely walk because every step I take is a reminder of his monster cock pounding me into a blithering, orgasmic frenzy.

Oh, and I'm pretty sure I'm in love with the guy.

Which is exactly what I *didn't* want to happen.

Earlier, I called Alex because she's the only person in the world I know who's been through something similar—with my brother, mind you. When I told her how fast things were going and how scared I am of giving Peter a real shot she schooled me. "Take it from me, don't overthink it. Trust your gut. Go get your man and see where it leads. Stop being afraid of what might or might not happen."

Her words were a much-needed jolt of reality. One text to Peter and now we're in the cozy ambience of The Pink Door sharing a tiramisu. Hands down, the best date I've ever been on. The conversation throughout dinner has been lighthearted yet flirtatious, filled with playful banter and subtle innuendos. Nothing too serious.

Peter feeds me the last bite. "The orgasmic look on your face when you eat chocolate." He grabs my hand across the table. "I'd give anything to see it every single day."

"What look?" I lick the last bit from the spoon. "When did you see me eat chocolate?"

"Uh...in Vegas, don't you remember? I fed you a Toblerone in bed. You have the same look of rapture now as you did when I licked your pussy." He squeezes my fingers between his and quirks an eyebrow.

And...my panties are wet. Of course I remember.

I remember everything.

"Peter." I take a deep breath because I'm taking such a huge risk and I'm scared shitless. "Without trying to DTR, the things you said last night and this morning. I want you to know my feelings for you are unlike anything I've ever experienced. I don't want to scare you off, but uh...I just..."

"I'm in love with you." He grips my fingers too tightly but I don't care. "Does that define the relationship?"

All the breath is sucked out of my body. Is this really happening? Is this what being in love feels like? I thought I loved Cameron, but no.

This. Is. It.

Alex was right. Life is short. It's time to be completely honest about my feelings and intentions.

He looks at me, waiting.

"I didn't mean to find a boyfriend. After Vegas, I came home feeling pretty humiliated. Cameron asked me out a few times prior to the trip, we lived in the same building at the time." I chew on my lower lip. Opening up isn't easy for me. "He asked me out and I went. At first, he reminded me of my pops. Tech guy. Nice. Goofy. Ambitious. The thing is, I've always been a relationship person. High school. Art school. The only one-night stand I ever had was with you. What happened scared me. I got tested. Was clean. Chose safe."

Peter's eyes don't leave mine, but there's a complexity in his gaze. A hint of confusion. Maybe a dash of worry. As though he's bracing for me to walk out without a backward glance. "Okay..."

"We were a couple for a long time and I never—and I mean *never*—felt anything close to what I felt for you in one night. I realized I didn't want to live my life being safe if there was nothing else, so I broke it off and took some time to figure out what I wanted. My mind kept returning to our night in Vegas. It's why I made my Tryst List. All because of you—or the *idea* of you." I know I'm babbling, but I can't stop.

I notice a change in Peter's disposition—by the smile playing on his lips, he's clearly delighted by my confession, but patiently waits for me to finish.

"I want to be honest about where I stand. I'm not interested in repeating my past mistakes." My shaky voice doesn't sound like my own. I'm nervous but force myself to continue. "I want something *real*. Something *meaningful*. And I think... I think I want it with you, and, uh...I'm in love with you too."

Peter's eyes widen. "Holy shit. Are we in *love?*"

"Oh, jeez." I pull my hand away and bury my face in my palms.

"Baby..." He pries my hands down. "No, don't hide from me. This moment is epic. We need to celebrate."

His words reassure me, yet I can't help but notice the slight tension in his posture. Like he's wrestling with something.

Of course, my mind immediately conjures up a million scenarios. All of which end in heartbreak for me. Taking a deep breath, I remember Alex's words and put my big-girl pants on. "Peter, I'm not hiding. I'm a woman in my thirties, who was in a long-term relationship with a man I didn't love. I'm realizing I've told the man I'm actually in love with how I feel—and I'm like a teenager who's confessed she has a crush on a boy. How emotionally stunted am I?"

"You're adorable when you babble." He grins from ear to ear. "As for me, I'm *not* a relationship guy and you're the first woman I've ever said the 'L' word to. If I have my way, you'll be the last."

I twirl a lock of hair with my finger. "So, here we are, a couple of immature idiots who had a one-night stand nearly a decade ago and can't seem to get over it."

"Sounds about right." Peter laughs. "Although, in our defense, we both have very successful businesses with multiple people working for us and have worldwide recognition in our professions, so..."

"Maybe we're immature geniuses." I can't help but join him in laughter.

Peter visibly relaxes. "Speaking of our businesses, tell me about your tattoo shop. I've read about you in magazines, of course, but tell me in your own words. What made you decide to hang up a shingle?"

My heart swells with pride at the mention of my shop. "The Salty Siren is my pride and joy. It's thriving, and I have plans to expand, maybe open another location. But, as the daughter of a tech giant, I want balance. I don't want my work to be my only focus."

"A family and kids?" He leans forward, genuinely interested.

"Sure." I gaze into his eyes and wonder what our children would look like. "I'm proud of what I've accomplished, but there's more to life than work."

Peter seems to ponder my words as his finger swirls around the rim of his wine glass. "Yeah."

"Not for you?" My heart catches in my throat.

He gives a small, somewhat forced smile. "Oh, I'd love those things. Right now, there are potential decisions about my future that could affect my company."

"It's none of my business but..." I lean back and study him. His vagueness piques my curiosity. I'm also concerned he's not ready to divulge whatever is on his mind after the conversation we had. Or am I just looking for red flags?

Peter shakes his head. "I'm up for a huge job. A life-changing situation for me and both my companies. I'm hesitant to talk about it because..."

"Superstition?" I helpfully finish, relieved it's nothing serious.

His eyebrow twitches. "Uh, maybe. What I can say is it's down to my company and one other. I spent the entire day working on a competitive analysis."

"Ah, you're probably tired." Part of me feels elated to have opened up to him, yet another part remains alert. He's clearly uncomfortable talking about this mystery project. Sadly, there's a slight tension permeating the romantic bubble of a few minutes ago. "Should we go?"

He nods and winks at me. "Yeah, we didn't get much sleep last night."

Peter insists on paying, which is nice. Leaving the restaurant, my stomach's in knots. On one hand, I'm filled with hope and excitement for what lies ahead with Peter. There's also a nagging uncertainty about the unresolved issue he's grappling with.

Yet, he's a man who makes me feel...well, like I'm the only woman in the world. Tonight, we confessed our love for each other, for God's sake.

As we walk through the Market, a bold sense of urgency surges through my entire being. I'm going to live in my own truth and if he can't handle it, Peter's not the guy for me.

Misinterpreting why I stopped in my tracks, he bends to kiss me, but I place my palm on his chest to stop him. "Look, I don't want to play games. We've already lost too many years." I keep my voice steady and clear. "I could play it coy, say goodnight, and catch an Uber home. But that's not what I want."

He watches me intently, surprise and anticipation flicker in his eyes.

"I enjoy expressing my affection physically, I've realized it's a huge part of who I am." I toe the ground but retain eye contact. "We've had sex—well, more than sex— and I don't see a reason to hold back. It's clear there's something you're keeping from me, and that's your prerogative. I still want us to explore whatever this is. Let's do my Tryst List. Hang out whenever we can." I narrow my eyes. "But leave declarations of love out of the equation until we're *both* coming from a place of commitment-level trust."

Peter leans forward. "I want to be with you and to understand all aspects of your life, and I want you to understand mine. I'm at a disadvantage because of my past behavior, my instinct is to lay out every single problem and flaw about myself and let the chips fall. On the other hand, everything between us feels natural and unforced. Honestly? I'm feeling a bit over my skis."

"That makes sense." Encouraged by his response, I lay out my vision for us in the short term. "We're both professionals with our own lives and obligations. Let's see if we can mesh our real lives. Take it one day at a time. When—and if—we're able to figure it out, we can put the 'L' word on the table again."

A smile spreads across Peter's face. "I understand, though I won't be able to help myself if it slips out." He kisses me. "But I agree. Let's not waste any more time. I want to know you, all of you. The professional, the artist, the woman."

Even as he speaks, I can sense a hint of hesitation, as if there's something he wants to tell me but can't find the words.

"Peter, are you sure there's not something else on your mind? You're saying all the right words, but you still seem a bit...conflicted," I probe, trying to be tactful but firm.

Briefly, a shadow crosses his face. "*No.* I'm not conflicted about you or us in any way, shape, or form. Please believe me." He grabs my hand. "I realized something about an important project that's bothering me. When I feel this way, I like to let it breathe. I'm sorry I haven't been better about hiding it—or maybe I'm not sorry since you want to be with me for some reason." He smiles. "Can we not worry about it tonight? I'd really like the rest of the evening to be about us."

His response piques my curiosity, but I decide not to press further.

"So, your place?" I rest my hands on his trim waist and blink up at him playfully.

He kisses my nose. "*Fuck* yeah. I thought you'd never ask."

The walk to Peter's place is filled with light touches and shared glances, a silent acknowledgment of the relationship we're both eager to explore. Despite the unanswered questions, I can't deny there's a sense of rightness in being with him.

An overwhelming feeling we're each other's destiny.

We arrive at his condo.

On the way up the elevator, I'm both excited and calm.

Could this be a new beginning for us?

Or, will Peter's secrets tear us apart?

Chapter Nineteen

My nerves are on high alert.

I'm en route to Jordan's family home in Medina, where her folks live amongst the who's who of tech bazillionaires, sports stars, and a couple of actors. It's not like the caliber of the celebrities she's related to intimidates me—I've worked with famous people for years. It's more like, embarrassingly, I've never met a girlfriend's parents before.

Today's my first time. I'm a parent-meeting virgin.

It's no wonder my nerves are practically vibrating. This isn't a normal family gathering; it's a high-profile wedding with security protocols rivaling any A-list celebrity event. Jordan's brother, Jace, is marrying his longtime love Alex on Valentine's Day, and it's quite the production.

As I approach the address on the invitation, I'm greeted by a security checkpoint complete with a guest list and bodyguards who look like they've stepped out of a Hollywood movie. One of them, stern-faced and armed, checks my ID against the list.

"Name, please?" he asks with no hint of welcome in his tone.

I try to sound like I'm used to this on a daily basis. "Peter Vander."

He scans the list, nods, allows me passage. The tone of his voice doesn't change, though his words do. "Welcome, Mr. Vander. Enjoy the wedding."

A valet intercepts me at the next stop. Once I relinquish my car, there's a metal detector and a cell phone drop-off point before I'm ushered through the gates onto the grounds of the forty-thousand-square-foot mansion, if my calculations are correct. Though it's been all Jordan's talked about for the past couple of weeks, it's only when I'm actually there the sheer scale of the event becomes apparent. I'm blown away her mother was able to pull this off in such a short amount of time.

The mansion itself is breathtaking, a sprawling testament to luxury and elegance, nestled beautifully on the shores of Lake Washington. The garden is transformed into a tented wedding paradise, delicate fairy lights creating a dreamlike ambiance.

I make my way along the path, feeling both at home and out of place amid the grandeur and the buzz of high-profile guests milling about. Some faces are recognizable—said actors, musicians, and tech moguls—mingling and laughing in their expensive suits and designer dresses.

A butler approaches me as I near the main gathering area. "May I assist you, sir?" In contrast to the guards, he has a polite, professional demeanor.

"Uh, yes, thank you. My name is Peter Vander, I'm looking for Jordan Deveraux." I scan the crowd, trying to catch a glimpse of her.

"Ah, yes. Mr. Vander. Miss Deveraux is part of the bridal party." His face lights up. "They're currently preparing. May I escort you to the waiting area for the ceremony?"

Nodding, I follow him, taking in the extravagant setup. Everything is meticulously organized, from the placement of chairs to the floral arch where the ceremony will take place. The view of the lake provides a stunning backdrop.

Without my phone, I'm unable to text Jordan, though I did let her know when I arrived at the first gate. Mingling amongst the wedding guests while I wait for her to find me, I accept a glass of champagne. Though I don't see Fiona because she's also in the wedding party, I recognize a few of my other clients in attendance, which makes me feel more at ease when I'm able to chat and make small talk.

Maybe I actually belong here.

"Holy shit, you're fucking gorgeous." Jordan, radiant in her bridesmaid dress, wraps her arms around me from behind. "You made it through the labyrinth. We've always had security, but today is next level."

I turn and take in her va-va-voom perfection. Her hair has been styled in some sort of elaborate updo. She wears a simple, satiny pinkish number leaving nothing to the imagination. "It was fine, baby. You're stunning. And, holy hell, this place is incredible."

"Ah, thanks, baby." She clutches my hand in both of hers. "I know, it's a bit much, but my family doesn't do anything by halves. I wanted to come see you, but the wedding planner will kill me if I don't get back to her. Sit anywhere and I'll find you after the ceremony."

She darts off and before long I find myself shuffled with the rest of the guests to get seated. I decide to park myself toward the rear on Alex's side of the aisle so I can see Jordan. The wedding unfolds beautifully. The vows, the setting, the emotion in the air—it's all picture-perfect.

I'm not gonna lie, I have a visual of Jordan standing up there waiting for me and it makes me happy.

After the ceremony, Jordan rejoins me, and we navigate the reception prior to dinner. Jace and Alex are surrounded by well-wishers, but I meet her sister Jen and Jen's partner, Becca, Jaylynn and her husband, whose name I've already forgotten.

We're guided to yet another location where Jordan's parents, Jason and Grace hold court. Jason, a formidable figure with a protective glint in his eye, extends his hand with a firm grip designed to assess my character.

"Peter, I've heard quite a bit about you." Jason's piercing gaze is intimidating, though I detect a hint of playfulness beneath his stern demeanor. It's kinda cute, Jordan shares this trait.

Trying to remain composed despite my nerves at meeting one of the most famous businessmen in the world, I manage to keep my voice calm. "It's a pleasure to meet you, sir."

"Welcome, Peter. Jordan speaks of you often." Grace kisses me on the cheek and clasps my hand with a warmth that counterbalances her husband's sternness.

As the conversation unfolds, I find common ground with Grace over our shared interest in design. Her insights into high-end interiors and the use of green technology are fascinating, and I feel myself relaxing into the conversation.

Jason, however, seems intent on keeping me on my toes. "So, Peter. VA/VT is quite impressive. I've been fascinated by your trajectory for quite a few years. I hear you're up for quite a prestigious appointment."

"Uh, yeah." I glance down at Jordan, who beams at me but quirks a brow. I still haven't told her about London, not because I'm hiding it. It hasn't come up.

Lies. I'm totally avoiding the topic. Which is why it hasn't come up.

Immediately, I feel like a piece of shit.

"Peter's firm is one of two in the running to design the new London pop culture museum and the infrastructure surrounding it." Jason nods approvingly to Grace. "Best of luck, it could put your career on the worldwide map. Cement your name in history."

And...just like that I'm outed by Jordan's dad. Jordan continues to smile at me to save face, but I see the hurt and confusion behind her eyes.

I have no choice but to acknowledge his comment. "Thank you, sir."

Grace gives her husband a gentle nudge. "We need to get inside." She touches my sleeve. "We'll chat more after dinner."

Jordan's lips set into a line, but with all the activity and people around us there's no time to explain. She and I are seated at the family table and tonight isn't about us. I'm quiet in the midst of the bustling dinner, hum of conversations and numerous clinking of glasses. The food and wine are probably delicious, but it's like acid in my stomach. I find myself longing for a moment alone with my girl.

Dinner finally wraps up a couple hours later. At the first opportunity, I tilt my head slightly, silently suggesting to Jordan that we sneak away. She understands immediately and nods her assent with an apprehensive sigh.

We slip out unnoticed, finding a secluded spot in the beautifully landscaped gardens of the mansion. The night air is brisk and the stars above are brilliant, casting a dramatic glow over the serene lake. It sucks to have this conversation during such a romantic celebration.

"Before you start in, *don't*." Jordan shakes her head. "We'll talk about this London thing tomorrow."

I stop in my tracks. "But..."

"I'm not an idiot. We're practically living together and it's obvious something at work stresses you out and it's not like you're quiet when you have calls." She rolls her eyes. "Besides, Pops told me all about London when I put you on the guest list. You must have a good reason for keeping this from me and tomorrow you'll tell me what it is. Tonight is our first Valentine's Day and I'd like to enjoy it and the rest of the wedding without fighting."

I take her hand, surprised at the grace she's giving me. "Why aren't you mad?"

"Peter, I grew up with my pops. It's not like he could disclose every little thing to my mom. He protected their relationship by not talking about work all the time and she trusted him to tell her about things impacting our family." She shrugs. "You and I are still new. I trust how you feel about me. Let's drop it and talk when we're alone and can get into it without a million people around."

I reach into my pocket, feeling the flat velvet box I picked up last week. "Okay. Thank you, baby. I'll give you the details later, I promise. How about I try to get the evening back on track. I have a Valentine's Day gift for you."

"What?" Her eyes widen with surprise. I open the box to reveal a delicate necklace. The pendant is a beautifully crafted mermaid made up of aquamarines, opals, and sapphires, shimmering under the twinkly lights.

"Oh, Peter, it's stunning!" Her hands cover her mouth in awe.

I carefully lift the necklace from the box, moving behind her to clasp it around her neck. "Taking inspiration from your mermaid designs I had this made. Beautiful, unique, captivating...like you."

"Ohmygod. This is so thoughtful." She turns around, her eyes glistening, and throws her arms around me. "Thank you, baby."

We share a tender, passionate kiss, the kind that makes the rest of the world fade away. A moment of pure intimacy, like most of my moments with Jordan. Sometimes I feel our emotions for each other expressed without words, and I want to do better. Be better. "Jordan...I know we said we wouldn't do this..."

"Not yet." She puts her finger up to my lips and shakes her head.

Sadly, I nod my understanding. She's right. We agreed to take the "L" word off the table until we were sure our lives meshed. With London looming, I don't know if they do. Instead, I gather her in my arms, and we sway under the stars, wrapped together. I can only hope my embrace conveys how I truly feel about her.

Eventually, we realize we've been gone a hair too long. Reluctantly, we make our way to the reception where everyone is dancing and it's not long before we encounter Jace and a couple guys from his band.

"So, Peter, enjoying the party?" Jace's knowing glance and slightly raised eyebrow don't escape my notice. He looks exactly like Jordan's father must have thirty years ago.

I grip Jordan's hand. "Yes, thank you for including me. Congratulations, by the way."

"So, he's the infamous Vegas guy," Jace says to his band mates while clapping me on the back.

Jordan slugs him in the arm. "Shut up, *ohmygod.*"

"What?" Jace puts his arm around her. "I've been there. To Alex, I was the infamous rockstar and now look at us…"

Alex taps him on the shoulder. "Say another word and we'll rewind this whole day."

The LTZ guys burst with laughter and continue bantering while I watch in fascination. They're so…free. I haven't found many friends I can trust—or be myself with. Jordan was the first. She's the center of attention and, considering how often they look over at me, I'm the main topic. The realization our history is common knowledge amongst her family and friends is both touching and overwhelming.

I *mean* something to her.

Throughout the night, Jordan introduces me to about a million people. We eat cake. Eventually, she and I find ourselves on the dance floor. As we sway to a slow song, I grapple with tomorrow's conversation hanging over me. It looks like I'll be in London for a few weeks as part of the final round of scrutiny for Project SoHo.

The thought of having to choose between two once-in-a-lifetime opportunities is unfathomable. A career in London? Or a committed relationship in Seattle with the love of my life?

I've let this go too long and it's not fair to Jordan. I need to be honest with her, even if it changes everything. I'm not sure how she'll react when she realizes I'll be away on business for weeks, let alone that I may have to move.

As the reception draws to a close and we say our goodbyes to her family and friends, the weight of my unspoken news feels heavier than ever.

Walking to my car with Jordan's hand in mine, I know without a shadow of a doubt I can't live without this.

Without her.

I'm in a hell of a conundrum, with no easy way out.

Chapter Twenty

Jordan

Good Lord, I needed a good night's sleep.

Stretching languidly, appreciating Peter's extraordinarily comfortable mattress, I roll over to find the bed empty beside me. I clutch the pillow and take a deep whiff, savoring the lingering warm, woodsy scent of his essential oil cologne. Surprisingly, I feel refreshed, though we stayed up most of the night making love.

Slipping out of bed, I pull on one of Peter's T-shirts and barefoot it to the kitchen to find him and get some coffee.

Peter's condo is modern and eco-friendly, with sleek lines and an airy, open-plan design. It's peaceful here. His dedication to maintaining a net-zero footprint is admirable, and while I always considered myself environmentally conscious, I'm learning a ton from him.

I pad silently across the cool, polished floor toward Peter's voice but realize he's on the balcony, engaged in what sounds like a heated phone conversation. I pause, not wanting to eavesdrop, but my curiosity gets the better of me.

Making my way to the kitchen, I stop to pour myself a cup of coffee then quietly step out onto the balcony. The Seattle waterfront view is breathtaking, with the morning sun casting a golden hue over Puget Sound.

Peter, wearing nothing but joggers, leans over the railing. His posture is tense, but the phone call apparently ended. Lost in thought, he doesn't notice me at first. In stark contrast to the usual calm-and-collected man I've come to know, his agitation is palpable.

"Everything okay?" I step closer to him and place my hand on his shoulder. Though it's still cold outside, the patio is heated using solar power, making it cozy even though I'm wearing barely anything.

Slightly stunned, he turns toward me, managing a half smile. "Oh, hey. Yeah, it's nothing. Just some family stuff."

"Family stuff with your mom?" I take a seat on one of his loungers and sip my coffee. He doesn't like to talk about it, but she seems to call him quite a bit.

He nods, looking out over the water. "Yeah, she... She can be demanding. It's complicated."

"You can talk to me about it, you know. Whatever it is." Part of me doesn't want to upset him, but the other part doesn't want him to keep things from me anymore. "Just like you can tell me about London."

Peter runs a hand through his hair. "It's the usual. She has this way of making me feel responsible for everything that goes wrong in her life, especially when it comes to my brothers. It's exhausting."

"That sucks." I can hear the frustration in his voice. It's a rare glimpse into the challenges he faces with his family. "I'm sorry you have to deal with it. But remember, you're not alone anymore. I'm here for you."

He turns to me and puffs out a huge breath. "I know, and I appreciate it. It's hard sometimes, trying to balance everything. They rely on me for money, and it feels like a never-ending cycle."

"Maybe it's time to set even more boundaries. You can't be everything to everyone." Hooking my fingers in his waistband, I tug him toward me, intending to offer what comfort I can.

He grins down at me. "You're right. It's not easy to change years of bullshit."

It's a moment of vulnerability for Peter, a side of him I've only begun to understand. I want to make him feel better. Peering up into his bright, blue eyes, I press kisses along the tight muscles of his abs down the smattering of silky hair under his belly button.

"Ah, babe. What are you doing to me?" Peter cups the sides of my face.

I peel down his joggers and his cock springs free against his stomach. "If it's not obvious, I'm doing a terrible job."

"*Fuuuuckkkk.*" He groans when I stroke him firmly in the way I know he likes. My man needs a little peace. To know I'll always be a safe place for him. I'll always be on his side.

Peter fists his hands at his sides, flexing and gripping as I get to work. His gaze is hot on me when I lift his shaft and suck his sac into my mouth. His nostrils flare when I run my tongue along the underside of his cock, following the pulsing vein to his crown. His entire body shivers when my mouth envelops him and I take him to the back of my throat.

"Jordan, your mouth is fucking heaven." He caresses my cheeks; his thumbs press against the corners of my mouth.

Relaxing my jaw and throat, I allow him to push deeper. When I swallow the tip, Peter groans and his head lolls. His thighs quake with the effort it's taking not to come. He pushes in deep, causing me to gag and choke. Saliva pools out of my mouth. He pulls free. "Sorry, baby. I'm too big. It's too much."

"I like it." And I do. Blowjobs aren't usually my thing. Then again, Peter is religious about eating clean. It makes a difference. He tastes amazing, I'll happily suck his cock any time he wants it.

I take him back into my mouth. This time, Peter covers my hands with his, threading our fingers as he slowly thrusts between my lips. We find a smooth, easy rhythm. He goes a little deeper each time and I drift into a dreamlike trance—savoring his taste on my tongue while he stretches my lips with each pass. His tempo slowly ramps up and I lean forward, changing the angle.

From his labored breathing and guttural groans stran-gling out of him, I know Peter's close. His cock flexes and he grips my hair. Flattening my tongue, I'm able to take him deeper.

"Jesus...oh, *Fuck*...baby..." Peter's hips snap forward when he releases down my throat. I swallow everything he has to give and suck and lick him until he's empty and slips free.

Chest heaving, Peter sags down, bracing his arms on either side of me. Gripping his ass, I ease him down and curl my arms around his neck until he settles. When his breathing returns to normal, he fits himself behind me and bands his arm around my waist, pulling my back against his chest. His other hand combs through my hair.

"Do you feel better?" I look up at him from over my shoulder.

Peter slides his hand down to my bare pussy and runs his fingers through my folds. "Much better. And I can tell you liked it too." He kisses me hard and deep and brings the finger coated with my arousal to our lips. "Taste."

"Mmmm." I suck myself off him and he dips his wet finger into my moisture.

No one can get me off as fast and as often as Peter can. The palm of his hand presses against my mound as he fucks me with his fingers, every so often pulling them out to rub my clit. When his free hand slips under his T-shirt and pinches my nipple, it's all over. Wincing, I cream all over him, clamping down on his wrist with my thighs, trapping him in place.

Peter laughs and drags his lips under my ear. "Greedy, greedy girl. Do you need another one?"

"Yes, please." I turn slightly in his arms to watch him rub my clit.

This man has ruined me. Well, he did that in Vegas years ago. It's only been confirmed over the past couple months of us being together. My body craves him. It doesn't matter what we do, he and I are molten.

"Hold up your shirt, baby. I want to suck on those delicious nipples of yours." I do as he asks as Peter sneaks his other hand behind me and works a finger inside my ass. He dips his head down and rakes his teeth along my breast and resumes fucking me with his fingers in both locations.

In seconds, I'm a blithering mess.

When I return to normality, Peter's kissing my forehead. "Welcome back, sweet girl."

"Not that I'm complaining, but you didn't need to get me off." I reach up and stroke his hair. "It was supposed to be about you."

He bends down to kiss me. "For me, it's always about you. Plus, we checked off another item on the Tryst List."

"Sex on a balcony. Right. Though it was just oral..." I wriggle in his lap.

He cups my tits and squeezes. "I thought we said we're using your list as a guide." He slips his cock into me from behind. "We're making progress. Washing machine was easy. I nailed you at the jobsite after everyone left. We film ourselves all the time. What do we have left? Somewhere public, mile high club, and nature?"

"Don't forget we knocked off my shop and your office." I watch him thrum my nipples as he thrusts up into me. "The limo was kind of public, wasn't it? We agreed your boat checked off both yacht and being stranded, right?"

Peter nuzzles my neck. "Yep. So, we have two left."

'Ohhhhhhhh.' I can't even comprehend what he's saying because my orgasm rips through me like a lightning bolt.

After Peter expertly fucks me into oblivion, we pull ourselves together and relax on the lounger entwined. The city's distant hum mirrors the buzzing in my head. As much as I'm tempted to get lost in this moment of closeness, it's long past time to address some unspoken truths between us. There's an undercurrent of things left unsaid. A disconnect I can't afford to ignore any longer.

"Peter," I try to convey tenderness with the seriousness in my tone, "we need to talk. About everything. London, your family... I shouldn't be hearing about these things from other people."

He squeezes his eyes shut. When he opens them, they're filled with a dawning realization he can't avoid this discussion any longer. His brows wrinkle with worry. "I'm not trying to keep things from you. I don't want to burden you with my problems. Especially not with my family."

"But that's just it." I prop myself up on an elbow. "If we're going to move forward, there shouldn't be any burdens we can't share. Let's start with this museum project. My pops told me the scale of it. Why didn't you?"

He scrubs his hand through his hair, his "tell" when he's uncomfortable, I've learned. "Truthfully? I... I wasn't sure how. The thought of being away from you and how it might affect us... It weighs on me. I want a future with you and..."

"...I need honesty." My tone is delicate yet firm. "If our lives can ever truly mesh, we need open communication. I can't commit to you if you're half in the shadows."

He nods and tightens his grip around my waist. "You're right, of course. I suck at this. Sometimes it's hard to open up when I'm afraid of what the reaction will be. It's always been a source of stress in my world."

"I understand, but I'd like it if you could start trusting me." I take his hand, offering a reassuring squeeze. "A committed relationship means sharing the stress. The worries. The fears."

He looks out over the Seattle waterfront. The early-morning light casts a mellow glow over his face. He doesn't answer for a while and I'm about to say something when he threads our fingers. "I *am* committed to you. Last night was a real eye opener for me. Your family is loving. Supportive. I can see where your expectations for a relationship were learned."

"And..." I encourage.

"My experience was very different. There's no room for error or there are accusations, snide comments, and gaslighting. Fights in the Vander household are no joke. I've always hated it. Felt like I was born into the wrong family." He lets out a big breath and looks me in the eye. "There's no excuse. I need to learn how to be honest with you about what's going on. I want to let you in, even if it means you'll be disappointed in me."

I lean against him, closing the distance between us. "I'll only be disappointed if you clam up. So, let's start. Tell me about London."

He takes a deep breath, turning to face me. "London... It's a huge opportunity, baby. The kind of project architects dream of. But it also means I'll have to move..."

Just like that, the world falls out from under me.

Peter's leaving me.

Again.

Chapter Twenty-One

The look on her face scares the shit out of me.

What's even worse— she's ripped herself from my embrace and stands over me with her arms crossed.

"Let me explain." This long-overdue conversation has been the bane of my existence. I'm not even sure where to begin. "Project SoHo is the code name. My team and I have been working on the submission and proposals going on three years. It started with over five hundred applicants. The review committee narrowed the field in stages. We've made it through all the cuts and we're at the end. I found out VA/VT was one of the three finalists just a few weeks before you started my tattoo.

Instead of understanding, devastation permeates her entire body.

"So, let me get this straight. You knew about this before you came in for your tattoo. Before you took me on the boat and said...all those things." She chews on her lip. "This entire time you've made me believe you and I have a future when you're fucking moving to *London*?"

"Yes, I've known," I admit, guilt gnawing at me. "Baby, it's not like I wanted to keep this secret. I was telling the truth when I told you I was superstitious. I didn't want to say anything about the move in case I didn't get the job."

"Well, that's a crock of bullshit." Jordan's face squinches with frustration. "For something this important you should absolutely tell the person you profess love for."

She's absolutely right and I know it. My hands clench into fists because my body is tense with desperation. "I know. I've messed up. But I do love you, Jordan. I don't want to lose what we have. At the same time, this is a massive opportunity for me and for the firm. If we get it, my building will be part of the London skyline forever. Sure, I may have to move to London for a few years, but it's not forever.

She tugs her T-shirt down. "So, what's the plan? When is all this happening?"

"My team and I are scheduled to go to London next month for a few weeks." I run my hands through my hair. "I've been struggling to figure out how I can balance our relationship and this job, but I absolutely should have—"

"Wait. You've been *struggling*?" She wraps her arms around herself like a protective barrier. "You're figuring out you can't balance a relationship with me and still do this project, aren't you? Because we're talking about *years*."

"No, that's not it at all." I reach out to her, but she steps away.

Jordan is shaking. Her voice warbles. "What is it?"

"I want to be with you, but this is my dream. I can't give up this opportunity." It's the first time I've said this out loud and the magnitude of my conflict drops to the ground like a cannonball.

"Of course you can't. I want you to have everything you've ever wanted, Peter." Tears well up in her eyes. "But where does moving leave us?" Her eyes search mine for answers I don't have.

All I can do is apologize. "I...uh. I'm sorry. I want us to be together so bad, but I was petrified of losing you."

And now I'll probably lose you anyway.

Jordan looks out over the waterfront, her expression torn. "To say this sucks is a fucking understatement. It's a lot to process. I need to think about what I want. What's even possible. I don't doubt your feelings." Her voice breaks slightly as she opens the door to go inside. "But in my world, love is about trust. Honesty. You've kept this from me, and it feels like a betrayal."

The warmth of the condo does little to dispel the chill settling over us. Jordan seems lost in thought, her movements automatic.

"I'm going to get dressed," she says quietly, breaking the silence.

I nod, watching her as she walks away. The sight of her in my T-shirt, which goes past her knees, usually brings me such joy. Now it makes me sad. I'm acutely aware of the emotional distance that's sprung up between us in minutes.

Left alone in the living room, I sink onto the sofa. The fabric of the cushions still holds our scent from making love last night. A reminder of the intimacy we shared moments ago on the balcony.

It's hard to reconcile.

Losing Jordan is unfathomable.

How will I survive without the best friend I've ever had? All the little moments we share? The secret glances. Eating together. Cuddling on the couch. Holding her hand. Our banter.

What's worse? Another man will taste her sweet nectar. Look into her eyes with his cock buried inside her. Smile as she walks down the aisle to promise him forever. Caress the swell of her belly.

Catastrophic.

Nobody's taking those moments from me.

A seizing pain grips my heart and takes my breath away. I've never felt anything like it, like my lungs are on fire and frozen all at once.

After a few minutes, Jordan returns, dressed in her own clothes. The transformation feels symbolic. Her expression is composed, but her eyes betray the turmoil she's feeling. She's pissed.

No. *Furious.*

She sits in the chair across from me. "What happened to the symbolism of your tattoo? Did you forget about it entirely? As far as I can tell, you've failed at prudence by not being able to discern the appropriate course of action. You're a fucking coward for not telling me, so fortitude's a wash. What are the other ones?"

"Justice and temperance."

"Ah, right." She teems with frustration. "What, exactly, is morally right about lying to me? What kind of self-control did it take to keep quiet? You told me the design was a reminder to embody all of the virtues."

She's fucking right. "I failed and I'm sorry. Can we talk about it?"

Our conversation continues for several hours. A back-and-forth filled with high emotions and solemn practicalities. We discuss logistics of a long-distance relationship, the impact on our careers, our personal lives. Unfortunately, the deeper we get into the weeds, the more it becomes apparent there are no easy answers. We love each other, but the reality of our situation is complex, filled with uncertainties and sacrifices.

As the day wears on, we're at a stalemate. Jordan is rightfully hurt. I've kept a significant part of my life from her, and it's threatening to tear us apart.

At the same time, it sucks I can't be excited about Project SoHo with her. A sliver of resentment snakes up my spine. I want her to be proud of me, not sad, resentful, and angry with no reprieve in sight.

Doesn't she realize I'll do anything to make our relationship work?

I'm exhausted. Frustrated. What I should do is table the conversation. Instead, my Vander genes kick in and I speak without thinking. "Jesus, Jordan. My life didn't stop after Vegas."

Her face drops. "*What*?"

"From the day we met, you were it for me. I realize I left you and you felt a certain way, but I'm not the one who immediately dove into an eight-year relationship with someone I didn't love just to feel safe. If you felt strongly about me..." It's like I'm in slow motion when I step in it further—I can't help myself. "Forget it. You're fixated on a move that may never happen. It's not like I was going to disappear off the planet. This entire thing should be simple. Having you in my life shouldn't complicate everything."

Jordan's expression, usually so animated and expressive, freezes. There's a sudden stillness in her features and her eyes widen in shock. Agony. The vibrant energy that usually radiates from her like sunshine visibly dims, replaced by a hurt so profound it's almost tangible.

Her glittery green eyes, always full of life and warmth, glisten with unshed tears, reflecting a deep sense of disbelief. It's as if she's struggling to comprehend how the person she's grown to love could destroy her trust and inflict such pain.

It's unbearable to witness, and it's all my fault.

"Oh, *shit*. That came out all wrong. Baby...I'm sorry." I move toward her.

Jordan's posture shifts in an instant. She wraps her arms around herself like a physical barrier to match the emotional one my careless words created. The vulnerability she's shared freely, even today, is hidden behind a wall of self-preservation. "*Don't. Fucking. Touch. Me.*"

The room grows silent except for the faint, ragged breaths Jordan takes as she tries to compose herself. She leans on the wall, as if she's trying to regain some semblance of control over the damage I've carelessly inflicted.

Seeing her like this, witnessing the direct impact of my words, fills me with a profound sense of regret and shame. I'm a fucking Vander through and through. I'm horrified. Ashamed. *Devastated*.

In this moment, I realize the gravity of the irreparable damage I've done to the person I love most in the world. The realization I probably won't be able to repair what I've broken looms over me like a daunting shadow over the bond we've built.

"Peter, I'm going home." Jordan's voice is steady but laced with an undercurrent of sadness.

The finality of her words sting, even though I understand her need for space and time from me to process everything. "I'm *sorry*. I was thoughtless with my words. It's not who I am, I'm ..."

"Today has been a lot." She avoids eye contact as she heads to my front door. "I need to think about all of this, and I can't be in your condo anymore."

More than anything, I want to reach out to her. Mend what I smashed to bits. Bridge the gap between us. Pick your fucking metaphor, but I don't do any of it. She should be able to process what happened in peace, no matter how much it hurts. At this point, my feelings are irrelevant.

"Can I call you later?" I say to her back, clinging to the hope this isn't the end of our conversation. Of us.

She still won't look at me and she's halfway out the door. "When I'm ready, I'll be in touch."

There's a finality in her words that makes my heart sink. When the door shuts behind her, the quiet of the condo feels oppressive. A stark contrast to the laughter and closeness we shared last night and this morning.

Fuck. Fucking *fuck*. I punch my fist against the wall. The excitement I once felt about Project SoHo feels overshadowed by the potential cost to my personal life. The possibility of losing Jordan this way, of hurting her so deeply, was something I didn't see coming.

Clutching my phone, waiting for Jordan to call, I don't move for hours. A loneliness more profound than I could ever imagine permeates my body with each passing minute. Tormented, I replay our conversation—every word and every expression of hurt on Jordan's face—over and over.

I've always been able to navigate the complexities of my professional life with confidence, but I'm a fucking loser when it comes to navigating the complexities of love.

That's the truth.

With a heavy heart, knowing I won't sleep a wink, I resign myself to the truth.

She's gone.

Chapter Twenty-Two

I've had something of an epiphany.

After feeling stuck with my mermaid designs for the past couple of years, I decided to change my attitude and remember why the sea Sirens inspired me in the first place. I'm pretty sure Peter's approach to his work rubbed off on me a bit. His eco-friendly designs are why he's successful, but he tackles each project with a sense of wonder and delight.

He leans into his gift.

I've been doing the same.

This morning, I completed a full leg sleeve—one of the most intricate and vibrant works I've ever created. My client, Emmie Lopez, is the guitar player for an up-and-coming band, Candy Crushed. I'm honestly not sure how she's able to afford a fifty-thousand-dollar tattoo, but who am I to judge.

Anyway, I'm thrilled with the outcome. The mermaid's eyes are a mesmerizing shade of deep ocean blue and convey the mysteries of the sea. Her hair, flowing and alive with shades of aquamarine and seafoam green, cascades down Emmie's thigh like a waterfall, blending seamlessly into the waves and currents forming the backdrop of the scene.

The scales on her tail are a kaleidoscope of ocean hues – turquoise, cerulean, and lavender – shimmering as if touched by the sun's rays filtering through the water. The sense of movement in her tail, with each scale meticulously shaded, gives the impression of a delicate swaying motion.

Surrounding the mermaid, the underwater world comes to life on Emmie's skin. Corals in vibrant oranges, pinks, and purples create a sense of depth and texture. I've painstakingly etched each detail and the result is a realistic portrayal of a thriving ocean floor.

As I worked on this particular tattoo, I remembered why mermaids inspired me in the first place. Every stroke of my needle and every blend of color is an expression of the passion I still hold for my craft. It's my finest piece. Everyone in the shop applauded when they saw the end result, which was humbling.

More importantly, Emmie is over the moon.

Though I'm filled with a sense of accomplishment, the adrenaline of a job well done is wearing off.

"Girl, I know you're not sitting here staring into space." Merc joins me in the breakroom where I'm doing just that.

It's hard not to rathole on the argument Peter and I had. His words echo painfully in my mind. The dishonesty hurts even worse. "He's been sending me texts, Merc. Apologizing, saying how much he misses me, how sorry he is. But I... I don't know what to do."

"Do you want to forgive him?" Merc frowns with concern.

I trace the rim of my tea mug. "I don't know. I wish I wasn't in love with him. It makes things complicated. We're not the same kids we were in Vegas—we've veered into commitment territory, and I don't know if I can trust him, let alone forgive him."

"Hmmm." Merc leans back, considering his words carefully. "Forgiveness isn't about forgetting, Jordan. It's about deciding whether the love you have is stronger than the pain he caused—and whether he's worth the effort in the end."

"Isn't that the fucking truth." I rest my cheek on my palm. "There's also the London thing. He's possibly moving there for years and he didn't think it was important information to tell me. I don't want to build a long-term relationship with someone who picks and chooses what he discloses about his life. Like I did to Cameron. Holy shit. I'm a monster. Is this karma biting me in the ass?"

Merc taps his long fingers on the table. "Well, that's dramatic AF because you can't compare the two. Cameron wasn't some safe little simp who you did wrong. He didn't support you or this shop. Plus, you didn't love each other enough to make it work."

"Fine, I'll give you that. The point is, I'm *not* leaving Seattle. This is my home and I love it. I don't want to be away from my family and business." I glance down at my phone, where Peter's daily texts stare me in the face. I show them to Merc.

Peter:

Jordan, I'm sorry. Keeping the London project from you was wrong. I should have been honest from the start.

Peter:

I've been thinking about everything I said, and I realize how much I've hurt you. It wasn't fair to you. I'm sorry for being such a dick. It's eating me up inside, and I wish I could take it all back.

Peter:

Baby, every day without you feels empty. I regret everything I've done to make you walk away. Please give me another chance. I made a mistake;, one I deeply regret. I'm sorry for letting you down and for the pain I've caused.

Peter:

I've been doing a lot of thinking. Not just about what I said, but about how I've handled everything from the beginning with you. I let my fears and ambitions get in the way of our trust and openness. That was wrong, and I'm so sorry. You deserved honesty and transparency from me, and I failed to give you that. I understand if you can't forgive me, but I want you to know how truly sorry I am and how much you mean to me. I love you.

Peter:

> Jordan, every morning I wake up wishing I could turn back time and fix the things I've done wrong. I was so scared of losing you, but in doing so, I ended up hurting you even more. I'm so sorry for everything. If there's any chance we can talk, face-to-face, I'd give anything for an opportunity. I love you more than any job and miss you more than words can express.

"Ah, he's groveling. That's good. Seems sincere." Merc quirks an eyebrow.

I shut my phone off and place it face down on the table. "Yeah...as heartfelt as Peter's texts seem to be, I'm taking my time to consider the entire situation. God knows, part of me wants to put myself in his shoes, be understanding and run to him. The weight of leading a major project like SoHo is probably overwhelming. It's possible the stress and pressure he's under clouded his judgement..."

Merc leans forward. "But..."

"A bigger part of me is petrified of being lovestruck and naïve. I opened myself to him once long ago and his behavior wounded me deeply. Now, I've given him a second chance and he's done it again. As they say, fool me once... Ah, whatever the stupid saying is."

He nods. "I get it. You believe he'll fuck up again and you'd only have yourself to blame."

"Yeah." I hang my head.

Merc snaps his fingers in front of my face. "Jordan. Eyes up here. Newsflash. He's going to fuck up. So are you. It's called life."

"What?" Merc's tough love bit surprises me.

He stands. "Baby girl, don't think I haven't noticed you've been dodging calls from your parents and friends too. Everyone's wondering who your date was at Jace's wedding and why you've fallen off the planet this past week." On his way out the door he looks over his shoulder. "I'm sure they think you're in some sex bubble somewhere, but it's clear you need support. You're surrounded by people who love you, lean on them if you need to."

"Oh *God*," I groan, rubbing my temples. "I know and I will. I can't deal with their questions right now. They all met him, liked him, and... What do I tell them? Vegas guy played me again? *Ugh*."

Merc blows me a kiss. "Tell them the truth—you're figuring things out. You don't owe anyone a perfect love story."

"Thanks, Merc. I don't know what I'd do without you." His words are a balm and I find myself smiling, despite the turmoil churning inside my head.

Merc's grin epitomizes his easygoing and sassy self. "Probably mope around and make bad tattoo decisions."

As I wait for my next appointment, Peter's words, his apologies, and the unresolved feelings between us dominate my thoughts. When my client arrives, the hum of the tattoo machine and the familiar scent of ink and antiseptic are comforting, but don't fully distract me from my dilemma.

When the shop closes and the last artist leaves, I sit alone. The quiet gives me time to think, free of distraction. No matter what I decide, this is a turning point in my life. My heart aches with love for Peter, but it's also guarded, bruised by his words and the uncertainty of our future.

My phone pings. Another text from Peter.

Peter:

I'm sorry for every pain I've caused you. I understand if you can't forgive me, but know I love you more than anything. You mean everything to me.

A tear rolls down my cheek. The sincerity in his words is evident, but so is the pain they bring. Forgiving him isn't about overcoming a single argument; it's about trusting him with my heart. About believing he and I can navigate a committed relationship.

My mind wanders to my family and the stable and loving environment I grew up in. I yearn for that kind of security and love in my life.

How much weight should I put on some esoteric attachment I feel with Peter—which started from the very first moment I saw him. Whether we're fucking or fighting or bantering or cuddling, he's feels like my home. My everything. Flaws and all. It crushes me to think of losing him forever.

Crushes me.

I suppose Peter and I need to have a come-to-Jesus talk before he leaves for London. Lay everything out on the table. For now, I need a few more days to process. It will give me time to heal. To think. To *decide* how and if we can move forward.

I lock up the shop, the weight of my heartbreak heavy on my shoulders.

When I step outside, I realize I'm not alone. Prickles of ice skate along my neck and race down my spine and I turn to face my fear.

"Jordan..." He steps in front of me.

It's Peter.

So much for having a few more days.

I guess we're doing this now.

Chapter Twenty-Three

In the week since the fallout with Jordan, my world has been a blur of introspection and regret.

Each day, I've battled the urge to reach out to her multiple times because I'm desperate to bridge the gulf of silence growing wider between us. Instead, I've opted for one heartfelt message per day. Her silence in response is a clear indication of her need for space. A boundary I've painstakingly respected but wish like hell wasn't there.

Being without her shreds me to the core.

She's the blood in my veins. Necessary for my survival.

But life, as always, has its own plans.

Developments with Project SoHo have taken a sharp turn. The trip to London has been expedited due to an urgent need to meet with key stakeholders and investors who have advanced their schedules unexpectedly. I'm faced with a departure in a few days, a time frame leaving no room to delay the conversation I need to have with Jordan.

With a heavy heart and a mind swamped with what-ifs, I drive over to The Salty Siren—a decision born of desperation and deep-seated fear. If I leave things unresolved between us, Jordan won't give me another chance.

Not that I deserve it, mind you.

The familiar sight of the quirky, artistic exterior of her shop fills me with apprehension because it feels like my future hangs in the balance of whatever happens tonight. I wait outside, watching as the lights inside the shop dim, signaling the end of her day. My heart pounds when I see her locking up, her figure silhouetted against the glow of the streetlights.

When she steps outside, I take a deep breath and approach her.

"Jordan," I call out faintly, not wanting to alarm her.

She turns, her expression of fear morphs into surprise when she recognizes me. "Peter? What are you doing here?"

"I didn't mean to startle you, but I needed to see you." I hate that I've scared her. "There's something important we need to talk about."

She hesitates, flicking her eyes around the area like she's trapped, looking for an escape. "Uh...I'm still not ready..."

"Please." I'm anguished, and it shows.

Her expression softens and she nods. "Okay. Just for a moment."

We move to a nearby bench by Alki Beach. It's a weeknight and the boardwalk is quiet with only the occasional passerby.

"Jordan, I'm leaving for London in a few days. My trip has been moved up." I watch her closely to gauge whether she cares.

She does. Her face contorts with a fresh wave of surprise and hurt. "Why should I believe you? Maybe you were leaving this soon all along."

"It was all finalized suddenly." I ignore her pointed barb. Tit for tat isn't going to get us anywhere. I'm focused on the bigger picture. "I came by because I didn't want to leave without seeing you. I've done a ton of thinking and I realize how much I've messed up..."

"Oh, I got your texts." She chews on her thumbnail and looks away. Her profile is bathed in the glowy light of the streetlamp. "I've been trying to process everything. It's a lot for me to digest."

"I understand and I'm sorry for ambushing you tonight. The thing is, I love you, Jordan. I wish I'd handled things differently." I want to reach for her hand or place my hand on her knee, but neither is appropriate, so I settle for clenching my fists.

"I love you too, Peter." She turns to me, her eyes searching mine. "But what does it matter if you don't live up to the values you're supposed to hold so dear? I honestly don't know who you are. Are you the man who loves me with all his heart and is thoughtful, caring and carries himself with integrity? Or are you the guy who gaslights me when he's confronted with behavior that genuinely sucks balls? It seems to me you don't know which man to be. It was never about choosing between me or your project."

I pause, the weight of her assessment feels like an elephant sitting on my heart. "I want to live up to my own values. I want *you* more than I've ever wanted anything in my life, but I can't deny this project is a once-in-a-lifetime opportunity. I don't know how to make it all work."

"You've neatly summarized the other problem." Jordan's sigh is weary. "You're assuming *you* have to make it work. We're supposed to be in this together. Discussing how *we* can make it work."

We sit in silence for a few minutes, the tension between us palpable. "I don't have all the answers," I finally admit. " I'm willing to do whatever it takes to figure it out. Even with the distance. If you're willing to try, that is. I love you so much, baby. It physically hurts to be without you."

"Oh, I get it. But, as I said a minute ago, love isn't always enough. Trust, communication, being there for each other—there are a lot of components to a healthy relationship. Judging strictly on your own track record, I'm not convinced you'll hold up your end of the bargain." She buries her face in her hands and her body heaves when she starts sobbing.

"Baby..." I pry her hand from her eyes and clasp it in mine. "Please don't cry. I'll *do* better. I'll *be* better. I know I've broken your trust. Will you let me try to rebuild it? I don't want to lose any more time with you."

Jordan looks down at our entwined hands and furrows her brow. "Every single part of me wants to jump into this and take the risk, which is why I'm being overcautious and taking time to process. You kept such a big part of your life from me. How can I be sure you won't do it again? Do you know how much it breaks my heart? Do you care?"

Her words strike a chord, and I feel the guilt and regret wash over me because I'm still keeping secrets about my family. It's time to open up. I've got nothing to lose and everything to gain.

"I understand your fear and I don't want to promise I'll be perfect." I rub the top of her hand with my thumb. "What I *can* promise is I'll be honest with you going forward about everything. No more secrets. No more half-truths. I want to build something real with you, no matter what."

Holding my breath, I wait for her response. Jordan looks at the ground and her expression changes about a million times before she finally looks up and meets my gaze. "I'll hear you out, but I still need time, Peter. Time to think about what I want for my future. Please don't pressure me into a decision tonight."

"I understand." I'm crushed, but I have no choice but to accept her need for space. I let go of her hand, defeated. "Take all the time you need. Whatever you decide, I'll respect it."

"Peter, you know I've always been fascinated by mermaids, right?" Jordan abruptly changes the subject. She leans against the bench and tucks one leg under her.

I'm confused, but she's still talking to me, so I'll gladly listen to whatever she wants to say. "Of course. We talked about it in Vegas. It's why your mermaid tattoos are more than art—they're a part of your very essence."

"Yeah." Jordan's eyes jump up to mine relaying what seems like fascination. "They are. Mermaids have always symbolized enchantment, seduction, and the power of femininity—representing both the beauty and the complexity of being a woman."

"The embodiment of raw, natural power and freedom." Immediately, I'm connected to this conversation. I think about the inspiration behind my favorite architectural designs. "Art has a way of mirroring your soul."

She reaches over and squeezes my knee. "I love tattooing mermaids because they're the epitome of feminine strength and independence. A reminder that sometimes what attracts us doesn't have to make logical sense. It's okay to be captivated by the mysterious. The otherworldly."

"Like you." Her golden-blonde hair flows behind her against the moon lighting up Puget Sound behind her. "I remember researching mermaids after we met and lost touch. Did you know they usually appear in the light of the moon or between dawn and dusk – times of magic and transformation. *You're* my mermaid, baby."

"That's a sweet thought, Peter, but, like a mermaid, I only show my true self to those who are sincere. Those who really *see* me." She releases my knee and stands as if she's ready to leave. "I thought you were my person. I felt it on such a deep level. And I hoped I could be *your* person so you knew I was trustworthy. Knew you could tell me anything and I'd keep you safe. But you *don't* feel that way. I'm finally facing the truth."

Stunned, I watch as Jordan starts to walk away. A deep sense of urgency grips my heart, compelling me to share the great shame of my family situation. I don't have a choice. "Jordan, wait. I told you I don't want any more secrets. I *do* trust you. I *do* see you."

She pauses and turns to me, seemingly annoyed but curious. "Well?"

"Uh..." I swallow hard, realizing my confession might further distance us. I hope the risk is worth it. I've got to have faith. "My family... I didn't grow up like you did. My upbringing—it's always been a source of turmoil. Choices I've made in the past created a lot of animosity. Choices my brothers continue to make...place a burden on my parents, who don't have the resources to get them help. As you know, it's fallen on me. I've financially supported the four of them for years. It feels like an endless cycle."

Jordan relaxes a bit. "Yeah. I know it's been difficult for you."

"It's more than the financial aspect." A knot of emotions stick in my throat. "In my family, information is power. It's something to be used, to hold over each other. In your family—sharing is about trust and support. In mine, it's a weapon."

She steps closer, her gaze searching mine. "Peter, you've said this all before. You're not really telling me anything new. By now you should know I'm safe. I'm *not* your family."

"Sure, I hear you." Her words mean a lot, but unless you've lived with a toxic family like mine, she has no way to comprehend how to deal with the repercussions. " What I haven't told you is, around the time we started the tattoo, I paid my mom a significant sum for all of them to stay out of my life. I even made her sign an agreement. It hasn't mattered. She still tries to pull me into the poisonous cycle every other day. God, the dread I feel every time my phone buzzes."

Jordan sits next to me, her gentle touch warm on my arm. " I hope you know it's okay to separate yourself from a toxic environment, you aren't tainted by your family's dynamics unless you allow it. You're your own person."

"I *do* know. I've always felt like I was born into the wrong family. They make me feel guilty for wanting more, like I'm betraying them." Her empathy compels me to share my innermost thoughts. "I haven't been entirely innocent, though..."

"...Peter, stop." She takes my hand and squeezes. "Stop beating yourself up. You're not betraying anyone by living your life on your own terms. You deserve to be happy and free from guilt."

Taking the liberty of hugging her, I feel a sense of comfort in her arms. "Thank you, Jordan. I've kept things from you out of fear—fear you'd see me as part of the dysfunction."

She pulls away. "I'm glad we spoke tonight. It doesn't erase the hurt or change anything about needing some time, but it helps me understand you better."

"I *love* you." I look into her green eyes, hoping she feels it. *Knows* it.

She hesitates then manages a small smile. "I love you, too."

We stand up from the bench and face each other. The distance between us feels both immense and non-existent. We're at a crossroads. Our future is uncertain. At least, for now, I can cling to the love we share as a beacon in the darkness.

"Goodbye, Jordan." My heart aching at the thought of leaving her.

"Goodbye, Peter. Safe travels." Her voice is laced with a sadness mirroring my own.

I watch her walk to her car across the street and drive away. Taillights disappear into the night.

Turning toward my car, I'm filled with a sense of resolve. This particular trip to London isn't only about Project SoHo. It's about figuring out my shit.

No matter what happens, I'll cherish the time Jordan and I had.

I won't give up hope for a future.

Hope she and I can find our way back to each other.

Chapter Twenty-Four

It's impossible not to have baby fever.

The atmosphere at my parents' house is one of joy and celebration. The guests of honor are the same as a few weeks ago—my brother Jace and his wife, Alex. Today isn't about weddings, though, it's the welcome party for baby Lennox, their son.

Honestly, it's a little déjà vu from the wedding a few weeks ago. The band is in attendance along with their wives. My folks, of course, as well as my sister Jen and her wife, Becca. Alex's parents and her siblings, and a smattering of close friends round out the guests. One person is missing, though.

Peter.

Outside, on the expansive backyard patio, I'm hanging out with the ladies, enjoying a beautiful spring day. The guys are playing pool downstairs, leaving us in a comfortable bubble of female camaraderie. Our conversation, which started out as a general catch-up session, is focused on me, much to my discomfort.

I get it. Everyone is curious about my relationship status with Peter, especially since they last saw us looking blissfully happy at Jace and Alex's wedding.

"So, Jordan, everyone's dying to know." Zoey nudges me playfully. "You and Peter were the picture of schmoopiness at the wedding. How are things?"

Hearing his name sends a pang to my core. "Peter's in London. He's up for a big project. Unfortunately, things between us are, uh...complicated."

"I keep telling her, long-distance can be tough but's doable if you're solid. Is everything okay?" Alex hands Lennox to her mom.

Hesitating for a moment, I pick at a loose thread on the cushion of my patio chair. In the past, I'd excitedly confide my problems to this group, knowing I'd be able to crowd-source a solution.

Now, things are different. I'm protective of Peter and our relationship. He's not Vegas guy anymore. He's a man I'm in love with, even if we're not in a good place.

As the weeks have passed, I find I'm not interested in complaining about our situation or making our issues all his fault. The last thing I want is for someone to put all the blame and responsibility on Peter. I don't need anyone telling me I'll be better off without him. It might be true, or it might not, but it's on me to stand behind whatever decision I make.

It doesn't mean I'll be able to hide from the people whom I love and trust implicitly. Nor do I want to. "Truthfully, we're working through some issues. Trust, communication. It's been a lot."

Everyone in the group is married, so they get it.

"Long-distance relationships test even the strongest bonds." Fiona understands more than most, given her history with Zane. "If it's important to the both of you, love will find a way."

My mom reaches over to squeeze my hand. "You're strong enough to get through anything, Jordy. You always have been."

Jen, who's been quietly listening, as is her nature, chimes in with her characteristic directness. "You want it to work, don't you? I mean, you two looked like you're in love."

My mind drifts to the recent texts Peter and I have been exchanging. Despite the constant communication, the time difference and his focus on the project often leave our conversations feeling strained, almost perfunctory.

"I dunno." I lean back in my patio chair. "I don't think a long-distance relationship is viable for us."

As the conversation continues, and the ladies share stories and advice, I find myself focused on the children playing nearby. The six older kids shriek and laugh in the play area. They're carefree and full of life. Watching them stirs my longing for a family of my own one day. Of sharing my life with someone I love.

Except, as I think about Peter and this project, we're facing years of separation if I don't move with him. My life is entrenched here in Seattle. I can't help but feel a sense of resignation.

I love him, yes, but love alone isn't always enough to bridge the gap of miles and conflicting schedules. We wanted to see if our lives meshed. Well, we're failing. Our relationship won't survive my trust issues and long distance.

It's sobering.

Becca tugs on my sleeve. "Earth to Jordan. Jen asked you a question. Do you see yourself with Peter long-term?"

I glance at the group of women who are my ride-or-dies. Tears fill my eyes. "I'd love a future with him, but I'm not sure it's possible. I'm *so* sad."

The ladies nod sympathetically, understanding the crossroads I'm at. Everyone's been there.

Zoey gives me a side-hug. "Sometimes the hardest—and stupidest—decisions are letting go if you don't want to. If I can give you some unsolicited advice, which would have saved me years of agony, insurmountable problems seem that way without communication. Make sure you talk to him until you've exhausted all available avenues. Don't stew on this alone. Fight with him, not against him before you decide to end it for good. I saw the two of you and there's something there."

Her advice is good, but my strained smile probably signifies to the group I'm tapped out because the next thing

I know the ladies have shifted focus to the upcoming LTZ tour. The laughter and chatter around me fade into the background as I grapple with Zoey's wise words and the growing realization Peter and I need to talk. *Really* talk.

"Excuse me, ladies. Gotta pee." I get up and dash inside the house, fully intending to call Peter.

Before I dial, I take a moment to gather my thoughts in the quiet of the foyer only to be interrupted by my pops, who skips down the stairs. When he notices me standing with my arms wrapped around myself, a look of concern blooms on his face.

For a man whose business acumen is revered throughout the world and is a role model for entrepreneurs everywhere, my dad always had time for me and my siblings. He once wrote about the importance of balancing work and family life in his best-selling book, a value he learned the hard way but now holds dear.

"Jordan." He embraces me and rubs my head the way he's always done since I was little. "I was hoping to get some father-daughter time to catch up with you. How's Peter? How are things in London?"

I'm slightly annoyed everyone in my inner circle is focused on my love life. Now my dad? Refraining from rolling my eyes, I shrug. "Things with Peter aren't great. We're on a break, I guess. The distance. His project in London...it's been tough."

"Project SoHo." He nods. "Did you know I'm on—or was on—the selection committee? I recused myself as soon as you two started dating."

I'm so surprised I nearly stumble. "Wait. You knew about the project because you're *part* of it?"

"That's right. Obviously, I couldn't tell Peter because of my fiduciary obligations." He wraps his arm around my shoulders and guides us into his study. "But, since you and I have father-daughter privilege let me say, the VA/VT proposal is one of the most impressive presentations I've ever seen. It's out of my hands, but I wouldn't be surprised if he's awarded the gig."

Holy shit. It makes sense. My pops does a lot of cool stuff all over the world.

"I'm sorry it's causing a strain between you two." He sits behind his desk, steeples his fingers and studies me.

I sink into the chair opposite from him. "No, it's more than the project, Pops. It's more about the lack of communication on his part. Our trust issues go way back to when we first met. He's a good man with a challenging background. He loves me. I love him but..."

"Jordan, let me tell you a story which might help, it might not, but humor your old man." He leans back and rests his feet on the desk. "When you were an infant, before Jen and Jace were born, your mother and I went through a very rough patch. After years of living in start-up mode with not a lot of money, my career was taking off. She was home with you and Jaylynn; I was getting a big head because everyone acted like I walked on water. I started to believe it. Rather than focusing on my wife and kids, I double and triple downed on work. Obviously, I couldn't find the right balance."

He pauses, a distant look in his eyes. "When your mom found out she was pregnant with you, we actually separated for a few months. She didn't want to be a single mother raising kids with a dude who worked 24/7. It was one of the hardest times in my life. Everyone in the world gassed me up. Told me how great I was. Except one. Your mom. She loved all of me, flaws and all. My ego liked the idea of being around the gassers. But, when the person who mattered cut me loose, it made me realize something crucial—a career is important, yes. But family and love in all its messiness, that's *life*."

"So, what did you do?" Leave it to my pops, the great Jason Deveraux, to find words to resonate with me. Tears well up in my eyes for the second time today.

His face settles into a sweet, reflective smile. "I changed my priorities. I wanted honesty, not praise. I made your mother and you kids my first priority. Sure, I still worked hard, but I never let it overshadow what truly mattered. Decades later our family is strong and thriving."

"I love you so much, Pops. Thank you for sharing. It makes me feel less of a loser to learn you and mom navigated similar issues. My situation with Peter is tough." I contemplate how to explain without revealing Peter's confidences. "I can't seem to get past why he didn't tell me about Project SoHo and what it meant for his future. It's such a huge part of his life. Even if he couldn't share details, why wouldn't he give me—the woman he's supposedly in love with—the heads-up he'd likely be moving to London. I can't help but wonder—if Peter thinks it's acceptable to withhold information about something so life changing, isn't it the hugest red flag? I'd be a fool to think his deception isn't a pattern. Right?"

"Jordan, sweetheart. Figuring stuff out is part of the journey," he says tactfully. "You're well aware there were many business transactions I couldn't tell your mother about. Granted, none would have had me uprooting the family. At the end of the day, you need to talk through your expectations and boundaries and so does he. If he's truly the man for you, you'll decide whether you're willing to make compromises. But remember, Jordan, it's a two-way street."

"Zoey gave me similar advice but I needed to hear this from you." A sense of clarity is finally beginning to gel into something actionable. "It helps to know even the strongest relationships have their trials. Mistakes shouldn't define a person; God knows I've made enough of them."

We stand to leave and he wraps an arm around my shoulders, giving me a reassuring squeeze. "Whatever the outcome, know you're strong and capable. You'll make the right decision for yourself. And no matter what, your mother and I support you."

Faced with a decision to call Peter or rejoin the ladies, I reflect on the advice I've received today. Love requires effort, compromise, and sometimes tough decisions. Today's also a reminder that, unlike Peter, I have a support system to face whatever comes next.

I'm about to walk outside into the warmth of the spring day and rejoin the laughter and chatter on the patio, but an overwhelming certainty of the path forward stops me in my tracks.

The clarity is astounding.

I have to see Peter. I can't live without him. I've been punishing him for hurting me by stonewalling his attempts at working things out.

It's time for me to take the lead.

Please, please, *please*, don't let it be too late.

Chapter Twenty-Five

Work saved me.

It's not the first time. Probably won't be the last. When everything in my personal life is shit, I focus on what I'm good at.

Hard, relentless work. It helps.

My team and I are seated around a cluttered conference table in our temporary London office. The walls are lined with conceptual drawings. Intricate models of the museum and ancillary structures are set up on round tables lining the walls. Collectively, all are a testament to the countless hours we've poured into Project SoHo.

We have a string of sixteen-hour days filled with meetings under our belt. The selection committee. The City of London. Environmental groups. Regulatory bodies. Historical societies. You name it. We've been put though the ringer and exhaustion emanates out of every one of us. Nevertheless, there's a deadline looming. There's no choice but to press on.

Over the past three weeks it's clear we've nailed the museum design and technology, but our competitor has wholly outshined us on the ancillary structures and the common spaces.

"Alright, team." My voice echoes slightly in the cavernous room. "We're at a critical juncture. Our competition has proved to be more formidable than we thought but, thanks to the hard work of everyone in this room, I believe we still have the edge."

Rose leans forward, her eyes scan over the revisions we've made to the garden design. "The updated plan to integrate the ancillary buildings with Smithfield Market includes living gardens with harvestable fruit. I'm concerned we haven't gone far enough. It's essential our design honors the heritage of the location while introducing modern elements."

"I suggest incorporating glass structures." Fabiola holds up her tablet to show us a prototype she's sketched.

"A timeless way to reflect the market's character and add a contemporary feel, blending the old with the new seamlessly."

Pip shakes his head. "C'mon. It doesn't take us far enough. There's a delicate dance—remember, the guy from the House of Lords demanded we respect the past while at the same time embracing the future. How will that incorporate our technology?"

"Look, our commitment to sustainability sets us apart," I remind the team. "But the selection committee is old school. The thing is, we have to stay true to our corporate mission. The energy-efficient designs and green spaces we propose are not architectural features. They're a testament to the past and our promise of the future. Somehow we missed the mark in conveying our vision."

And therein lies the problem. Working this hard for so many days in a row without any breaks is killing our creativity. VA/VT is comprised of the four of us while our competitors have about thirty people on their team. I'm used to being the underdog, it's why we've been successful. Part of me wonders if we should take the night off and reconvene after a good night's sleep.

Rose sips her iced coffee. "Here's the thing. Winning the hearts of the local community is crucial. We need to engage them, make them a part of this transformation. Let's get a focus group together this week."

"We can't, Rose." I scrub my chin with my fingers. "There's no way."

Fabiola holds up a finger. "How about we commission art installations involving local artists and select creators from around the world. It could symbolize England's link to its local roots as well as the rest of the world. We'd develop criteria for submissions to ensure the pieces reflect the area's history. Wouldn't that be transformative? It could create a dialogue between the space and those who inhabit it. Didn't you do something similar on that Vegas project, Peter?"

"Yeah, it's going well." The idea of art installations make me think of Jordan.

Who the fuck am I kidding. She's *always* in the back of my mind. Despite our frequent texts, the time difference and my absorption in this project have strained our communication. Her absence is like a shadow, always present, reminding me of what's at stake beyond these walls.

"Let's revisit the art installation idea tomorrow. I'd like to stay focused on the physical garden concept." I stand and draw the team's attention to the detailed renderings tacked up to the wall. "It's ambitious, but highlighting ecological balance will be a key."

Pip tries to cover his yawn. "It's bold and we'll need expert input to ensure its viability. I'll look into finding some resources first thing tomorrow."

"Make sure they understand this garden isn't just for show; it's a living, breathing part of the community." Rose takes the words out of my mouth.

We continue to go round and round on the intricacies of expanding the green space when my phone buzzes. The first vibration I dismiss, assuming it's an annoying robocall. When it buzzes fifteen minutes later, I tense up. Probably my mother. When it goes off again half hour later, I can't help but take a quick glance.

To my surprise, I have three texts from Jordan.

Jordan:

Hey…can you talk?

Jordan:

You must be swamped. Call me when you can.

Jordan:

> Okay, it's past eleven p.m. in London, now I know you're ghosting me. In all seriousness, can we talk? And, if you're ghosting me, stop it please. I need to hear your voice.

My heart beats wildly. Seeing her name on my screen stirs a whirlwind of conflicting emotions. Our recent phone conversations have been sparse and strained. I'm the one who's initiated contact, desperate for her to forgive me. Willing to do anything to bridge the gap between us. Her responses have been consistent—cautious and guarded. She's given me no indication we have a future, but no indication we don't.

It's a shitty stage of limbo for which I have no one to blame but myself.

On the other hand, this is the first time she's reached out since our, *um*...falling out, which gives me a glimmer of hope.

Unfortunately, I have people counting on me. I quickly shove the phone into my pocket to refocus on the meeting. Rose brilliantly describes her concerns about the community engagement plan and Pip interjects with suggestions about sustainable infrastructure integration for the green space. I should help guide the discussion, but my thoughts keep drifting to Jordan and the desire to call her back.

Fabiola tugs on my sleeve. "Peter, are you with us? Pip asked if we should expand the green spaces up toward the theater?"

"Well...let's see how it looks on the model." I rub my eyes. "Truthfully, I'm wrecked. Let's reconvene at eight tomorrow morning. We all need fresh eyes rather than going around and around saying the same thing. It's imperative we present a tangible plan, not a bunch of pie-in-the-sky ideas."

As the meeting draws to a close, my team assures me they're confident we'll pull everything together in time. I'm not as sure, but I paste on an encouraging smile as they leave.

Now alone, the silence of the room is a stark contrast to the flurry of ideas and discussions filling it moments ago.

Usually in these quiet moments I have time to be objective. Tonight, however, I feel pretty down. My confidence has taken a beating. Our proposal has been brutally scrutinized by the various stakeholders, which was to be expected. Nobody wants a project of this magnitude to move forward without understanding the risks. What's more concerning is they've uncovered miscalculations on the fees we'll receive—which can only be chalked up to my inexperience in bidding for a job like this.

Fuck. I'll call it like it is—I've overlooked the obvious in my quest to have my name on this project and it's costing me a small fortune.

First of all, the travel is through the roof—we've been flying back and forth to London on the company's dime and staying in pricey hotels, not to mention meals for all of us. I've also diverted significant corporate resources to this project. Everything from paying for 3D models and other renderings to supporting the hefty salaries and benefit packages of my staff, who've been singularly focused on this nonpaying gig for the past year. Each time we make it through another round, the costs ramp up.

I totally understand why some of the candidates dropped out. It's fucking expensive to throw your hat in the ring for something which, increasingly seems like nothing more than a vanity project.

Worse than all of the financial stuff, I've learned the processes, timing and permitting—as it pertains to my technology—will require a lot of hand-holding. No matter who wins this job, building a landmark and its surrounding public spaces is political. This isn't an international commute situation. I'll have to move to London, and not temporarily.

Easily a decade. Or more.

If London becomes my permanent home, the odds of working things out with Jordan are zilch.

Shit...Jordan.

I haven't responded to her yet. I pull out my phone and stare at her texts. The urge to call her rather than text is overwhelming because she needs to know about all of this. Regardless of the consequences. How can I ask her to give up her life in Seattle to move overseas with me?

Fuck. I question whether this monumental project aligns with my personal aspirations anymore. Except, now I'm in too deep financially to pull out.

"Peter, I know this is a big moment for you." Rose's voice scares the living shit out of me. "I've seen your dedication to this project, your passion. I also see the conflict it's causing you."

I turn to see her approach me tentatively. In her eyes, I see the same ambition that once fueled my every decision. "It's not about the project, Rose. It's what it means for my life—all of our lives."

"I understand." Rose sits next to me. "I want to offer my help. I believe in this project, in its potential. I'd like to take on the role of managing it. It's a once-in-a-lifetime opportunity, and I'm ready for the challenge."

It's funny. A few months ago her offer would have pissed me off. Now, her words offer a glimmer of possibility. Could this be the solution? Could her leadership give me the space to balance my professional and personal life? "Rose, what a generous offer. I promise to think about it. Thank you. *Truly*."

"Of course." She nods, stops as if she's going to say something, then departs with a wave.

Huh. The possibility of allowing Rose to take a leadership role under my guidance is tempting. It's definitely something I'm going to consider should we land this appointment. At the end of the day, we're so close to the finish line and the investment I've made will be wasted if we don't see it through. Besides, there's really no going backward at this point.

It's time to get some sleep.

Luckily, the hotel is two blocks away and it's only about ten minutes before I dial Jordan's number.

My heart thrums with apprehension as the phone rings.

This call could change everything.

Chapter Twenty-Six

I'm so fucking nervous.

At least I'm no longer confused.

Or scared.

Well, that's not true. I'm petrified I've stiff-armed Peter for too long and he's given up on me.

I'm wearing out a patch of the plush carpeted hallway waiting for Peter to call me. Pacing. Kicking the floor with my toe. Pacing some more. It's been hours since I tried him. Now, it's past midnight in London and he hasn't responded, which is surprising. I thought he'd call right away.

When he didn't, it called for drastic measures with a dash of stalker. Maybe he's—

As if I've conjured him out of the ether, Peter's name flashes on my screen.

I let it buzz twice before answering to gather my wits. "Hey."

"I'm sorry it took me so long to call." He sounds tired. Beaten down. "Today's been a bitch. I've been swamped with meetings and finally got to the hotel about ten minutes ago. How are you?"

I suppress a giggle as I watch a room service attendant knock on his door. "I'm good, just thought I'd check in. Is everything going alright?"

He opens the door barefooted wearing a tight black T-shirt and a pair of charcoal joggers. He turns and gestures for the staffer to follow him in but he's laser focused on his phone and doesn't notice me shuffling in behind the food cart. "Yeah... extremely hectic. This project is such a massive undertaking. I've been meaning to talk to you about it."

"Oh?" I step out from behind the cart and look at him, knowing he could hear my voice through the phone and in person. My heart pounds in my chest.

He turns, phone still to his ear, and his eyes widen in shock. "*Jordan*? Wait. What...how are you in London?"

"Surprise! I thought I'd drop by. Can I come in?" I step closer. Judging by his stunned expression, I'm the last person he expected to see.

Peter shuts off his phone and tosses it on the bed. "You're *already* in. I can't believe... This is amazing."

He signs the check and the delivery gal takes off and I close the door behind her.

In the quiet of Peter's hotel room, the air is charged. Standing a few feet apart gazing into each other's eyes, we're caught in a moment of uncertainty. My surprise arrival leaves us both unmoored. I'm present but can't figure out how to bridge the gap between us.

Peter's eyes reflect a storm of swirling emotions. He takes a half step forward. Stops, unsure whether to close or keep the distance. I mirror his hesitation, though I long to run and jump into his arms. The space between feels like a vast expanse, charged with the potential of what could be and the fear of what might not be.

"Do you want to sit down?" Peter breaks the silence and gestures to the couch, where his food has been set up.

I nod. "Yeah, that would be good."

We tentatively move to the sofa. We're close enough to touch, yet we both refrain from invading each other's space just yet. The physical proximity only seems to amplify our awkwardness. He's close, yet so far.

Gulping down my fear, I tuck a strand of hair behind my ear. "I wasn't sure if I should come, but I needed to see you."

"I'm glad. Jordan. I... I wasn't expecting this." Peter runs a hand through his hair, his gesture of unease. "I thought we'd talk once I got home."

We're navigating uncharted waters, trying to find a way back to each other while being acutely aware of the hurdles in front of us.

"Yeah." I smile and place my hand on his knee. "I couldn't wait another day, though."

My bold move helps dissipate our initial awkwardness. Our physical affection, though slight, is a reminder of a bond distance and time don't seem to erase. The uncertainty of the moment lingers, but it's tempered by a cautious hope—at least for me—of reconciliation.

"I... Jordan, before we go any further there's something important I need to tell you about the project." Peter's discomfort is palpable. "I've realized it's much bigger. Ah, *fuck*. It's at least a ten-year commitment."

I hold his gaze. "I know. My pops filled me in on the expectation. I'm not in London to tell you goodbye. I came to tell you home is wherever you are. I don't want to lose you over this."

Relief washes over his features. "You have no idea how much I needed to hear you say that."

"My pops also made me realize something even more important." I move closer and take his hands in mine. "If we really want this, we'll make it work, no matter the distance or time—or obstacle. I love you. I want a future with you, if you still feel the same way."

Peter's eyes search mine. "Are you sure? This is a big move. I don't want to hold you back."

I squeeze his hands. "First, thank you for giving me the time and space to process. In answer to your question, yes. I'm sure. There's more. Merc and I have talked about opening a branch of The Salty Siren in London. If I need to relocate, we can figure it out."

"Wait, you'd *relocate*? For *me*?" A look of astonishment settles on Peter's face.

I shrug, feeling a surge of hope. "I believe in us, Peter and despite my...standoffishness for the past few weeks, I'm willing to take this chance. As long as we're honest with each other going forward and there are no more secrets. Except for presents. Presents can remain secret."

Peter yanks me into a tight embrace against his broad chest. "I love you so much, baby. No more secrets. I promise. We'll figure this out."

As we hold each other in his hotel room, I feel a sense of rightness. Despite any challenges ahead, I think we can be—no, are—something beautiful.

"I need you, baby." I stroke the stubble on his face. "Please..."

"On your back." Peter presses against the cushions, unbuttons my jeans and yanks them down with my underwear like a man possessed. "Goddamn, baby. I can smell you. I'm starving for your sweet little pussy."

He kneels between my legs, dips his thumb into my wetness and drags it up to my swollen clit. When he gives it a little pinch, I practically levitate off the couch. "Christ, Peter."

"You have no idea..." He groans as he shoves the denim pooled around my ankles off and to the ground.

Peter pries one of my legs up and sets it on the back of the sofa, opening me up. His palms caress my inner thighs to press them even farther apart and he dives in. I cup his head in both my hands and cry out as he licks the entire length of my slit with the flat of his tongue. He spreads my lower lips apart with his fingers and licks slower this time, as if he's savoring me. Needing more, I raise my hips to push my pussy against his mouth.

"Now. Now, baby." Peter palms my lower belly to press me back down and rubs his thumb over my swollen clit. "Let me take care of you. *Relax*."

He resumes feasting on me until my thighs quiver on either side of his head. My blunt nails rake across his scalp when he wedges both thumbs into my channel, spreading me wider to bury his tongue deep inside. My hips rock into him, I'm gasping and grinding as he explores everywhere. All the while circling my clit with a finger. Flicking it with his nails. Lapping up the arousal pooling out of me.

"I'm close…"

Peter looks up at me from between my legs. "I can taste it." He hums against my clit before sucking it hard between his lips.

Manic pulses overtake my body like low-level electrocution. Keeping suction on my little nub, he thrusts two fingers into me hard and curves them upward to my sweet spot, making me gasp and try to scramble up to get away. "It's too much..."

"Never. You're going to come all over my fucking face," Peter growls, pressing his forearm across my belly to keep me still before latching his lips on my clit.

He fucks me faster with his fingers. I cry out like a banshee and dig my fingers into his scalp.

"*Peter*!" My voice is anguished with rapture. He lifts his head and watches me quivering and quaking. Doesn't stop stroking into me. Doesn't stop sucking on my clit. My walls are tight and wet. I'm bucking and lashing, grinding my pussy on his face.

Deep, soulful eyes stare into mine. "Look at me. Watch me while you come."

I nod frantically, squeezing his fingers with each stroke. Peter lowers to me, his gaze synced with mine. Never looks away as he strokes my G-spot harder and savors my throbbing clit with his tongue. He's coaxing the dirtiest, wettest sounds from my pussy and my nipples are so hard, they're practically poking through the fabric of my black bustier. My entire body begins to shake and arch.

"I *said*, look at me," Peter commands, pausing until I comply.

Time stands still for a fraction of a second until he shoves his fingers inside me again. It's so much. My thighs clamp around his ears but he keeps driving into me and flicking his tongue on my clit. I try to shove his head away, but he holds me in place with his strong arm.

I turn my face into the cushion, shaking. "I can't..." He doesn't stop finger-fucking me or letting up on the pressure. "I *can't*..."

"You *can*. Listen to how wet and ready you are. Your pussy is so fucking beautiful," he growls against my core.

"*Ahhhhhhhhh*," I sob when the pressure releases explosively, flooding his mouth.

What was too much a minute ago is now *everything*. I'm eager for more. I lean up on my elbow and arch into his strokes. With my free hand, I undo the laces on my top and shove down the cups to free my breasts. My nipples are distended and aching. I pinch them and pull the peaks as he adds a third finger and fucks me hard. Twisting and turning them inside me. Dragging them over my stimulated nerve endings. Then he gives my clit one long, hard suck.

My pussy clenches and I rocket upright, screaming through another flood of release. I keep coming and he keeps licking me up as I shamelessly fuck his face, riding out every last wave until I slump down, splayed and satiated.

Peter, who's still clothed, kneels between my legs and cups my heavy tits. "Are you ready for my cock?"

"So ready." The tip of his shaft is wet with pre-cum and pokes out of the waistband of his joggers. Pulling his pants down with one hand, I grasp him with my other and stroke. "Fuck me, Peter. I can't go another minute."

When he guides himself inside me, I'm not prepared for the rush of emotion.

Or the overwhelming certainty.

This is the man I'm supposed to be with.

Nothing else matters.

Chapter Twenty-Seven

S inking into Jordan's like coming home.

Gripping her hip to keep my cock from slipping out, I reach behind my head with my free hand to yank off my shirt. After I toss it on the floor, I allow myself to ogle my girl. All splayed out on the couch with her tits bursting free of her sexy little top. Impaled on my dick.

Fucking stunning.

How it should be, always.

Unable to resist, I lean down and nip one of her exposed nipples and follow it with a slow, languid suck. Cupping her breasts, I continue to bite and lick her taut peaks, edging back when she squirms and locks her feet around my thighs in an attempt to get me to move.

"Fuck me, baby. Stop teasing." She reaches around to cup my ass and pulls me deeper.

I like driving her a little mad, so I pull out slooooowly and ram into her.

"Ohhhhh." Her pussy contracts around my cock.

I like feeling her clenching around my shaft even more.

"I think you like being teased, baby. You're creaming all over my dick." I pull out briefly to plant one foot on the floor.

Jordan bites her finger and smiles. "Am I? Prove it. Give me a little taste."

Holy shit, this woman.

"Only for a sec, I need to be inside you." I tap my dick on her lips.

Jordan fondles my balls as she swallows my crown. "*Mmmmmm*," she hums with a twinkle in her eye.

"Jesus, baby." I pull free. "You're a shocking, greedy girl."

She giggles. "Duh. I flew nearly five thousand miles to fuck you."

"Well." I slam inside her hard. Pull out. "If this is our reunion fuck, let's make sure you feel every inch of me."

Gripping her hip, I press her legs together and roll her slightly to the side. Her pussy lips, swollen and wet, peep out from between her thighs. Looming over her, I squeeze her ass. Run my fingers along her exposed slit. With one swift thrust, I'm once again immersed in her hot, velvet heat. I drag my hips backward until I nearly slip free. Slam into her. Repeat.

By the fifth or sixth time, Jordan's eyes squinch shut. "*Ohhhh...*"

"You like a hint of pain, baby?" I pound into her, harder and faster, using one hand to hold her in place, the other to pinch her already taut nipples.

She moans, "*Yessss.*"

I notice Jordan's green eyes are open, but she's not looking at me. Her focus is on the mirror on the opposite side of the room where she watches me manhandle her.

"Ah, you like watching me fuck you." My mouth hovers against her ear as my fingers delve between her ass cheeks.

Jordan looks at me through the mirror. "No, I *love* watching you fuck me. It should have been on my list."

"From now on, everything *we* do is the list." I slap her ass. "The next thing on my list is to make you come within a minute."

Jordan presses her cheek into the pillows, still watching us. Gasps for breath as I go into overtime. I take her as though she can withstand anything, because she can. And *does*.

Her entire body quivers through her climax but I don't stop. Instead, I flip her over on her stomach to take her from behind. Jordan tries to push herself up to her knees, but I grip one wrist, then the other and hold them in one hand against the small of her back. She's at my mercy. In this position, her pussy is tight as hell and I'm able to slide in deeply—it's like the holy grail.

"*Ohmygod*, Peter...." I know exactly when my cock hits her spot because her thighs start shaking uncontrollably. Doubling down, I use the leverage from my bent knee to pummel into her relentlessly. I want to mark her. Imprint her from the inside out. My jaw locks hearing her beg, "Come inside me, baby. Fill me. Claim me."

Jesus. She squeezes my dick so tightly I can barely breathe. I draw back and sink home one final time, wincing as I try to stave off my own release. But I can't. I'm too far gone.

"Go over with me," I order, exploding inside her.

Jordan obeys, crying my name out over and over as she milks every lost drop out of me. I nearly weep with joy.

God, I missed her. I missed this. I won't be without her another day, that's the fucking truth.

Collapsing from exhaustion, I manage to hold my full weight off her body until my hips stop pumping. I release her wrists and roll us to our sides, banding my arm around her stomach to stay connected for as long as humanly possible. In the aftermath, the world stills except for her aftershocks and our heavy breathing.

Lying beside Jordan in the quiet of my hotel room, the day's ups and downs stir up a whirlwind of emotions. The closeness we've shared isn't just physical, it's a divine camaraderie. Spiritual in its intensity.

Like it is every time when we make love.

We manage to get up from the couch to ready ourselves for bed. I turn the lights off except for the bedside lamp, which casts a serene light, bathing the room in a golden glow. We slip into bed, facing each other.

"Jordan, baby." I caress her cheek and trace her hairline with my finger. "There's something I need to say—I love you more than anything. I'm sorry for the hurt I've caused you and for not being open with you. Losing you, even for a moment, felt like losing a part of myself."

Our lips meet and part slightly as we kiss. There's a sacredness to this moment. A reverence for what we have going forward...and what we nearly lost.

Jordan's eyes brim with a love so pure it's humbling. "I love *you*. I'd apologize for taking my time to process, but the truth is I needed it. For the record, I'm a thousand percent sure about my love for you but it took more time for me to reconcile my heart with the noise in my head."

We kiss sweetly. Deeply. Passionately. Both of us stroking and caressing each other. Our conversation unfolds like a trickling stream, flowing with dreams and hopes for a shared future. Every word feels like a step toward the life we both want badly—a life together.

Each word weaves a stronger bond between us.

Each word heals the fractures of the past.

"One of the reasons I love you is because of your strength and your unyielding passion." Jordan runs her fingers along my bicep. "You see the world in ways that inspire me as an artist. Your business acumen is astounding. Mostly, it's the way you love me. You're it for me."

Her words wash over me, bringing me peace and a feeling of joy I can't describe. *I belong to her.* "Baby, you've brought a vibrancy to my life I didn't know was missing. You inspire me and challenge me in all the best ways. A world without you is unimaginable."

As the night bleeds into early morning and our eyes grow heavy, I'm filled with a new understanding. We've crossed a crucial threshold. Our past mistakes have been transformed into lessons, forging a deeper, more profound bond.

Unbreakable.

"I'm happy we're together," I whisper, holding her close.

"Me too." Her breath is warm against my skin. "We have something truly special. Something worth cherishing and fighting for."

As we both drift to sleep, I'm enveloped in a profound sense of peace. The challenges ahead no longer seem insurmountable. Here, in this moment, I feel an unshakeable sense of belonging and a renewed commitment to our love.

For the first time, I *believe* we're more than two individuals.

Jordan and I are a union of hearts and souls.

It's a hair after five a.m.

Lying beside me, Jordan stirs, her eyes fluttering open. She reaches out to trace the line of my jaw. "Morning," she murmurs, her voice thick with sleep.

"Hi, my beautiful girl." My heart swells at the sight of her in my bed. "I didn't want to wake you, but I've got an early start today."

She yawns and props herself up on one elbow, the sheets slip to reveal the curve of her breast. "How are you feeling about it?"

"Honestly? I'm determined. More than ever. Last night, with you...it's given me a new inspiration." I kiss her nose. "I want to win this, not only for me, but for us. Are you okay on your own for a couple hours?"

Jordan threads her fingers in my hair and kisses me. "I have no doubt you and your team will nail it, baby. And don't worry about me. I'm planning on flying home this afternoon after breakfast with an old tattoo friend from Amsterdam. I'd like to get some intel on the local market. If there's time, I may slip in some shopping. All you need to do is focus on winning this bid. When you're in Seattle next week, we'll figure out our next steps."

"God damn, I love you." I catch her hand and press a kiss to her palm. "Having you with me, even for a night, has reenergized my focus. Knowing we're in a good place—it's everything."

She has a mischievous glint in her eyes. "Well, I do aim to surprise and impress. If you're up for it, we can do something about your morning wood, but if you need to get going..."

"Fuck, baby." My mostly-hard dick twitches against her thigh. "I'm always up for it."

Jordan pulls back the sheets and lets her knees fall open. "Good, because I'm wet for you..."

And...I'm fully erect.

Twenty minutes later, we're satiated for the moment. I jump in the shower and watch as she brushes her teeth. Then we switch. The simple routine of getting ready seems to match the energy of our renewed commitment.

As she zips up her little carryon, I wrap my arms around her from behind and bury my face in her silky, blonde hair. "I'm going to miss you."

She turns in my arms and places her palm on my heart. "I'll miss you too. But this isn't goodbye. It's a 'see you soon.'"

"I know." I lean down to capture her lips. "I'll FaceTime you every day. Once I'm home, we'll make *all* the plans. Seattle, London... Wherever we are, as long as we're together."

Her eyes shine with affection. "*Together.*"

With one last kiss, we depart the hotel and part ways.

Jordan's off to meet her friend and I'm going to kick ass in this final stretch of Project SoHo. As I watch her walk toward the cafe, I've never been happier. My drive to succeed professionally is more meaningful knowing I'll be building a future with the woman I love.

With Jordan by my side, even from across the ocean, anything feels possible.

Chapter Twenty-Eight

God, he's so fucking hot.

Emerging from the bathroom in only a bra and thong, I gaze at Peter, who's standing in front of the full-length mirror in his walk-in closet.

Captivated, I watch him fasten the cuffs of his crisp, white shirt. He wears a bespoke suit in a deep, midnight blue, which drapes over his muscled frame with precision. The fabric catches the light with a subtle sheen, outlining the strong breadth of his shoulders tapering down to his trim waist.

Peter's dark-blond hair, usually a sexy, tousled mess, is slicked back—though a couple of renegade pieces have broken free. He's so effortlessly handsome. Sharp jawline, high cheekbones counterbalanced by sparkling blue eyes and an expressive brow.

Our eyes meet when he catches me watching him in the mirror adjusting his tie. I'm transfixed by his fingers as they deftly maneuver the silk—an hour ago, those fingers made me come so hard, I'm still rattled.

As if he can read my mind, he smiles at me through the glass. Quirks an eyebrow. "Are you planning on wearing clothes to dinner?"

"I didn't want to get makeup on my dress." I slink in behind him and caress his package through his slacks. "I'm happy to get lipstick on your cock, though."

Peter spins around and clasps me to him, holding me firm at the small of my back. "You're a *bad* influence, baby."

"We have time." I skate my hand to his zipper, but he encircles my wrist with his free hand.

"We don't." He brings our hands to the slip of a waistband on my panties. "But, if you can get yourself off in under three minutes, we can try double penetration with the dildo tonight."

My thighs clamp together at the thought and I'm pretty sure I'm soaked. "If I don't?"

"I'll lick you until you beg me to stop." He drags our hands to my mound and releases his grip. "I'm waiting."

Never one to shy away from a challenge, especially one where I win no matter what, I slip my fingers into the side of the scrap of cloth disguised as underwear and pull them to the side so he can see my swollen lips. Leaning against the doorframe, I get to work. Slicking my finger through my arousal. Rubbing tight little circles on my clit.

Peter's eyes are laser focused on me masturbating and I'm pleased to see his pants start to tent. "Ohhhhh," I moan with deliberate exaggeration for his benefit, though I'm already seconds away from detonating.

"*Fuck*, baby. Not fair. Not fair." Peter's hips shift and cant watching me pinch my nipple through my sheer lace bra with my free hand.

Seconds later, his pants are down to his ankles and he's lifted me onto his cock. It only takes a few deep, hard thrusts and we're both moaning through our respective orgasms.

"I'm sorry, I've made us late." My arms are wound around his neck and my legs are hooked around his waist, though he always holds me up effortlessly.

"Don't be sorry." He shuffles us into the bathroom, with me still speared on his shaft. "It's worth it. Grab a hand towel, baby so I can get us cleaned up. The last thing I want is for your folks to see spunk on this suit."

Carefully, he sets me on the counter and wipes up the evidence. While he redresses, I change my underwear, slip on my black sheath dress and step into my black wedges.

Fifteen minutes later, we walk hand in hand to the Metropolitan Grill, which is only a couple blocks from his condo.

I'm glad we slipped in a quickie. Peter's nervous because tonight isn't merely a casual dinner—he and I have catapulted the dating stage into full-blown commitment. With our new status solidified, I want him to get to know my family on more than a superficial event-laden level. It's also important, with two famous members in my immediate family, for him to know firsthand what he's getting into.

No matter how tonight goes, Peter's my guy, but I can't help but hope for my mom and dad's approval. I may be a grown woman with my own business, but my family is important to me. I want them to see the Peter I know and love. Not the one who broke my heart years ago without even realizing it. Or the polite party-going guy from the wedding.

"If I didn't say so before, you look stunning." Peter squeezes my hand.

I lean into him. "Thank you, baby. You're not so bad yourself. Are you ready for this?"

"Yeah." Peter gives a reassuring nod. "I've actually been looking forward to this. I'm guessing it'll be a far cry from dinner with my family."

The hostess leads us back to the private dining room where my parents are waiting. My pops predictably wears his techie uniform of jeans and a sweater. My mom looks beautiful in a simple burgundy dress and black flats. Always charming hosts, they engage Peter in a conversation about Project SoHo immediately. Peter holds his own, infusing both humility and pride in retelling of the late nights his team endured trying to get the final submission in on time.

By the time our food arrives, the conversation flows effortlessly on a ton of different subjects, including my decision switching from fine art to tattoo art. My parents share a mortifying story about my childhood. When I was four, I threw a temper tantrum in a hotel parking lot and threatened to run away in a purple Volkswagen Beetle.

Peter takes it all in. He's attentive, respectful, and present, but there's a sadness behind his eyes as he experiences the support and love my parents have for me.

Amidst the lively hum of our conversation and a delicious steak dinner, Peter's phone starts buzzing, vibrating the table. I know why he has it out—the selection committee is supposed to call this weekend. Trying to be discreet, Peter silences it and attempts to tuck it away, but the persistent buzzing draws everyone's attention.

My pops taps the table with his finger. "Sounds like someone trying to urgently reach you, Peter."

"Uhh..." Peter glances at his phone, a flicker of annoyance crosses his face. "It's nothing. It can wait. I prefer not to let phones interrupt personal time."

His phone, however, has a different plan. Minutes later the buzzing starts once more.

With a resigned sigh, Peter glances at the screen and mutters, "It's my mother."

"You should take the call, Peter. Family is important." My dad knows nothing about the problems in Peter's family and gestures for him to get up and answer the phone.

Peter glances at me before he reluctantly excuses himself and steps outside the private room. The moment he's gone, my parents look at me curiously.

I take a deep breath. "Peter doesn't talk much about his family. He has a...complicated relationship with them."

"*Hmmm*. Must be tough for both of you." My mom's eyes crinkle with empathy.

My nose wrinkles inadvertently. "Well, I haven't met them yet."

Rather than chastise me, my pops knows how to get his point across without putting me on the defensive. "It's important to understand these dynamics, Jordy. Especially given our family's public profile. If this guy's going to be an important part of your life, you need to understand what you're getting into."

"I know. I'm convinced Peter's trying to protect and shield me from something." I chew on my thumbnail. "But you're right. I'll talk to him later."

My pops tilts his head thoughtfully. "Just make sure there's nothing...sketchy going on. It's always good to know the full picture."

"You know something." A realization dawns on me. "You've already done a background check on him, haven't you?"

There's a glint in his eyes. "Let's say I like to be informed about the people who are important to my daughter. I'll be interested to learn how this plays out, but I'll also point out your mother and I didn't cancel."

I shake my head, amused and weirdly reassured by my dad's protective nature. Whatever it is, my pops isn't bothered. The bigger question is, will Peter be honest about his family situation. Is he hiding something else from me?

The door opens and Peter returns, looking slightly unsettled but composed.

"Everything okay?" I reach for his hand as he takes his seat next to me.

His smile is strained. "Yeah, family stuff. Sorry for my rudeness."

"*Peter.*" My pops says his name as a command, though his tone is thoughtful. "Family matters can be tough. I know a thing or two about it, unfortunately."

"Yes, they can be. It's...complicated." Peter juts out his chin defensively, though I can tell he's curious as to what he has to say. Jason Deveraux, after all, is more than just my father. He's one of the most respected minds on the planet.

Dad steeples his fingers under his chin. "Family matters always are. Do you mind if I share an experience I had with my estranged biological father, around the time I first found success?"

I lean in, surprised by his openness. Knowing my pops, there'll be a point to the story. He's alluding to whatever intel he has on Peter's family. "Really, Dad? I thought Grandpa Emil was your bio dad."

Pops squints and looks off into the distance for a moment before returning his attention to me and Peter. "No. Grandpa Emil is actually my stepfather, but I've always thought of him as my real dad. Bio-dad Doug was never in the picture, until I started making a name for myself, of course. Then he suddenly reappeared, thinking he could claim a part of my success."

Mom strokes my dad's hair lovingly. "Was a big shock."

"It was. When Doug tried to blackmail me, I thought he was a stalker." Dad's voice is steady, despite the gravity of his words. "He dug up some old family secrets. Threatened to reveal a couple things from high school I wasn't proud of." He crosses his arms and leans back. "The shit hit the fan, though. He threatened my mother."

"Grandma Elsa?" My hands fly to my mouth.

He pats my hand. "Yes. He planned to go public with dirt he had on her from Sweden unless I paid him off."

I sit in stunned silence, processing this revelation. Peter, meanwhile, is riveted by my father's story.

"How did you handle it?" Peter's voice is tinged with curiosity.

My pops shakes his head. "It wasn't easy. I was torn between protecting my family's privacy and not giving in to his demands. In the end, I decided not to pay him. It resulted in a brief, ugly spat, which caught the media's attention, but it eventually died down. I took care of him later."

"*Jason.*" Mom grips his hand. "Legally, you took care of him *legally.*"

My pops smiles tightly. "Of *course...*"

"Must have been a tough call to make." Peter taps his chin, so deep in thought I'm not sure he's caught on to my pops's power.

"It was." Dad folds his napkin and tosses it on the table. "But it taught me an important lesson about integrity and standing up for what's right. No matter how difficult it may seem. It's not the challenges that define us, but how we choose to face them."

Peter looks at me, his mouth a grim line. In this moment, I know he's aware my father's done a background check. His expression tells me we'll talk about it later.

As we stand up to leave, my pops grips Peter's shoulder. "I shared my story because I want you to know you're not alone in dealing with family complications. And, more importantly, these issues don't define your future or your worth. Good luck in figuring it out."

"Thank you, Jason. Your advice means a lot." Peter's eyes shine. "I've always felt like a complete asshole for distancing myself from them." He grits his teeth. "It's so fucking...uh...*sorry*." He realizes how fired up he sounds. Swallows and regains his composure. "What I meant to say is it's helpful to hear I'm not the only one who's gone through it."

We depart the restaurant. While we wait for the valet to bring my parents' car around, Peter takes my hand. When they leave, we head back toward his place.

Walking beside him, I feel a deep sense of closeness.

Peter and I have made so much progress in such a short time.

He and I are solid.

As long as he tells me what the fuck is going on with his family.

Chapter Twenty-Nine

Saturday is always a great day to catch up on work. For years, I've come into the office and sorted through emails, tackled administrative tasks and focused on client development. For the past few months though, most of my Saturdays have revolved around Project SoHo.

Of course, since Jordan...well, my weekends have been tackling Jordan's Tryst List and adding additional trysts.

There's really no contest as to what I prefer.

Today, however, Jordan has a booking with an actor who's commissioned an intricate back piece. He's leaving on a five-month shoot on Monday, so today was his only opening. He also doubled Jordan's fee, so she could hardly say no. With approximately ten hours to kill, I decided to come into the office. Mainly, to keep my mind off things.

Two weeks after the Project SoHo committee were supposed to make their decision, it's been radio silence. After putting so much energy into the submission, the wait is *agonizing*.

In the meantime, I'm vigorously scouting for new projects closer to home in an attempt to keep the company's momentum going and money coming in. My efforts have paid off and VA/VT is on deck to helm a new mixed-use commercial building project in downtown Seattle.

Lost in Revit, the software program we use to create designs, I'm shocked to find Rose standing in the doorway.

It's unusual to see her on a weekend unless we're working on Project SoHo, but Rose has always been dedicated, so I don't think much about it.

"Hey, Rose. Didn't expect to see you today." I wave from my desk. "C'mon in."

She steps inside, her expression serious. "I'd like to talk about Project SoHo."

"Okay..." I lean back in my chair, sensing I'm not going to enjoy this conversation.

She hesitates for a moment. "As I mentioned in London, I want to be the project manager for SoHo. I know I can handle it."

Her determination is evident, however, the scale and complexity of Project SoHo is unlike anything we've tackled. "I appreciate your enthusiasm, and I've thought a lot about what we talked about. SoHo is a massive undertaking. It's not only about managing the project, it's about navigating the political landscape, public opinion, international standards—"

"I know what it entails, Peter." She cuts me off, her tone firm. "I've been with this company for years. I've managed complex projects. I deserve this chance."

I narrow my eyes. Her approach surprises me, there must be something going on. "I'll make the decision at the appropriate time. As I was saying before you cut me off, there are a lot of factors at play. My plan is for you to have a leadership role, but it depends on what the committee says."

"Peter...I didn't mean..." Rose looks crushed.

It's time for me to cut her off. "Look. I'm not questioning your capabilities or your dedication. I'm saying SoHo could be a ten-year commitment. It's not purely about technical skills; it's about long-term vision, adaptability to an international stage. As you're aware, this is something I'll likely personally oversee."

Her expression tightens. " The thing is, I met someone. I *want* to relocate to be with him."

"Ah." I realize the reason for her unusual behavior. "Duly noted. Let's wait until we hear back. I promise you'll be at the top of the list for a prime role."

Rose puffs out a breath. "I hope so. I've given a lot to this firm. I've earned this opportunity."

With nothing more to say, she leaves my office. Mentoring staff is tough. I often find myself torn. On the one hand, I want to support and uplift my team. On the other, it's my responsibility to make the right call for my business.

As the minutes pass, her visit weighs heavily on me. I'd hate to lose Rose, she's been my rock throughout this process. As between her and the rest of my team, she's definitely the person I'd trust the most to lead this project if it wasn't me. Something about her approach rubbed me the wrong way.

Which sucks. No matter what the outcome, my decisions will leave a bitter taste for someone.

Ah, the perils of being a boss.

My thoughts are interrupted by the ping of my phone. I'm almost afraid to look, but I do.

Holy shit. It's my brother Lance. It's been years since he and I spoke directly. Fear stabs at my heart. Has something happened to one of my parents? *Fuck.* With a sense of foreboding, I dial his number. The call connects, and I brace myself for what's to come.

"Lance, what's going on?" I strive to keep my voice even.

His voice slithers through the phone, the same old mash-up of greed and malice I remember. "*Petey*! Good to hear your voice."

"Is Mom okay? Dad?" I pinch the bridge of my nose at his disrespect of using a nickname I hate. Ten seconds in and I'm aware of what a bad fucking idea it is to talk to him.

Lance sucks in a drag on his cigarette. Or joint. Or vape. Who knows. "Yeah, yeah." He blows out loudly.

"Bro, I hear you're with Ms. big titty hot-as-fuck tattoo chick, Jordan Deveraux. Amiright?"

"How the fuck do you know Jordan?" My blood turns to ice at his insulting reference to the woman I love. This is my worst fucking nightmare. "And, who says we're together?"

His sinister laugh makes me sick. "Ah, brother. You're so fucking predictable. Defending a juicy piece of ass. Don't you know by now I know every fucking thing about your life? Just like I know with Jason Deveraux backing you, it's time you shared the wealth. Your debt to the family doesn't end, and you know why."

Jesus. My brother—a man who lives with his aging parents with no job and no legitimate prospects—has watched too many mob movies. However, the implication of this call hits me like a tsunami. Is he seriously threatening to use my past against me with Jordan and her family?

"I've made it clear to Mom, there's no more money. That's not up for discussion." I'm so mad my hands shake.

Lance's voice grows cold and emotionless. "Oh, Petey. Petey. *Petey*. You stupid little *fuck*. Always playing the righteous card. Let's not forget, you haven't always been Mr. Perfect. Remember your little felony scam back in college? How do you think sexy Jordan Deveraux would feel if she knew? Not to mention her rich daddy. You know what? I should report it. You're no better than any of us. Maybe a stint in jail will knock you off your high horse."

And just like that, my instincts are confirmed.

"You wouldn't dare." A cold chill runs down my spine. He wouldn't dare expose me, would he? "There's no way you'd risk your gravy train drying up."

Lance is completely unbothered. "Seems to me, you've sealed your own fate. You may think you're so powerful hiding behind your stupid company and all the publicity you get for being such a woke fucking pussy man. Don't forget, you're living in a glass house, brother. It won't take much to shatter it. A nudge in the right direction, and your perfect little world comes crashing down."

"How the fuck did you get this way." I clench the phone tighter, anger and disbelief coursing through me. "Do you have a decent fucking bone in your body?"

"Business is business," he replies coldly. "All you are to me is a good opportunity. One I intend to capitalize on."

I hang up on him, disgusted. Ever since I gave my mother the 250K, her attempts to contact me have been persistent, but I've held firm to my boundaries.

This is different. Lance is likely coming after me, the woman I love, and her family.

Fuck. I shouldn't be surprised but...maybe I've always known it would come to this.

I'm left staring out the window, the cityscape below suddenly feeling distant and unreal.

Flashes of the past flicker in my mind, taking me back to my days in graduate school at the University of Washington. I was deep into my academic journey, pursuing a double master's degree in architecture specializing in Sustainable Systems and Design and Materials and Fabrication. The rigorous program demanded seven years of higher education, and I broke my back paying for it.

Working three jobs helped, but I still had close to two hundred thousand dollars in student debt with two years to go.

When a golden opportunity arose—an invitation to study abroad in Rome—not only was it a dream come true, but an opportunity to learn from three European masters. A real resume builder in a competitive field.

Unfortunately, three weeks before I was supposed to leave, I hit a financial roadblock. My student aid ran out, and the expenses for the year overseas loomed large, threatening to derail my plans.

Desperation led me to make a decision that haunts me to this day. I falsified a student aid application, forging my father's signature to secure a loan. In the moment, it felt like the only way to keep my academic and professional dreams alive. The consequences of my decision didn't hit immediately.

No. The shit hit the fan the morning after I met Jordan. My father, already strained by the constant trouble my brothers got into, tried to borrow money to bail them out of jail. The truth came to light—I forged his signature on a loan I was still paying off, his application was denied, and my actions created a rift that's never fully healed.

I had no idea the forgery was a felony until that morning. I've paid my parents back ten times over but the indiscretion looms like a shadow, threatening to take me down at any given time. Every time they need money, they threaten me. And I pay.

Always under duress...the threat of being turned in, or else.

Filled with a deep sense of shame and regret, I sit in my office until darkness falls. My sordid past weighs heavy on my shoulders and the extent of the vulnerability I've opened myself up to feels catastrophic. A moment of desperation in college, born out of a fierce desire to succeed and grow, has come back to haunt me in ways I couldn't imagine in the two seconds it took to forge my dad's signature.

I'm not stupid. If my forgery and loan fraud is made public, it will not only tarnish my professional repu-tation, but will destroy my relationship with Jordan. I haven't lied to her, she knows about my family stress.

But I left one important detail out.

Because I didn't trust her enough.

No, because I didn't trust *me* enough.

The irony isn't lost on me—the very thing I did to secure my future is threatening to unravel it.

I close my eyes, grappling with the emotions swirling within me. Guilt. Fear. A deep sense of betrayal from my own family. My past, which I thought I'd left behind, is a weapon in the hands of my own relatives who should be my refuge but are actually my enemies.

The entire situation is a bitter pill to swallow.

I've got to do the right thing.

No matter what the consequences.

Chapter Thirty

The sun spills through the windows, casting a warm, inviting glow across the room.

Despite the beautiful morning, I'm uneasy. Unsettled. A little freaked out.

Yesterday had been such a cool experience. Tom Hardy, an actor who starred in a movie which featured LTZ on its soundtrack, finally had time to finish the back piece I've been working on for a couple of months. After we finished, Jace and I took him out to dinner. He was so funny and self-depreciating. We had a great time.

Peter was supposed to come, but backed out, claiming a headache. By the time I got back to the condo, he was sound asleep and I didn't want to disturb him. But I woke up ten minutes ago and he was gone. No note. No explanation. Nothing.

It's not like him.

Scratch that.

It's not like him *now*.

Or maybe it *is* like him and I'm an idiot.

Fuck this. I won't go down this rabbit hole again. I will *not* let my emotions rule my mind.

Tuning into my body, I realize I'm starving. I don't bother putting on clothes and pad out to the kitchen to fix myself a light breakfast—a bowl of Greek yogurt topped with a sprinkle of granola and a drizzle of honey. The thought of coffee roils my stomach, so I pour a glass of orange juice instead.

It's too bad every bite seems tasteless. Maybe my mind is too preoccupied with thoughts of Peter to enjoy my food.

God, I can admit it. I'm worried. I'm also frustrated. His behavior over the past couple of weeks makes it hard not to wonder if he's slipped. Ever since dinner with my parents, it seems like he's keeping things from me again. Did he get bad news from London? Is it something with his family? This mysterious act isn't cool. I don't like getting iced out. Too many of our problems stem from his reluctance to confide in me.

It makes me feel like he doesn't trust me. I'm not going to put up with it.

I decide to send him a text, a simple, "Good morning, everything okay?"

No response, which only heightens my anxiety.

Aborting the mission on breakfast, I focus on getting ready for the day. Peter's walk-in shower is gorgeous, but he's so water conscious I usually follow his lead and keep them short and sweet. Unsupervised, I relish my time and let the warm water cascade over me for easily twenty minutes. My little act of rebellion helps alleviate some of the tension.

Feeling better, I step out and reach for my towel and see I've missed a call from Peter. Relief washes over me, followed swiftly by a resurgence of my earlier annoyance. Wrapped in a towel with water dripping from my hair, I'm about to call him back but a sharp, unexpected chime spooks the shit out of me—someone's at the front door.

Thinking Peter locked himself out, I hurry to the door without getting dressed. Taking a deep breath to steady myself, I slowly turn the handle.

His colleague Rose is the last person I expect to see. She stands there wringing her hands as she rolls off a litany of apologies. Alarm bells instantly permeate my brain. Her demeanor is fraught with tension—I'm partly legit worried about her and partly mortified at being essentially naked in front of one of Peter's employees.

"Jordan, I need to talk to Peter about yesterday. I might have said some inappropriate things... I wasn't in the right frame of mind," Rose avoids looking at me, adding to my discomfort.

My heart skates a few laps around a hockey rink as I try to maintain a calm exterior. "What do you mean?"

She hesitates, flicks her eyes around the room, at anything but me. "I...um...I may have gotten a bit too personal with him about Project SoHo. I've been so invested in it, and I think I let my emotions cloud my judgment."

Vague much? Her unspoken implications are petrifying.

"Personal *how*, exactly?" I try hard not to betray the mounting sense of dread inside me.

"I've grown close to Peter, all of us on Project SoHo have. I guess I let my familiarity spill over into our conversation yesterday." Rose's usually chipper voice is laced with an ambiguous regret. "I feel so stupid."

Peter and Rose were together yesterday.

An icy chill runs down my spine, causing me to inadvertently shiver. Oh, I know her words could mean anything—but it's hard not to jump to conclusions.

"What happened?" I throw a fishing line out.

Rose turns beet red. "I might have crossed a line and I want to clear the air. Make sure we're still good professionally."

What the actual fuck? Rose hit on Peter? How she's speaking makes me want to rip her hair out. She knows I'm his girlfriend...why would she tell me this?

As for my boyfriend, is this why he didn't come to dinner? Is this why he's avoiding me this morning?

"Peter's not at home. I'll let him know you stopped by." I mask the urge to claw Rose's eyes out. What good will it do?

Rose finally meets my gaze. "Thanks, Jordan. I appreciate it. Sorry to interrupt your shower...and for any confusion."

Relief floods me the second I close the door behind her.

Jesus. So fucking strange.

I'm engulfed in uncertainty. Months ago, Peter brought Rose to the restaurant opening. He said she was a colleague who dated women, but did Rose develop feelings for Peter? My gut tells me no.

My gut sometimes doesn't do its job.

God, I hate moping around Peter's condo with a nagging suspicion and a heavy heart.

Hate. It.

Tamping down the urge to call Peter back, I sort through the tangled fears Rose's vague confessions have stirred up. Combined with his family shit, the trust we've worked so carefully to build feels fragile. Threatened by unspoken words and unseen actions.

Every part of my body aches with sadness. I'm devastated to think our hard-earned stability might be on shaky ground. Has Peter forgotten his values once more? With a heavy heart, I decide to go home and lick my wounds. As I'm getting dressed, lost in my thoughts, the sound of the bedroom door opening startles me.

I turn to find Peter holding my favorite coffee and a breakfast sandwich. "I brought breakfast because we need to talk. I've done something so horrific you probably won't forgive me."

My blood turns to ice. He fucked Rose. Our relationship is over.

"Okay, let's talk." I hoist myself up on the counter in his island wearing only bra and panties.

If he's going to confess some sort of situationship with Rose, he'll do it while looking at my banging half-naked body.

Peter sets the sandwich and coffee next to me and leans against the tile. "A choice I made in college is coming back to bite me in the ass. I've been honest about my family troubles, but I didn't tell you my role in why that is."

"Okay..." This is going in a different direction than I anticipated. I'll hear him out.

Except, I'm not expecting anything near to what he confides. Recounting an incident from his time at the University of Washington, Peter describes how financial desperation led him to forge his father's signature on a loan application. His words are heavy with the weight of a mistake that has haunted him for years.

"Lance is threatening to expose me if I don't give in to their demands," he concludes, a hint of despair in his eyes. "He knows I'm with you. Knows about Jace. Your dad..."

My heart breaks for Peter. Though he's a billionaire, it wasn't always the case. Though I'd like to think I'm down to earth, I've lived a privileged life. I've never stressed about money or how to pay for my education, let alone food and housing. I sit in silence for a moment, absorbing the gravity of his confession. The man I've come to know is honorable, hardworking—his revelation doesn't change what's true. His family dynamics definitely bring complexity to our situation.

Trying not to judge him, I still won't sweep a breach of the core of our relationship—honesty—under the rug. "I'm not about to chastise you for a bad decision you made a long time ago. Lies are a deal breaker, though. When we promised each other to tell the truth. I meant it. Keeping things from me is no longer an option if you want this relationship to continue. It can't happen."

"I know, and I'm sorry. When we had the talk before London on the beach, I tried to bring it up, but the moment passed." Peter looks down, a shadow crossing his features. "Doesn't matter. I'm so ashamed of what I did and how it's impacting my life."

In this moment, I picture a younger, naiver version of Peter and his determination to make something of himself. "We don't need to share every little detail of our pasts but with something this significant—like your family blackmailing you—I need to know the truth."

He doesn't say anything. Just nods.

"I can't stress this boundary enough. I won't stay with someone I can't trust. Now's your chance. Are there more secrets looming over us?" I hope and pray he'll say something about Rose. Because if he doesn't...

Peter's eyes meet mine. "There's *nothing* else, Jordan. I promise. Well, one nuance might give you context about what happened in Vegas." He takes a big breath. "The main reason I left so abruptly was because my dad discovered I forged his name and he lost his loan because of me. The stress caused his heart attack. I had to leave. There was no choice. I've never felt as shitty about myself as I did in that moment, so I decided I wasn't the right guy for you. Which wasn't the truth but, at the time, I thought you deserved someone who wouldn't sell out his family to bolster himself."

"Thank you for trusting me, Peter. I'm sorry you carried such a heavy burden." Upon hearing the raw pain in his voice, my heart aches for him. "What you did was wrong, but it was a long time ago. You're not the same person anymore."

He looks at me, hope mingling with trepidation. "You forgive me?"

"I want to, but something weird happened when you were gone. Rose stopped by. She was...apologetic. Insinuated the two of you had a fight." I jump to the floor and pull on a T-shirt.

Peter's genuinely confused. "She came to my *house?*"

"As I said, it was weird. She didn't give details but confessed the two of you had a rough conversation yesterday. She wanted to clear the air." I cross my arms and wait.

He scrubs his face with his hand. "Yesterday, she was at the office and asked to take over the London project. She was pretty assertive and it pissed me off, if I'm honest."

"That's it?" I tilt my head and cross my arms. "It seemed more personal."

"Did she say something physical happened between us? If so, I have a bigger problem to deal with." Peter is stunned.

Ahhhhhhh. My body sags with a profound sense of relief. "No. She was flustered. I guess I read into it and thought..."

"Wait—you thought I would...?" Peter's horrified gaze tells me everything.

I'm an idiot. Nothing happened. Ever. I'm sure of it.

I close the gap between us and take his hands in mine. "*No.* Never mind." I lean up and kiss him. "I misread the entire situation. Look, here's the thing. We both have pasts to cloud our judgement. We've both made mistakes we're not proud of. This thing with your family has got to stop. You've paid them back tenfold. Now, let's brainstorm and figure out how to deal with Lance and this stupid threat. *Together.*"

"*Together.*" For the first time this morning, Peter's eyes fill with resolve. "Fuck. Yeah. I won't let them use my guilt for one more day. I'm allowing them to hold this over my head and I haven't done enough to stop it. I want to put an end to this. Once and for all."

Running my thumbs over his knuckles, I decide to use this moment to also give Rose some grace. "For the record, consider what Rose had to say. It's not easy for a woman to climb up the corporate ladder in a male-dominated industry. You're such a progressive thinker, try expanding your mind into the possibilities of her taking a bigger role."

For the rest of the day, Peter and I brainstorm possible ways to tackle the situation. We workshop everything from seeking legal advice to confronting Lance and the rest of his family. As we talk, a sense of cohesion solidifies between us.

Peter doesn't have to solve his problems on his own.

We can face everything as a team.

Chapter Thirty-One

How the fuck did we get here?

Jordan and I sit with her parents in the Deveraux's spacious living room overlooking Lake Washington.

The atmosphere is tense but not unfriendly.

Earlier today, I left Jordan sleeping in my bed and, honestly, things could have gone two ways.

She could have kicked me to the curb, and rightfully so. I promised her there'd be no more secrets, knowing this one is a fucking doozy. It's no excuse, but I've been living with the shame of what I did for so long, I'm not sure if it even registered as a bonafide "secret."

My fateful decision became part of me. Lord knows, if my dad hadn't found out about it a decade ago, I wouldn't have told a soul. What does that say about me? Do I have a character flaw? Am I really any better than Lance?

Luckily, Jordan's given me grace. *Again*. We talked all morning and came up with what I thought was our final plan—me confessing what happened to the selection committee and the university and trying to handle it quietly.

Somehow, we're at her parents' house. Jordan convinced me to run everything past Jason. I went along with it because I know this isn't about seeking advice. For her, it's about gaining the trust and support of her family.

For me? I feel like a goddamn child and I'm uncomfortable as hell. As much as I respect Jordan's dad, I don't need his fucking permission or advice. I'm my own man and I know how to do the right thing.

Do you?

"Peter, as you've probably surmised, I've been aware of your...situation for a while." Jason's eyes, as green as Jordan's, pierce mine. "Your past doesn't define you, but how you handle it does. Jordan mentioned you've come up with a game plan. Do you feel comfortable sharing?"

Goddamn him. Why does he have to be so...uh...perceptive and deferential. I nod, my throat tight with nerves. "Truthfully, until Jordan and I did some research today, I had no clue about the severe legal ramifications. Somehow, over the years, I've compartmentalized it. Figured out how to justify what I did for the greater good. It was selfish and I should have found another way."

When I say the words, something miraculous happens. I feel lighter. Freer. Jordan sits beside me and notices. She smiles and her hand finds mine, offering silent support.

"Your track record in business speaks volumes about your character and your work ethic." Jason leans forward on his elbows. "Unfortunately, when it comes to personal matters, especially with Jordan, you allow your ego to cloud your judgment."

"Pops! Don't say that." Jordan's angry. She drops my hand and crosses her arms over her chest.

I swallow hard. As much as it sucks to hear it, he's nailed it. "It's okay, baby. He's absolutely right. But I recognize it and I'm committed to doing the right thing.

Especially with you, Jordan. I love you. Want a future with you. There's nothing I won't do. I...I don't want to let you down."

It feels like the air's sucked out of the room at my admission.

Jordan has tears in her eyes. "I want a future with you too, baby. I know you're uncomfortable, but I wanted you to know how it feels to be surrounded by a family who unconditionally supports you in times of trouble." She looks at Jason. "Right, Pops?"

"Yes, sweetheart." Jason leans back. His eyes fill with affection when he looks at his daughter. He flicks his eyes back to me and he's all business again. "Actions speak louder than lip service. Only you can decide how you're going to face the music. Jordan is a grown woman who can make her own decisions, but I'm counting on you to do the right thing. If you two have your own family one day, I'd expect you'd have this exact same discussion with your child's partner as well."

Grace leans on Jason's shoulder. "Peter, to translate Jason's gruff delivery, as long as you're with Jordan, we claim you as one of our own. Sometimes, families have to close ranks and this, my dear, is one of those times."

I feel the weight of their words. I look at Jordan, who is so beautiful and good. Long, blonde hair flowing over her little black t-shirt. She's so strong and capable. It's not like she *needs* her parents' approval, she merely respects their opinion and counts on their guidance.

For the first time since we arrived, I'm able to understand this visit is a gift. Jordan knows I don't have parents I can turn to so she's loaning out Jason and Grace. "I give you my word. I'll do whatever it takes to be the man Jordan deserves, to be someone you can trust as part of this family. I love your daughter and intend on doing her proud for the rest of our lives."

Jordan squeezes my hand. "Dad, Mom. I know Peter has made a pretty big mistake, but it was a long time ago. We've talked about everything and we're ready to face the fallout."

Together, Jordan and I describe our plan, which involves a lot of disclosure, accountability, and a fair bit of groveling.

"Let me tell you something." Jason leans back on the couch with his arm wrapped around his wife. "When I went through my own bout of shit right after Jordan was born, I felt a lot like you do. It's not easy to know what the right thing to do is if you don't have anyone modeling it for you. In my opinion, you must stand up to extortion. Exposing something you're not proud of is far easier than living with the fear of it being exposed.

Grace leans forward and pats my knee. "It's true. Because none of us is perfect. What's important is how we grow, learn, and move on. When our family faced a similar situation, Jason's head of security told me giving in to blackmail only leads to more demands. It's a never-ending cycle, as you've seen for yourself the past few years."

I nod. "I have. Though there could be repercussions, if I take away the leverage, I'll be able to reclaim my truth."

"We're not going to let anyone use a mistake to destroy you." Jordan nods definitively. "Standing up to them is the only way."

I feel a surge of gratitude for everyone's support. "Thank you. Sincerely. I've let this fear control me for too long. I'm ready to face it head-on."

The conversation continues for a couple hours. We discuss potential legal steps and strategies. Particularly, with respect to the fraudulent financial aid. It's important for me to disclose and settle any potential claims which could be brought against me first. Deal with my family later. As we wrap up our discussion, I feel a renewed sense of purpose and determination.

As Jordan and I drive back to my condo from her parents' house, the car is—once more—filled with a contemplative silence. Today's discussions are a reminder of the tumultuous journey we've been on. I can't help but feel a sense of resolve, a readiness to confront my past and rebuild, as long as Jordan is by my side.

Yet, I find myself grappling with a question that's been haunting me. "Baby, I have to ask...after everything, why do you stay? What do you see in me?"

"Oh, Peter." Jordan's gaze is steady and full of warmth. "I see *you*. Not just your hotness. Or success. Or your magic cock. Or your mistakes, even. I've always seen who you are at your core, even if you couldn't see it yourself. It's so fucking sexy you're not running from your past. It means you accept yourself for everything you are—attributes, flaws, whatever."

I shake my head, still struggling to understand. "Sure, but with everything coming to light, I might lose so much. My reputation, my career..."

"What if the situation were reversed?" She squeezes my thigh reassuringly. "You'd say, whatever obstacles come up, facing your past, being willing to make amends and learning from the experience are what matters."

I let her words sink in. Jordan's so fucking perceptive. "What about the repercussions? What if I have to start over?"

"Then we'll face it head-on." Her faith in me, unwavering and sincere, fills me with a sense of peace I'm not sure I've ever known.

I bring her fingers to my lips and kiss her knuckles. "I don't know what I did to deserve you, baby. I realized something in there. My tendency to hold back, to hide things...it's how I've always protected myself from the people closest to me. Until I met you I didn't realize how fucked-up my approach was."

"I'm glad you finally see it." Jordan smiles warmly.

"I want to start therapy." The words feel both scary and liberating. "I overheard Ty talking about his own past and, truth be told, the abuse I've endured may not be physical, but I can see it for what it is. For the good of our relationship, I'm committed to work through my issues so I don't fall into these shitty patterns. I want to be a better partner to you and, once we get through all of this, a good parent someday. Your mom and dad are awesome."

As we continue our drive, Jordan and I talk about our dreams, fears, and hopes for the future. We discuss the practicalities of potentially moving to London, of starting over if necessary, and of building a life reflecting who we are and what we value.

The road ahead may be uncertain, but as I listen to Jordan's voice, steady and sure, I feel a profound sense of gratitude.

Every day we're together, life gets better.

I'm committed to becoming a better man.

For her, for myself, and for our future.

Chapter Thirty-Two

Jordan

I'm bone tired, but I wouldn't miss tonight for the world.

My girlfriends and I haven't hung out in months because our schedules are getting crazier and crazier. Tonight, all of us happen to be in town so, even if it's only a couple of hours, I'm not going to miss the opportunity to catch up.

Merc locks up while I set the alarm. I sling my arm through his and as we walk two blocks to The Nook, a cozy neighborhood joint, the friendly banter starts almost immediately.

"So, Jordy, remember when you couldn't stand the sight of Peter?" Merc's ever-present mischievous grin is in full force. " Look at you two, all 'solid as a rock' and shit."

I roll my eyes playfully, unable to suppress a smile. "Oh, come on, Merc. It feels like a lifetime ago."

"Yeah, yeah." Merc chuckles, nudging me with his elbow. "I'm fucking with you. But you gotta admit, it's kind of a wild turnaround. From fury to forever love in under a year."

My laugh echoes down the quiet street. "Well, if you put it like that, it does sound pretty dramatic. But, hey, we've had a hell of a time checking off items on my Tryst List. I couldn't have planned it any better."

"Ah, to find my own Peter. Someone who can turn my disdain into undying devotion." He sighs dramatically, flipping his braids over one shoulder and placing his hand over his heart.

I nudge him back. "You want a bit of hate sex. Tell the truth."

Merc grins wickedly. "Guilty as charged. But honestly, it's great to see you so happy. You and Peter have been through a lot but have something very special."

We reach the bar and the warm glow from inside spills out onto the street, welcoming us.

"Thanks, Merc. And don't worry, your 'Peter' is out there somewhere. Just you wait." I duck under his arm. "Are you happy to be one of the girls tonight?"

"It's taken long enough." He sniffs and makes a beeline for the oversized couches flanked by wingback chairs, where Zoey, Alex, Fiona, and Ronni await our arrival.

The Nook, our chosen spot for the evening, is a cozy, two-story lounge with a magnificent, handcrafted bar made from three different slabs of wood. Rustically charming, with kitschy nostalgia like an old rotary phone and a 1920s radio, I like it because it's cozy and private. The antique lighting fixtures bathe the space in a gentle, inviting glow, while shelves of twinkling antique glasses add a touch of elegance. Soft music plays in the background, a blend of classic hits and soothing tunes, loud enough to be heard but not so loud it drowns out conversation.

"So, Jordan, spill the tea! How's everything with Peter?" Fiona rests her hand on her protruding belly, her eyes sparkling with interest.

I smile, taking a sip of my drink. "Well, it's been a rollercoaster, but we're in a good place. Peter came clean about his past and while he lost a couple of jobs in

Seattle, it hasn't been catastrophic to his business. Quite the opposite. He's got so much work he hired two new staff members."

Merc leans in, eager to be part of the gossip. "Don't forget the reason he's in London."

"Well, I'm sure you've heard. VA/VT was a finalist to design the new museum in London," I practically gush, because it was such a major accomplishment to be considered let alone get down to the final two. "They weren't awarded the primary bid, but VA is handling the green energy aspect of the project and VT is doing a technology integration. Peter and his team are so passionate about zero carbon emission work, I think he realized it's more about the legacy of global impact rather than the glory."

"So cool." Alex, who gave up a lucrative travel influencer career to run a horse rescue has been so supportive. "Finding what truly motivates you is key."

Ronni taps the table. "Wait, so are you guys moving to London?"

"No. The plan is for Peter to commute for the all-hands-on-deck meetings a couple of days a month until the project's complete. He promoted his project manager, Rose to oversee the project on a day-to-day basis." I sigh happily. "She's doing amazing. I'd like to think I nudged him in the right direction, and he realizes how important it is to support women in such a male-dominated industry. He's confident it's a permanent solution. She loves living in London and got engaged to her boyfriend a couple weeks ago."

Zoey leans forward, which is logistically challenging because she also has a baby bump. "So, what does this mean for you two? Any big plans for the future?"

The question hangs in the air, and I feel everyone's eyes on me. Inside, I'm smiling to myself because Peter and I have a surprise up our sleeve. Tonight's not the night I'm revealing it though.

"Well, we're taking things one step at a time." I sip my drink. "We're stronger than ever, and I'm excited about what the future holds."

"Code for 'we're still fucking like rabbits,'" Fee mock whispers to Ronni.

"Oh, please. You're *all* still fucking like rabbits," I fire back.

Everyone laughs.

Because it's true.

Merc raises his glass. "To fucking like rabbits."

We settle into the cozy warmth of the bar and conversation flows effortlessly among us. The atmosphere is charged with laughter and shared stories as we catch up on our lives. Nobody knows it, but I'm not drinking any alcohol tonight either. Instead, I sip on a mocktail, soaking in the joy of being with my friends.

"So, ladies, isn't it nice to have a kid-free night out?" I raise my glass in a mock toast.

Zoey pats her baby bump. "Absolutely! As much as I love being a mom, a break is always welcome. Plus, it cracks me up knowing famous rock stars are on daddy duty tonight."

"Zane probably brought Mia over to your house and she's taken over." Fiona chuckles about her precocious daughter. "She'll run them ragged, I swear she's an eighty-year-old in a ten-year-old's body. I should have set up the nanny cam."

"Oh, I've got you, babe." Zoey proudly holds up her phone. "Check it out."

We all huddle around her phone and watch with great amusement as Mia puts makeup on Ty and Zane, who sit side by side on the couch. Baby Oliver is sound asleep in a bassinette next to Ty.

Alex shudders. "I can't unsee it, can I?"

"Take a look at this." Ronni, who's barely showing, turns her phone so we can see Connor chasing his twin sons around their bedroom, trying to put on their pajamas. "Those guys command a stage in front of fifty thousand fans who would probably give anything to see this."

We all laugh, enjoying the images of real-life rockstars trying to keep up with the demands of parenthood.

"Hey, Jordan, I heard you're selling your condo," Alex prods me. "Big move, huh?"

"Way to steal my thunder, Ms. Inside Information. Peter and I bought a beautiful place on Beach Drive. He's fast-tracking renovations to his standards so we're living at his house until its finished. It's right on the water – the view is incredible." I can't help but picture the home, which will be perfect for us.

Ronni whistles appreciatively. "Beach Drive, fancy! So you two are really setting down roots?"

"It's not Hunt's Point, but we like it." I get in a jovial dig about the fancy neighborhood where Ronni and Connor live.

"When will it be done?" Zoey leans back in her chair and shifts positions.

"A few months. In all seriousness, it feels right, you know? We both wanted a place of our own. We're keeping his place downtown because it's awesome, but the new house will be our main house." I feel a flutter of excitement at the thought of Peter and I moving in officially to *our* home.

Especially because of my little secret.

Merc grins, bumping his shoulder against mine playfully. "Look at you ladies. Every one of you all grown up and domesticated."

"Peter's a good guy." Fiona leans her head on my shoulder. "I can't believe how perfect you are for each other. I mean it."

"He's perfect for me," I agree, feeling a warmth spread through me at the thought of my man. "Despite some serious setbacks, he's shown me time and again how committed he is to us, to our future. This move...it's like starting a new chapter."

If only they all knew.

The night winds down and I'm grateful for the time we've had tonight. The next few months are going to be a whirlwind, and it's hard to know when—and if—another night like this will happen anytime soon.

In any case, the sense of camaraderie and support fills me with warmth. With friends like these, life is pretty fucking great.

Half hour later, I'm relaxing in bed, watching some YouTube videos on my iPad. As the clock inches toward eleven, fatigue starts to set in. First-trimester pregnancy is no joke, but I'm trying to rally because I'm eagerly waiting for Peter's call.

I decide to haul my ass out of bed and pack a couple of boxes. Peter wants me to hire movers, but I've lived in this house for a long time and I want to go through everything myself. There's no reason to bring a bunch of crap to our new house because it's purging season. I'm actually looking forward to a fresh start.

As I'm folding some clothes, my phone finally buzzes. It's Peter on FaceTime. A smile spreads across my face as I answer. "Hey, sexy. I miss you."

Peter's handsome face fills the screen. "Hi, baby. Today is going to be busy, we've officially submitted the drawings for preliminary review. Everything's moving forward."

"Fantastic! I'm so proud of you." I make a kissy face to the screen, genuinely happy for him.

He looks to his left and right and makes a quick kissy face back. "I'm on the Tube so don't make me do anything embarrassing."

"Would it be inappropriate of me to ask to see your cock?" I wink when I mouth the word "cock."

"What am I going to do with you." He tsks, shaking his finger. "I can't wait to come home. Neither can my cock. Speaking of home, I have a surprise for you."

My curiosity is piqued. "A surprise? What kind of surprise would be better than riding your cock?"

Peter chuckles. "You'll see. Just pack a bag for a weekend getaway. We're leaving as soon as I get home. I'll text you the instructions. It's going to be something special."

"Instructions? How fun!" I can't help but feel a rush of excitement at his words. "I love surprises! I'll be ready."

We chat a bit more about our days. I tell him about the girls' night out, the laughter, the stories, and the support.

He listens intently, which is one of the many reasons I love him. He genuinely cares about every little detail of my life.

Another reason my love for Peter has deepened is witnessing the integrity he's shown in dealing with his past. As we suspected, it's affected every aspect of his life—personal, and professional—but he's come out the other side lighter and happier. Lately we find ourselves naturally recapping the recent upheavals and resolutions in his family situation. It feels like a necessary step. He's got to process everything to close a painful chapter before we fully embrace the new journey ahead of us.

Especially because I'm almost three months pregnant. A happy surprise for both of us.

"So, it's your first trip away after resolving the shit with your folks. How do you feel? It seems like a good chance to finally breathe and focus on what's important—us and the baby." I rest a hand on my miniscule bump.

Peter nods. "Absolutely. It's been a rough ride, and I couldn't have gotten through it without you, baby."

"I'll always believe in you." My heart hurts for Peter, I can't imagine having parents who exploited me. "It's hard for me to understand how they can still stand up for your brothers after everything."

He looks away from the camera for a second. I know all of this is an open wound, but his therapist has encouraged us to talk about it. "When I think about our baby, it actually makes me sad for them. They have no interest in me, you, or our child, and it's their loss. I guess some people like to keep themselves grounded in misery. Quite honestly, I don't feel much of anything for them anymore. I've paid my debt—they have a new house and money in the bank. I'm done. It helps having a new lawyer. Joe Finney made clear—any further attempts to extort money from me will be prosecuted. They're out of my life, maybe forever and I feel free for the first time in years."

"We're creating our own family." I smile at him.

He smiles back, but there's a hint of sadness in his eyes. "Kyle's in rehab and Lance is back in jail, this time for a long stretch. Stepping back from the chaos has been so good for my well-being. Changing my phone number was the first step. I don't get low-level anxiety every time it rings."

"It's the right decision," I say thoughtfully. "You need peace."

"Yeah." He's so handsome, gazing at me through the screen. "It's really all behind us and we can concentrate on our future. A new house. Our baby. I'm still shocked my situation with the bank turned out so well. Joe did an excellent job banging out the terms of the settlement. Work is good. My team at the firm didn't even bat an eye, Fabiola's the only one who's moved on."

Despite the potential fallout, Peter called a meeting and told his entire staff the truth, apologized and offered them six months' severance if they wanted to move on. "Your leadership really shone through, Peter. Your team believes in you, like I do."

Peter beams. "How are you feeling? Still barfing up everything you eat?"

"No, I've moved into starvo mode." I can't help but nudge about a deeper commitment. "Did you look at the link I sent you? What do you think about getting married at the courthouse and doing a bigger wedding after the baby's born?"

Peter's eyes twinkle with a secret I'm not yet privy to. "Oh, we can do better. Let's just say I've got some ideas up my sleeve. We'll talk about it in person."

"God." I laugh. "You and your surprises. I can't wait to see what you have planned."

As our conversation winds down, I'm hormonally emotional. "I can't wait for you to be home. These video calls are great, but I miss you so much."

"I know, baby." His voice is tender. Sweet. "I miss you too. We'll be together very soon, and I promise this weekend will be worth the wait."

We hang up and I miss him immediately.

Looks like I'll be counting each minute until he gets home.

Chapter Thirty-Three

The morning air is crisp and filled with anticipation on the way to Jordan's house.

I touched down from London an hour ago, but I promised a special surprise for my girl so I'm retrieving her and we'll be off on an adventure of a lifetime.

Last night, I texted her instructions to pack for a weekend getaway—casual clothes and something fancy for dinner—deliberately leaving the details tantalizingly vague. I'm sure she's losing her shit, wondering what I'm up to. My Uber pulls into her driveway and my heart leaps when I see Jordan on the porch waiting with her suitcase. She's so beautiful in a simple gray tunic and black leggings, her hair long and loose. I get out of the car, I rush over to her, eager to breathe her in.

"Baby!" She throws her arms around me. "I've missed you so much!"

I band my arms around her, keeping her snug against my body. "God, I missed you too. More than words can say."

We stand there for a moment, simply holding each other. Giving each other little kisses and caresses as the world around us fades into the background.

Knowing we'll have plenty of time for affection all morning, I force myself to step back. "Ready for our adventure?"

"Absolutely, but you have to tell me where we're going!" She practically jumps up and down like a little kid.

I grab Jordan's suitcase and lead her toward the car. "Nope! You'll love it. At least I hope you will."

"Can I have a hint?" She's giddy. Unable to contain the excitement.

I smirk. "Not a chance. You'll find out soon enough."

After helping her into the car and scooting in next to her, she leans against me and the driver starts the engine. The familiar streets of Jordan's neighborhood pass by in a blur and my excitement builds as we make our way, not to the commercial airport, but to Boeing Field, where a private jet experience awaits us.

I know the second she catches sight of the Falcon 900LX, an eco-friendly private jet I chartered.

"What the fuck? Peter?" She presses her face to the window, taking in the sleek aircraft before us.

"I know you've flown private many times." I'm not usually one to indulge, given my propensity for conservation. "But this one is special, it's one of the most eco-efficient jets out there. It's indulgent, but we'll travel with a lower carbon footprint than a commercial plane, even though you and I are the only passengers today."

She kisses me sweetly. "You've taught me to be mindful of our impact. This is super cool."

As we board the jet, the luxurious and intimate interior greets us. The cabin is spacious, with private sleeping quarters in the back. Decorated in creams and grays, the attention to detail in the design is evident, blending comfort with elegance. Settling into the plush seats, I can't help but feel a sense of pride.

"This is beyond anything I could have imagined." Jordan grabs my hand. "I'm looking forward to having you to myself all weekend."

Once we hit cruising altitude, I squeeze her hand gently, ready to reveal the first of many surprises. "So...in case you hadn't realized it, we're down to the final item on the Tryst List. What do you say..."

"Mile high club!" Jordan squeals, then clamps her hand over her mouth and looks around the cabin nervously.

I lean over, my lips nip at hers as my hand skates up her ribs to cop a feel of her tit. "You can be as loud as you want, baby. It's only us and the pilots for a little over two hours."

"Where are we going..." she starts to ask, but I silence her with a kiss.

I flick my thumb over Jordan's already taut nipple. "The only place you need to think about is the bedroom. I want you so bad I can't wait another second."

Standing, I take Jordan's hand and lead her to the back of the plane where I've arranged for rose petals to be sprinkled all over the fluffy, white duvet. I close the door behind us and her hands fall to my chest then rise to my shoulders.

"I'm so fucking horny. I've worn out the batteries on my clit stimulator since you've been gone." She unbuttons my shirt and slips her fingers under the fabric, slowly moving it over my shoulders and down my arms. I shake it off to the floor and kick it into the corner.

And...my dick tries to bore out of my jeans as I lift Jordan's shirt over her head. "God, me too. I beat off four or five times a day every time we're apart," I whisper against her lips.

Heated eyes trained on each other, we hastily take off our clothes. Jordan pulls down her leggings and kicks off her shoes while I fumble with my zipper, which is taut against my erection. The second I manage to free myself, Jordan grips me tightly while I step out of my boxers and jeans.

It's nearly too much. "*Fuck*, Jordan."

I pepper her with whispery kisses as she strokes me from root to tip, moving down her collarbone to pull her hard little nipple in between my lips.

"Yes," she keens, pumping me faster. "God, I've wanted to fuck you on a plane for so long."

Continuing to suck and nibble her nipple, I cup her other breast and squeeze. Glide my hand down to the teeniest swell of her belly. I can't help but pause for a moment, before slipping my fingers through her folds and plunging them into her channel.

"Fuck. You're soaking." I drag my wet fingers to her clit.

She squirms. "And very, *very* sensitive."

"*So* sensitive." Amping up my rhythm on Jordan's needy little nub, my tongue dives into her sweet mouth and swirls against hers. Her hips seem to have a mind of their own, bucking and grinding against my hand. I feel her core muscles tense up, and I know exactly what to do. My fingers slide through her slickness and furiously circle her clit, exactly the way she likes it.

Soon, she's panting against my mouth and clutching at my hair. "Peter, I'm coming...oh *God.*"

I'll never get tired of Jordan gushing all over my fingers. Her entire pussy vibrates as she melts against me. Moaning. Writhing. Panting. I've got her, though, holding her upright until she catches her breath. Then, I ease her down on the bed.

"Good girl." Gripping my cock, I stroke myself to get a little relief, rotating and pulling. Occasionally swiping my thumb over my crown.

"It's so hot watching you jack yourself." Jordan's knees fall open, revealing her glistening, pink pussy. She reaches between my legs and gently squeezes and rolls my balls between her fingers. Bites her lip. Pinches her nipple with her free hand. "Put your thick cock inside me."

Since her dirty little mouth doesn't specify where, I tap my shaft against her lips. "I love you craving my cock."

"I *always* crave your cock, you should know." Jordan traces the contour of my abs with her finger.

Before I can react, Jordan's mouth engulfs the head of my dick. Her hands rest on my hips to hold me steady as she licks and sucks me like a pro.

"*Jesus*," I hiss and wind my hand around her hair. I look down at my cock in her mouth. Her eyes water every time I hit the back of her throat, but she *loves* it. "*Fuck.*"

If I'm not careful, I'll come too quickly so I pull free and scoot in next to her. Grip her cheeks in my palms and press my mouth to hers. Our kisses are messy. Desperate. Needy.

"I *really* want you in my pussy," Jordan moans against my mouth.

"Yeah. I can't wait another second." I roll Jordan to the side so her back is to my chest. Cupping her breast with one hand, I snag her chin with the other to carefully pull her head back against my neck so our tongues can meld and dance. Then I lift her leg up and to the side, so my cock can slide along her slit and rub against her clit. I kiss across Jordan's neck to behind her ear. "I'm going to fuck you hard, baby. Are you ready for it?"

"So ready." She grips my cock and positions it at her entrance. "*Ohmygod.*" Her head lolls back against my shoulder. "Put it in me, I'm so wet for you."

With one snap of my hips, I plunge inside with one robust thrust. "Like that?"

"*Yessss,*" Jordan cries out, draping her thigh high over my hip. I hold her leg in place with one hand and circle her clit with the other.

In and out, my cock disappears inside her body. There's no better sight. No better feeling. We're both lost in the sensation of being joined after a week apart. Changing angles. Shifting positions slightly. The only objective is our connection and how good it feels.

Jordan's entire body begins to quiver from the intensity of her building orgasm. "Peter, right there. Yes. *Yesssss...* Oh, God, I'm gonna come so fucking hard."

"Fuck, baby. You're sucking me dry." Her pussy suctions my cock so tightly, my eyes roll back in my head.

I lift her leg higher, which allows me to go even deeper. The sensation of sliding against her velvety walls nearly sends me over the edge. Jordan's writhing like a woman possessed so I double down. Thrusting. Gyrating. Anything to prolong her orgasm until I have no choice but to let go, grinding against her until I've pumped every last drop into her body.

Minutes later, still lodged deep, I move my hand over Jordan's belly. Smoothing. Gliding. Stroking. She wraps her hand behind my neck and coaxes me to her. Gives me a sweet kiss on my lips. "I'm showing a tiny bit," she whispers.

"I can't get over it." I lean across her and kiss the slight swell before lying next to her on the pillow. "No one but us would ever notice. It looks like you ate a big meal."

Jordan strokes my cheek, her thumb passing over my bottom lip. "We'll know if it's a boy or a girl in a few weeks."

"As much as I want to talk about our baby, I need to ask—are you up for round two?" I tweak her nipple. "You did say you're exceptionally horny, it's a short flight. We might as well get our money's worth for this mile-high experience."

Jordan giggles. "Oh, I'm up for it. Who knew being pregnant would be like female Viagra?"

"Good. You know what's coming. I want you to sit on my face." I wind my arm around her waist.

She tilts her head. "What? Here?"

"Don't get sassy. You know it's my favorite thing." She's so tiny, before she knows it, I've maneuvered her to straddle my stomach. "I want to eat my come out of your pussy, then lick you until you come. Then I'm going to fuck you and fill you back up."

Jordan's eyes dilate. Her nipples pucker. "You know how wet it makes me when you give me a play-by-play."

"Oh, I know, baby." Grabbing her hips, I lift her effortlessly until her pussy hovers over my mouth. I spread her lips with my fingers and lick up our release.

"Oh *fuuuuuck*." Jordan falls forward and presses her hands against the wall for leverage. Her tits dangle over my head, nipples hard as marbles. I reach up and twist them between my fingers as I lap at her pussy with long, languid strokes. She swivels her hips, rocking and riding my face, creaming all over my tongue. "How do you *dooooo* that?"

"There's nothing I love more in the world than to make you come, baby." I decide to slow things down a bit. Instead of devouring Jordan like a starving man, I release her tits and grip her hips, tenderly flicking her clit with the tip of my tongue. Controlling her movement entirely, I rock her slowly against my lips as I suck and lick until her inner thighs tremble around my ears. She's whimpering. Breathily panting.

In a move of desperation, she cups her breasts, which are at least a cup size bigger than normal, lifts them to her lips and—sucks on her own fucking nipples. One after the other.

"Holy Jesus." My eyes bug out. It's the most erotic thing I've ever seen in real life.

My cock is so fucking hard, I'm pretty sure I can feel every ounce of blood moving through my veins straight to my dick. I can take no more, so I lift Jordan off my mouth and slam her down on my shaft. Hold her firmly by her sweet ass so I can pump up into her from below like a madman. The slaps of our bodies fill the little bedroom along with our increasingly feral moans of passion.

Thank Christ I had the foresight to dismiss the flight attendant.

White-hot heat zings down my spine and up my shaft, but I'm not ready to come so I stop to let Jordan choose her pace. She braces herself on my chest with her hands, rolling her hips faster and faster, seeking some sort of friction a hair out of reach. Helpfully, I reach between us to spread her lips apart so her clit has direct contact with my pubic bone. It only takes a few more gyrations until she cries out and I press on her lower back so she can't retreat from the stimulation. Then I bite her nipple. Sharply, but not too hard.

"Ohmyfuckinggod." Jordan floods me, squeezing my cock as she comes.

I'm right there with her, erupting as I fall over the edge. Jordan collapses on top of me. After a few deep breaths, I'm able to speak. "Are you okay, baby?"

"More than okay." Her voice is dreamy as she melts into me. "As okay as you can get."

"I'd love to cuddle you and sleep for a bit, but we're probably landing any minute. Let's get cleaned up." I kiss her temple but make no effort to move.

She brings my palm to her belly. "Are you gonna tell me where we are? I mean, we obviously haven't gone too far."

"I'll give you one clue. I thought it was high time we returned to the scene of the crime." I stifle a laugh.

"Scene of the crime?" She looks up, confused. "I have pregnancy brain. Riddles aren't fair."

I trace her hairline with my finger. "I'm pretty sure this one will come to you. It's not difficult."

Jordan pushes herself up to a seated position and tucks her feet under her. Tries to open up the little porthole window, but I catch her wrist. "No cheating."

"You're so mean." She harumphs. Crosses her arms over her luscious tits.

I get up and toss her clothes to her but hold up her panties on one finger. "These, I'm keeping with me."

We dress as she mumbles to herself, "Scene of the crime. Scene of the crime."

I know she's figured it out when her eyes widen dramatically.

"Vegas. We're in Vegas." She pushes on my shoulder. "*Peter*!"

I pull her into my arms. "You hit the jackpot, baby."

Little does she know, today's surprises have only begun.

Chapter Thirty-Four

I have no idea what to expect.

The private jet comes to a smooth stop on the tarmac and the thrill of Peter's surprise fills me with a childlike excitement. I glance over at him, hoping for any hint of our plans, but he remains delightfully mysterious.

And smug.

Peter helps me down the steps as we disembark, a warm breeze at our back, and I catch sight of a driver dressed in a black suit in front of an elegant electric Bentley. "You're too much," I say as we approach the car. "You're driving me crazy with all this secrecy. Can't you give me a tiny clue about what you've planned?"

His eyes twinkle with mischief. "Where's the fun in that, baby? You'll find out soon enough. For now, it's on a need-to-know basis."

I swat him as we settle into the buttery leather seats. "Are we staying at the Venetian? Going to a private residence? Come on, give me something."

"*Nope.*" Peter shakes his head, feigning a stern look. "Not a word. You'll have to wait and see."

Our car glides through the streets, its electric engine whisper-quiet, as we make our way toward the unknown destination. My anticipation is almost tangible, which I realize is part of Peter's plan. I try a different tactic. "Okay, how about a hint? Are we going somewhere we've been before?"

"I promise, it'll be worth the wait." He slings his arm around my shoulder.

Nothing prepares me for the awe-inspiring sight that greets us as we arrive at The Mansion at the MGM Grand. Even from the outside, its discreet façade whispers of the opulence that lies within. I've heard about it—both my pops and brother have stayed before—I'm psyched to take in the art.

"Wow, Peter, this place...it's like another world!" I can't help but gawk at the grand entrance, and I've seen my share.

Peter smiles, his eyes reflect my wide-eyed enthusiasm. "Just wait until you see inside."

The Mansion is a private group of residences nestled discreetly within the MGM Grand casino. It's an invite-only sanctuary shrouded in an air of exclusivity and mystique. Franco, our designated host, greets us and offers to give us a tour. As we enter, I'm struck by the architectural grandeur of the place.

"It's modeled after an 18th-century Florentine villa." Peter notices my fascination. "Isn't the attention to detail incredible?"

"Yeah. Like your Florence-inspired tattoo." Jordan grips my bicep.

Franco guides us toward a display of art. "I'm told the lady is an artist. While you're staying with us, please feel free to enjoy our collection. We're honored to have over eight hundred exquisite pieces by artists such as Henri Matisse, Pablo Picasso, and Salvador Dali.

"It's like walking through a private museum," I marvel, nearly reduced to tears.

"This property has quite a few villas, we have you staying in the main mansion where you'll have your own private pool, and I'll be around to take care of your every need." Franco leads us through a temperature-controlled atrium. "This is where you'll dine, we've arranged a series of delicious meals over the next few days."

I can't help but be overwhelmed by the sheer decadence of it all. "Peter, this is unbelievable. It's like we're in Tuscany, not Vegas."

Peter takes my hand, weaving our fingers as we follow Franco toward our villa. "I thought it would be the perfect place for us to unwind, to be away from the hustle and bustle of the Strip. Maybe reimagine Vegas to tell a different story for us."

"I dunno." I lean up to kiss him. "Our story has turned out pretty fucking awesome."

But as we settle into our villa, overlooking the lush Italian-style garden atrium, I realize this weekend is more than a getaway. It's a celebration of our journey, a testament to our love and the life we're building.

Amidst the grandeur and splendor of The Mansion, I find a profound sense of peace and happiness, knowing

I'm with the person who means everything to me in the place where we met nearly a decade ago.

***

A few hours and many orgasms later, after a blissful and romantic afternoon spent naked in our twelve-thousand-square-foot villa, Peter coaxes me to get ready for dinner.

"The chef is incredible; I've arranged for something special tonight." He's so handsome, his eyes shine with excitement.

Once we're showered, I'm taken by surprise as we dress in our evening attire. Peter's arranged for me to have hair and makeup, and a gorgeous floaty seafoam green gown hangs in the wardrobe.

"It's beautiful." I let the fabric slide through my fingers. "This is so much fun."

I'm primped, plucked, and styled and the anticipation of the night ahead fills me with a sense of delight. A wardrobe attendant helps me put on the dress and leads me to the foyer where Peter, looking dashing in his suit, offers his arm.

"You're the most beautiful woman I've ever known, Jordan." He bends to kiss me, gently touching my mermaid necklace. "You have no idea how proud I am you've chosen me. I'm the luckiest person on the planet."

"It's always been you, baby. From the first time our eyes met." I tuck myself under his strong arm as we step out into the plaza to stroll the grounds before dinner.

At night, the Mansion's grounds are even more breathtaking, a serene oasis amidst the vibrant energy of Las Vegas. We wander past beautifully manicured gardens, each turn revealing another stunning piece of art. The atmosphere is imbued with a sense of tranquility and timeless elegance. Peter seems to know exactly where we're going as he guides me toward a high wall obscured by a large tarp. Two men dressed in butler uniforms stand guard.

Curiosity piqued, I turn to Peter. "What's this?"

With a mysterious smile, he gives a subtle nod to the men, who proceed to pull down the tarp. My breath catches in my throat as it falls away, revealing a magnificent mosaic spanning the entire wall—ten feet high and ten feet wide. It's one of my mixed media mermaid pieces, brought to life in vibrant, shimmering tiles.

I'm overwhelmed, speechless at the sight. It nearly brings me to my knees. "Peter, this...how? It's my design!

I thought I'd lost it. All of this collection went missing a few years ago."

Peter takes my hand, his eyes reflecting the mosaic's hues. "Jordan, you're my mermaid, and your art is as beautiful as any fresco in Italy. I wanted to celebrate your talent, to immortalize it forever. I've been working on this project as a surprise as part of my collaboration in modernizing The Mansion with contemporary artists' works."

"But, how?" I'm so confused.

Enfolding me in his arms, Peter divulges a few surprises. "After our night in Vegas, I still found myself captivated by the most magical woman I'd ever known. I respected your relationship, but everything about our night made it impossible to forget you. Every now and then I'd Google you, or your brother, to pick up information about what you were up to. I was able to piece together a bit more about your background in fine art."

"A little stalkerish, but so far I'm with you," I tease, nestling against him.

"Don't be a little shit." Peter nuzzles my neck. "Anyway, around the time I got brought into The Mansion project—a year or so before you started my tattoo—I stumbled upon an old podcast you did with Dave Navarro. You spoke candidly about your career in the tattoo industry and how difficult it was for a woman to break through. You also spoke about your upbringing. Values. I began to understand what made you tick a little more. What resonated most was what you said about embracing the dual influence of your mom's creative nurturing and your dad's business acumen. It led you to open The Salty Siren where you combine your artistic talent and entrepreneurial spirit in a more accessible way."

I turn in his arms. "Yeah, yeah, yeah. I remember the podcast. More importantly, how did you get my piece?"

"Listening to those interviews made me fall in love with you even more." Peter presses his forehead to mine. "You perfectly articulated how the arts are continuously devalued in a world of instant gratification which, as you know, breaks my heart. In your case, stunning original mermaid artwork by Jordan fucking Deveraux—was lost. Sold. Stolen. Misplaced. Didn't matter. Somebody devalued your priceless creations, and allowed it to happen, which means they devalued *you*."

"Yeah." My eyes mist up. "I can't believe you remember all this when I'd nearly forgotten. I loved those pieces.

My entire experience with the gallery turned me off working in fine art for good. I still wonder what could have happened to my art babies."

Peter kisses the top of my head as we face the stunning rendition of one of my long-lost pieces. " I know what happened to your artwork. I bought it. *All of it*. I popped into Amsterdam on one of my trips to London. Found the gallery. Made them search their storage and there they were. Shoved away. As beautiful, haunting, and magical as you described."

"Wait, what?" I'm shocked senseless. Tears of joy and disbelief well up in my eyes.

"I planned on telling you at my first appointment but then...well, you know our story." He smiles at me. "Knowing how skeptical you were of my intentions, I didn't want to love bomb you right away. So, I decided to keep them safe. Even though we had a rough road, something inside me always believed we'd find our way to each other. Either way, I bought them back for you to have."

I sigh happily, this is the single coolest thing anyone has ever done for me. The mosaic is a stunning interpretation of my work, each tile meticulously placed to capture the essence and beauty of my design. "I can't believe it, baby. It's the most beautiful gift. To see my art on such a grand scale, in this place... It's more than I ever imagined."

"You're an incredible artist, Jordan." He wraps his arms back around me, and we stand there, in front of my mosaic, lost in the moment. "Your art deserves to be seen and celebrated. You inspire me every day, and I wanted you to have something to always remind you of how extraordinary you are."

As the evening sun casts its golden light over the grounds, illuminating the mosaic in a radiant glow, I realize this moment is more than a gesture of love—it's a testament to our journey, to the depth of our attachment, and the shared appreciation for art and beauty binds us.

Lost in the beauty of the moment, Peter suddenly steps back, his expression turning solemn yet filled with love. To my utter surprise, he drops to one knee, a small velvet box in his hand.

The world seems to pause around us.

"Jordan, baby." Peter's voice is steady but filled with emotion. "You're my inspiration. My partner. My only love. The mother of my baby. With you, I've found joy and peace I didn't know existed. Will you marry me?"

He opens the box to reveal a stunning ring, sparkling with diamonds and aquamarines, my birthstone.

It's perfect.

Tears of happiness fill my eyes as I nod vigorously. "Omigod, yes, Peter, *yes*! I'll marry you!"

"So, what do you think? Does this make the list?" He grips my cheeks between his palms and plants a kiss on my lips.

I tilt my head, then it dawns on me.

"Yes." I laugh. "It's the ultimate Tryst."

"The *best* Tryst." He nibbles on my lips.

"For now." I gaze up at him. "We're going to have a lifetime of trysts and I look forward to each and every one of them. With you."

Jordan thinks our surprises are done for the night.

Why wouldn't she?

An art installation. A marriage proposal.

The thing is, I'm not waiting another day for our forever. There's one final surprise.

I slip the ring onto Jordan's slender finger. Then stand and take both of her hands in mine. "How about we get married tonight?"

"*Uh...*" Jordan looks deep into my eyes to see if I'm serious. Then she frantically looks around. "Tonight would be amazing, but... my family isn't in Vegas."

My cue. I turn toward the garden path to signal our butler. "I thought you might say that baby."

One by one, Jordan's friends and family members step out from the shadows. Her parents, Jace and Alex, Jen and Becca, Jaylynn, the LTZ guys and their wives, Merc, Kali, Ryuji and Luna from The Salty Siren. Joining them, Pip, Fabiola, and Rose come forward with a few of my staff.

Everyone witnessed the unveiling of her art and my proposal. All are checked into the villas for the wedding.

Our wedding.

Clearly overwhelmed, tears stream down Jordan's cheeks. She's half-laughing. Half-crying. "*Ohmygod*. Peter, you did all this for us?"

I nod, happiness bursting from deep inside me. "I wouldn't surprise you like this unless all the people we care about could join us."

"Let's do it." She kisses me. "Let's get married. Right. Now."

While the hotel staff expediently assemble the wedding elements, Jordan and I are whisked to the back. Jason and Grace join her while I take my place by the justice of the peace at the altar, which has been set up in front of her mermaid mosaic.

The guests mingle and laugh as they take their seats in the hastily set up chairs. Music fills the air with a joyous hum. As I wait for my bride to walk down the aisle, I reflect on the whirlwind of planning leading to this impromptu—yet perfect—wedding ceremony.

Admittedly, orchestrating this surprise for Jordan wasn't the tough part. Keeping it under wraps while coordinating with her friends and family has been nothing short of an exhilarating challenge.

The first step was seeking Jason's blessing.

I remember sitting across from him a few days after we found out she was pregnant, the gravity of the conversation weighing heavily on me because he didn't know about our pregnancy at the time. "Jason, I love your daughter more than words can express, and I want to spend the rest of my life with her. I would be honored to have your blessing to ask Jordan to marry me."

The sincerity in his eyes when he gave us his blessing, along with a few words of fatherly advice, is a moment I'll cherish forever.

Then came the secret coordination with her family and friends. It was like orchestrating a ballet, each move carefully planned and executed with precision. I reached out to each of them, explaining my plan to surprise Jordan with a wedding. Their enthusiasm and willingness to be part of my secret mission was overwhelming. We had group chats and covert meetings, discussing everything from travel arrangements to the perfect timing for the big reveal.

Arranging for everyone to stay at The Mansion's various villas was easier. The staff go out of their way to ensure every detail is perfect—from the luxurious accommodations to the discreet arrival of each guest.

Of course, the most complicated part was keeping it all from Jordan. Every text message and phone call was a potential slip-up. I had to be cautious, ensuring nothing gave away the surprise. The joy and anticipation in planning this for her, for us, made every secretive step exhilarating.

We're finally all here. Our wedding is about to begin. The color scheme, flowers, music—every element was chosen to reflect Jordan's taste and our love story. Watching it all come together, seeing the look of surprise on Jordan's face as she realized what was happening, has been a moment of pure magic.

It's taken us a decade, but we're where we need to be.

Jason and Grace flank Jordan as she walks through the garden toward me. A sense of enchantment fills the air as everyone stands and turns to see her approach. As for me, my eyes seem to have sprung leaks.

She's so incredibly beautiful. My mermaid. My Siren. My *everything*.

Hand in hand we say our vows, surrounded by our loved ones in this magical place. I realize this is more than a wedding. It's a celebration of love, of journeying through life's ups and downs. It's a promise of new beginnings and our future—including parenthood, which imminently looms around the corner.

I can honestly say I couldn't be happier than I am right now. Under the starlit sky in Las Vegas, the city where I met the woman I love, vowing to love her forever.

This is our moment.

It's perfect.

Fifteen minutes later, we're officially husband and wife. Wonderful energy abounds and we move on to the next part of the evening—our wedding reception.

Everyone moves into the grand hall, which is beautifully adorned with fragrant flowers and warm lighting, while Jordan and I sign our paperwork and take a moment to ourselves.

"Hi, wife." I kiss her nose. "Did I do okay?"

She swats me playfully. "Hi, husband. I was kind of freaking out you hadn't asked me to marry you. This is incredible. So perfect for us. Thoughtful. Adventurous. Spontaneous..."

"*Uh*..." My eyebrows furrow.

Jordan combs her fingers through my hair. "Kidding. I know how much work went into this. Who knew you'd have a second career as a wedding planner. Seriously, baby. I love you so much. I'm so proud to be your wife."

Our lips meet and, quite honestly, we lose track of time until I hear a loud cough behind us.

"I, uh...hate to interrupt." Jace looks everywhere but at our disheveled selves. "Everyone's waiting."

Jordan spins around and points at him. "Don't get it twisted, baby bro. I'm allowed to make out with my husband."

"No judgment." He holds up his hands in surrender and backs away. "Trust."

Hand in hand we follow Jace. When we enter the dining room, our family and friends erupt into cheers. Jason and Grace are the first to embrace us, their eyes shining with happiness. "Congratulations, you two!" Jason claps me on the back. Grace wipes away a tear, adding, "Welcome to the family, Peter."

"You're in the club, big bro!" Jace teases while Alex hugs Jordan tightly. "You two are going to love being married."

Jordan's sisters Jaylynn and Jen and Jen's wife, Becca offer hugs and congratulations. The other members of Less Than Zero and their wives wish us well. Our staff gather too.

Rose, of course, thinks Jordan is both the stars and the moon after her advocacy and they've become close.

Merc, ever the life of the party, makes his way to the dance floor. "Come on, everybody up! This is a celebration!"

For the rest of the evening, the air is filled with the sound of laughter, music, and clinking glasses. The dance floor pulses with energy, everyone, including the kids, flail around to hits from the nineties and two thousands. LTZ guys—well, mostly Zane—occasionally take the stage, their impromptu performances add an extra layer of excitement to the night.

During a slower song, I pull Jordan close and we sway together, lost in our own world. "I can't believe I pulled it off. I tricked you into marrying me," I whisper, looking down into her eyes.

"I'd marry you a hundred times over." Jordan leans up to kiss me. "Can I tell you a secret?"

"Absolutely. But I'll point out, we're not supposed to keep secrets." I beam down at her.

"Says the man who surprised me with a wedding...*never mind*." She nestles into my chest.

"You gonna tell me," I tip her chin up to look at me, "the *secret*?"

She blinks her eyes coquettishly. "My secret is, if you'd asked me to get married the last time we were in Vegas, I'd have said yes."

"Oh yeah? I planned on asking. If my family situation hadn't exploded, I was fully planning on convincing you to let Elvis marry us." I kiss her nose.

From behind us, someone tings a spoon on a wine glass. Jordan and I spin around to see Merc standing by the destroyed wedding cake.

"Before you all leave, darlings, I wanted to give Jordan and Peter my gift." He raises an eyebrow and stares down the crowd. "And I don't want anyone to laugh."

Of course, everyone laughs and Merc shoots everyone faux glares. "As we send Peter and Jordan off tonight, I'd like to leave you with this poem I'll call 'A Mermaid's Tale.'"

Beneath the moon's soft, silvery glow, a mermaid's whisper swayed,
In depths of love, like stars above, where Jordan's dreams were made.
Peter, in quest, his heart confessed, drawn to her Siren's call,
Their souls did meet, in harmony sweet, a love to outlast all.
From vibrant seas to life's tapestries, they wove their tale so bright,
In each embrace, they found their place, beneath the ocean's light.
Together they swim, through currents grim, their love a beacon true,
A mermaid's tale, where love prevails, in waters deep and blue.

Sappy. Heartfelt. Perfect.

It's a weddinglicious mic drop moment.

A sweet sentiment that perfectly sums up our love story.

Want more Jordan and Peter? Scan for a bonus scene.

Want to read more about the men of LTZ and their strong women. Start with Endless.

For all things Kaylene subscribe to my Newsletter.

Behind the Scenes

Let's start out by saying, I placed the Easter Egg for The Tryst List way back in Limitless.

Remember? When we learned Jace has a sister who's a famous tattoo artist? Well, Jordan Deveraux intrigued me back then and OMG...she was a joy to write.

First, let me tell you a bit about my inspiration for Jordan. Back in the day, one of my favorite shows was LA Ink with Kat Von D who was a bad-ass female owner of a tattoo shop. Kat is a controversial figure, but I loved the idea of a woman owning a business and rising up the ranks in a male-dominated industry.

The idea stuck with me, but the role didn't seem to fit any of the LTZ wives. But, it did fit Jordan Deveraux. She's not your typical tattoo artist or business owner, which I love. It's fun to write characters who don't fit in any one box.

As with all my Spicy Standalones, I'm exploring strong female main characters who own their sexuality without apology. What I love about Jordan is how "real" she is. I think all of us have insecurities at times. You can feel beautiful and invincible one minute and face a self-esteem crisis in the next.

Peter, on the other hand, shares something in common with all my male main characters—a difficult upbringing and family life. One of the things I most relate to in Peter is that sense of familial obligation. The idea that you should step in and help no matter what the cost to you or your own values. It's something I struggled with for a long time, so helping Peter break the pattern is cathartic in a way.

Above all, Peter and Jordan share a connection that transcends everything—it's mythical. Magical. I like to think of their story as a fairytale with obstacles and misunderstandings keeping them apart even though both of them know, deep in their heart, they belong together.

Hence, my mermaid theme. I'm fascinated with mermaids and Jordan was always meant to be my mermaid heroine. She's the siren, the coveted woman for Peter. The only one he'll ever love.

The Tryst List itself comes out of a game my friends and I used to play back in my rock promoter days. We'd list all the creative places we'd gotten busy in and make bets on who'd be first to get the job done in other places.

The idea popped in my head last year and I thought – wouldn't that be the perfect way to get over a breakup? By making your own Tryst List?

Hence...Jordan and Peter's story.

I hope you love it!

Kaylene

Acknowledgments

Cover/Graphic Designer: Regina Wamba

Editor: Grace Bradley Editing, LLC

Proofreading: Letitia Delan

Formatting: Willow Yanarella

PR: Wildfire Marketing

Publicity: Next Step PR, Xpresso Tours

Website Maven: Sherri Kiarsis, Sublime Creations

My Right Hand: Willow Yanarella

YAY to KAYLENE'S KREW!!!

About the Author

Kaylene Winter is an Amazon best-selling author of steamy, contemporary romance.

Each character-driven novel is filled with snappy dialogue, pop-culture references and enough steam to make you fan yourself. Kaylene weaves authenticity, emotion and angst into a turbulent rollercoaster ride of love, passion and soul-searing romance always ending with a delicious HEA.

Kaylene lives in Seattle with her amazing Irish husband and gorgeous Siberian Husky. She loves creating art of all kinds.

Other Titles